MY LAST
INNOCENT
YEAR

MY LAST INNOCENT YEAR

A Novel

DAISY ALPERT FLORIN

 HENRY HOLT AND COMPANY   NEW YORK

Henry Holt and Company
Publishers since 1866
120 Broadway
New York, New York 10271
www.henryholt.com

Library of Congress Cataloging-in-Publication Data is available.

ISBN: 9781250857033

Our books may be purchased in bulk for promotional, educational, or business use.
Please contact your local bookseller or the Macmillan Corporate and Premium
Sales Department at (800) 221-7945, extension 5442, or by e-mail at
MacmillanSpecialMarkets@macmillan.com.

First Edition 2023

Designed by Kelly S. Too

Printed in the United States of America

1 3 5 7 9 10 8 6 4 2

For my mother, who taught me about beauty,
and my father, who taught me to tell stories

In retrospect it seems to me that those days before I knew the names of all the bridges were happier than the ones that came later, but perhaps you will see that as we go along.

Joan Didion, "Goodbye to All That"

MY LAST INNOCENT YEAR

1

IT'S hard to say how I ended up in Zev Neman's dorm
room the night before winter break. It was a bitter night—
December in New Hampshire—and on our way back from
the library we'd been arguing, this time about whether
windchill was a legitimate meteorological phenomenon, as
Zev believed, or a ruse cooked up by weather executives to
distract us from the threat of global warming.

"Weather executives?" Zev said. He had a light Israeli
accent. "Isabel. That's not even a thing."

"It is so," I said, stepping over a pile of dirty snow.

Zev stopped under a streetlight in front of his dorm
and crossed his arms; his face was craggy in the shadows. "I
never took you for a conspiracy theorist. A left-wing agi-
tator maybe, but conspiracy theorist?" He shook his head.

"But it's worth considering, right?" I tried to read his

expression, but Zev was forever inscrutable. Wind blew my coat open, bit through my jeans to the skin.

"Either way, it's pretty fucking cold." He jerked his head. "Want to come in?"

I shrugged and followed him into the squat cinderblock building.

So I guess that's how I ended up in Zev Neman's room: he invited me and I didn't say no.

Zev's room, a single overlooking the river, was neat. Bed made, no clothes on the floor; it even smelled clean. Nothing like the other boy bedrooms I'd visited in my nearly four years at Wilder College. I attributed the cleanliness to Zev's two years in the Israeli army defending the Jewish homeland—my homeland, as he liked to remind me. He threw off his parka and flopped on the bed. Books were piled on the only chair so I walked over and studied his bookshelf: economics textbooks, books in Hebrew, a couple of paperback thrillers thick as doorstops. I wanted to skip this part, the part where you wondered when the thing you'd come to a boy's bedroom to do would start happening, when you could stop making small talk that only revealed all the ways this boy, any boy, would never understand you. To pass beyond language straight into touch.

I picked up a dog-eared copy of *The Executioner's Song*. Next to it was a framed picture of a girl standing on a beach wearing a black bikini and mirrored sunglasses.

"Who's that?"

Zev was tossing a Nerf basketball back and forth between his hands. "My girlfriend, Yael," he said as if we'd just been speaking about her when in fact he'd never mentioned her, never mentioned having a girlfriend at all.

I picked up the picture. Yael was pretty. Beautiful actually. Long legs, olive skin, sun-kissed amber hair. I wondered if that's what I might have looked like if my ancestors had made a left instead of a right on their way out of Russia. I was surprised Zev had a girlfriend, but I was more surprised she was so pretty. I glanced over at him stretched out across the bed and realized Yael gave him a currency he hadn't had before.

"How come you never told me about her?"

"Why?" he asked. "Are you jealous?"

"No," I said, placing the picture back on the shelf. What I felt wasn't jealousy, more curiosity about how you became the kind of girl who let someone take your picture in a bathing suit. Or how you could have a girlfriend, a girlfriend like that, and never even mention it. If I had a boyfriend, I was certain I'd never stop talking about him.

Zev was still tossing the basketball between his hands, faster and faster without missing. "Why would I tell you about her?" he said. "Besides, she's there and I'm here, so." He aimed the ball at a hoop hanging over the back of his closet door. "Score!"

I looked out the window at the river glistening in the moonlight. It was the sort of thing you took for granted in college: a bedroom with a river view. I couldn't explain to Zev why I thought it was strange he'd never mentioned Yael without making it sound like I cared, which I didn't. Or maybe I did. Either way, I thought the whole point of having a girlfriend was so you didn't have to do this anymore.

This. I was acutely aware of Zev's presence: the rasp of his breath, the creak of the mattress as he shifted his weight. I ran the charm on my necklace back and forth along the chain and listened for a shift in his breathing or some other signal that he was about to touch me. After a minute or two, I heard him stand up and walk toward me, slow steps across the linoleum floor. I felt a hand on my shoulder. I turned and there he was, his mouth hanging open slightly as if he had a stuffy nose. I held my breath as he clumsily leaned in and kissed me. I fell back into the bookshelf and heard Yael's picture tumble to the floor.

I'm not sure what I thought was going to happen, or what I even wanted to happen. I was mainly relieved to know which way the night was going. I might have been as relieved if Zev had asked me to leave because he had a headache or had to study for a test, even if he had told me to get the fuck out. As I settled into kissing him, feeling his tongue probe the recesses of my mouth in a way that wasn't entirely unpleasant, I started thinking about what it would be like to fuck Zev Neman and if I even wanted to. I imagined telling versions of our origin story at future dinner parties. "We met as freshmen but didn't start dating until senior year," I would say, turning a glass of merlot thoughtfully around in my hands as Zev stroked my knee under the table. I thought about Yael, facedown on the floor by our feet, and wondered how she might fit into the narrative. Yael, the inconvenient girlfriend whose heart Zev had to break so he could find his way to me. Zev stuck his hand under my shirt. His tongue was still going, the dinner party beginning to fade. If I had any say in the story I would one day tell about myself—and, at twenty-one, I wasn't sure I did—I didn't know if this was how I wanted it to begin, or if the ending was something I wanted either.

It occurred to me then, as Zev squeezed my breast a little too hard, that I wasn't sure what I was doing there. I'd come to Zev's bedroom more out of curiosity and boredom than desire, because the library, where we'd bumped into each other, was closing early and I didn't feel like going back to my room yet, and because, despite my strong opinions vis-à-vis windchill, it was pretty fucking cold out. In short, I'd wandered into this encounter the way you wander into a dark room: with one hand outstretched, feeling your way as you go, unable to see what's on the walls or how exactly you might get out.

IT WAS STRANGE to think I'd known Zev longer than almost anyone at Wilder, longer even than Debra and Kelsey. We met on the first Friday of freshman year at a Shabbat dinner at Hillel House, the small beige building on the edge of campus where Wilder's skeletal collection of Jews gathered. Like many elite colleges, Wilder had a long history of institutional anti-Semitism, as well as a more recent scandal involving fraternity brothers forcing a group of barefoot pledges in striped pajamas to carry heavy stones across the green. The Holocaust imagery was undeniable, and the incident attracted national attention. But things had settled down and, a few years back, a group of Jewish alumni raised the money to establish a Hillel House on campus, so Jewish parents were finally comfortable sending their children to

Wilder. My father had had no such qualms; I'd spent my whole life around Jews and he wanted me to go to Wilder precisely so I could get away from them.

I went to the dinner with Sally Steinberg, of the Bethesda Steinbergs, whom I'd met earlier that week in a step aerobics class. Sally was the coddled only child of older parents who'd met at Brandeis, where they desperately wanted her to go, but Sally had insisted on Wilder. Her parents relented, as they did with everything, and as a prerequisite to enrollment, they'd made her promise to attend weekly Shabbat dinners.

Zev was there when we arrived, sitting at the long dining table. The rabbi, a young man wearing a Boston Red Sox yarmulke, introduced us, and Zev held out his hand. This was something people at Wilder did, I'd discovered, they shook hands, something I'd only ever done with adults, and rarely. "Pleased to meet you," he said, taking Sally's hand and then mine. His grip was strong, his fingers stained yellow at the tips.

"Let me guess where you're from," he said to me as girls in long skirts fluttered around us carrying handfuls of plastic silverware and jugs of grape juice. "New York."

"How'd you know?"

He pointed at my scuffed Doc Martens. "But you're not an uptown girl. Not West Side either. Downtown?"

"Impressive. Lower East Side." He asked what my father did for a living—something else people at Wilder did—and I told him he owned an appetizing store.

"An appetizing store? Really? Wow. I didn't know Jews like you still existed."

"Jews like what?"

"Jews who sell smoked fish and seeded ryes. I thought all those stores were gone."

"A lot of them are gone, but there are still a few." I named them—Guss' Pickles, Yonah Shimmel knishes, Kossar's bialys, Russ & Daughters.

"Cute," Zev said. "Like something out of a Malamud novel." He reached for a piece of challah. "So, what? Your father pinned all his hopes on you? Sent you here to fulfill his dream of upward mobility?"

I didn't know what to say. I'd never heard my father's ambitions summed up so succinctly, or so crassly. Zev was looking at me like I was a unicorn but I couldn't tell if it was wonder in his eyes or if he wanted to lure me closer to cut off my horn. Before I could answer, the rabbi began reciting the prayers welcoming in Shabbat.

Dinner was chaotic and long. There were many courses, each one interrupted by more prayers and candle lighting. The long-skirted girls, one of whom was the rabbi's wife, cleared plates and poured seltzer while the rabbi's two young sons ran around dressed like miniature actuaries. I hadn't been around so many Jews since I got to Wilder; not that there were a lot of us—the room felt crowded mostly on account of it being small. Sprung loose from Scarsdale and Great Neck, the Jews of Wilder had to stick together. During dinner, I found out Zev was a freshman like me, but older because he'd spent those two years in the army. He was short and stocky with close-cropped black hair, and a nose that looked like it had been punched in. He'd been born in Iran, he told me, but moved to Israel as a child after the revolution. He smelled like cigarettes and body spray. We bonded mainly over our mutual disdain of everyone else, including Sally, who announced, loudly, that she'd come to the dinner because her mother told her it would be a good place to find a husband. (She would go home that night with the boy seated to her left, Gabe Feldman, whom she would indeed eventually marry.) Over the years, I would discover that Zev's disdain for people extended to most everyone at Wilder, perhaps even to people in general, but that night, making fun of the people at Hillel House was the most fun I'd had since I arrived.

As the meal came to a close, one of the girls who was clearing dropped a stack of dirty plates. "Mazel tov!" Gabe shouted. Sally laughed. The girl looked like she was about to cry. I felt an instant kinship with her and moved to help, but Zev grabbed my wrist.

"Don't," he said. "Let them do it. Stay and talk to me some more." His grip was strong, but I liked it, the press of it, the force. I couldn't remember the last time anyone had looked at me with such intensity, or if anyone ever had. I sat back down and talked to him for the rest of the night.

Zev and I stayed friends after that, although friends might not have been the right word. Whenever we saw each other, in the dining hall or library, he would seek me out and we would talk, not about little things like what his parents did for a living or if he had a pet, but big things like politics, economics, God, the Middle East. Zev challenged me to articulate my beliefs, to explain why I was a feminist or a Democrat. I wasn't a debater by nature and somewhere along the way had come to believe that what I felt, if it couldn't be articulated or defended, was invalid. Maybe that's why I thought I had to listen to Zev, who was clear in his beliefs and never wavered. When we talked, I could feel my mind stretching to take in this new worldview—his worldview— but mostly I was trying to figure out if he liked me, if he thought I was pretty, if he ever thought about kissing me. It only occurred to me later that Zev didn't have any friends besides me, that whenever I saw him at a party or lecture, he was always alone. He sought me out because he had no one else to talk to, because no one else could stand him.

Debra, for one, hated him. "You don't have to be friends with him just because he's Jewish," she said, but that wasn't the reason. There was something dangerous about Zev that felt exciting to me, a cold, bitter exterior I was determined to crack. He was exactly the sort of man I would avoid when I was older and knew better, but we usually learn that the hard way.

"He just wants to fuck you," Debra said, but I wasn't sure. Other than grabbing my wrist that night at Hillel House, Zev never touched me. Sometimes, after we'd been arguing for a while, I found myself waiting for the feel of his hand, unfamiliar, uninvited.

THE HEATER IN the corner rattled loudly, like something or someone was trapped inside. Zev's hands were rough and chapped and everywhere—under my shirt, pawing at the space between my legs. A line from a poem ran through my head—*Then all night you rummaged my flesh for some body else.* I felt as though I'd been dropped into the middle of a sexual encounter that had been going on for a while. I placed a hand on the wall behind me, tried to catch my breath. I thought about asking him to slow down when he pulled me toward the bed.

Zev was strong, his body taut like a drum. He lay down on top of me and pulled up my shirt. I heard a couple of buttons pop off, which, for some reason, made me laugh. Zev didn't laugh though, and for the first time that night, maybe in my whole life, I felt scared.

"Whoa there, soldier," I said as he started to unzip his pants. From this close up, his skin looked oily, his eyes too close together. "Could you maybe slow down a little?" Despite all the kissing and touching, I was barely aroused.

Zev was breathing hard, as if he'd run up a flight of stairs. "I don't think I can," he said, slipping my hand into the opening of his boxer shorts. It was damp and humid in there. "Come on," he breathed into my neck. "Why'd you come up here anyway?"

Why had I come, I thought as Zev threaded a hand up the back of my shirt and unhooked my bra. He pushed me down on the extralong twin mattress, and I thought about telling him I had my period. I heard voices in the hallway, people walking by, enjoying their night. I wondered if I should call out to them, but there was nothing remarkable happening. I'd been here before—not in Zev's room per se, but under boys who smelled like sweat and dirty hair. Zev reached for a condom, and I thought about my mother on a long-ago first day of school, the slap of her Dr. Scholl's sandals against the sidewalk. "Be a good girl, Isabel," she'd said, bending down to kiss me on the nose. "It'll be over before you know it."

I was still dry, so Zev licked a finger and placed it inside me before easing himself in. Then he moved his dick back and forth slowly, trying to find a comfortable rhythm. I tried to pull my shirt closed because I didn't like being shirtless in front of a man, but he grabbed my wrists and held them above my head.

My eyes were open but Zev's were closed, his eyelids fluttering as if he was watching something play out inside them. Maybe a scene from a Western, and I was the stallion he was riding across the dusty plains. Or maybe we were riding across the voluptuous deserts of Israel. Did Israel have deserts? All I could picture from that part of the world were scenes from Operation Desert Storm. With each thrust, my head pressed against the metal headboard. I tried to think about something else, anything else, like the paper I'd just turned in about Russian Jewry in the nineteenth century. I watched the shadows move across the popcorn ceiling, listened to the buzz of the fluorescent lights out in the hallway, as Zev moved faster, ramping up to the big finish. And then, finally, after several shuddering thrusts, he sputtered and came, quietly, like every boy I'd slept with who'd only ever had sex in places where he had to be quiet. Part of me was disappointed he didn't scream or cry out so I would know if he liked it, if anyone liked it.

"What are you doing for break?" Zev asked after he peeled off the condom and tossed it into the trash, where it landed among old copies of the *Wall Street Journal* and strings of dental floss.

"Not too much," I said, buttoning my shirt as best as I could. "Working in my dad's store mostly. How about you?"

"I'm going to Washington with a couple international students. There isn't enough time to go home."

We talked for a minute or two about Washington and what he should do while he was there. He should definitely visit the Vietnam Veterans Memorial, I said, since I knew he was interested in monuments to mass tragedies. I told him about the time I went to DC in high school and a group of kids got sent home for doing Whip Its.

"Have a good break," I said. Then I grabbed my things and left. It was really cold out now, the wind whipping with such force I began to reconsider my position on windchill, if I'd ever really held a position in the first place. *I'll tell Zev he was right the next time we talk*, I thought, before remembering that I was never going to talk to him again.

I OFTEN WONDER what would have happened if Debra hadn't been in our room when I got back, as she so often wasn't. But there she was, sitting on the papasan chair eating a bowl of Sugar Corn Pops. Kelsey was already gone, on her way to Sun Valley, where she'd spend a few days skiing with Jason and his family before heading home to New York for Christmas. Debra and I were leaving the next day. She'd drive me as far as Scarsdale, then her parents would put me on the train to Grand Central.

"Where were you?" Debra asked as I sat down on the sofa. Something hurt, deep in some place I couldn't see or name. I shifted slightly until the sensation lessened.

"With Zev Neman," I said, reaching for a handful of cereal. My voice sounded shaky. I found it hard to say his name.

"Well, praise Jesus. Did you finally fuck him?"

I thought about telling the story the way Debra would, as another crazy one-night stand, the kind she had with boys and girls she barely knew, people she picked up and discarded with ease. But I couldn't frame what had happened with Zev in those terms. There was a darkness to it, a heaviness, like the way my body felt right before my period. The cereal had become a sickly sweet paste in my mouth, and I wondered if I might vomit.

"Isabel." Debra pushed herself up awkwardly in the strangely deep chair. "What the fuck. Did something happen?" She set her bowl down on the steamer trunk we used as a coffee table and rested her hands on her knees.

I don't remember exactly what I said. Only that, as I spoke, Debra stood up and started pacing, her thighs jiggling each time her foot hit the creaky wooden floor. Her dark hair had dried into the kinks she tried to tame into submission. They stuck out of her head now, making her look as if she'd been electrified. Maybe that was how she summoned her indefatigable energy, I thought, as I rested my head on the arm of the sofa. There was a tender spot on the back of my skull. I reached back and pressed on it.

"Holy shit," she said. "I always hated that guy."

"Well, you were right. He's a dick."

"He's more than a dick. That guy *raped* you."

"Oh, Jesus. Debra, come on."

"I'm sorry." She stopped pacing. "What would you call it?"

"I mean, it happened a little faster than I would have liked, but he didn't *force* me."

"Did you even want to?"

Did I? I couldn't remember. In so many ways, the night had been a blur, while some parts were sharp and defined. I rubbed my forehead, trying to untangle the knot that had formed between my eyebrows. "I don't know. I guess not, but . . . I mean, c'mon . . . Like that's never happened to you."

"No. It fucking hasn't."

I'd asked the wrong person.

Debra started pacing again. I could feel her footsteps vibrating through the floorboards as I rolled my head back and forth on the armrest, passing through the bruise each time. Debra's anger was palpable, a living, breathing thing. Part of me wanted her to calm down, but another part was happy she was angry so I didn't have to be.

"We have to show him he can't get away with this," she said. "We should call the police. Or the dean—what's his name again?"

"Hansen," I said. "But Debra—"

"You're right. Fuck Hansen. What's he gonna do?" She chewed her finger. "We can't just sit here."

"I don't want to make a big deal about this. It's not worth it."

She looked at me. She had on an oversized Lilith Fair T-shirt, a pair of men's boxer shorts peeking out beneath the hem. "When you say that, Isabel, what you're really saying is you're not worth it. And is that what you really think?"

I sighed heavily and curled onto my side. It was almost 2 a.m. I felt detached from what had happened to me, Debra's anger reminding me how I should be feeling, but didn't. What was wrong with me, I wondered? Why didn't I react to things the way other people did, in ways that were normal? I opened and closed my hand, watching the mechanics of tendon and bone. Was this really my hand? If so, how was it connected to the rest of my body? What was my body anyway? What made it mine?

Debra was still talking, pacing, fuming. I hadn't wanted to sleep with Zev, she said, and he knew that but forced me anyway, right? I'd told him no, hadn't I, but he hadn't listened because he never listened. He'd tricked me into coming up to his room so he could rape me because that is what he did, isn't it, he raped me, raped me, raped me. I closed my eyes, wondering how it would feel if I let Debra's words find purchase inside me, if I grabbed onto them and made them fit. Because I was angry even if I didn't show it, even if Debra was describing a night I didn't quite recognize. And the more I listened to her, the angrier I became. Especially when I thought about Zev and the way he pressed his fingers into my flesh like wet clay, the slick of his tongue in my ear, the way he'd rummaged around inside me like a bag of old clothes.

But really, it was Debra. She had a way of making you believe something, making *me* believe something.

And so, for the second time that night, I found myself climbing the stairs to Zev Neman's dorm room.

AT TWENTY-ONE, DEBRA was already an experienced vandal. As editor of her high school yearbook, she'd embedded messages throughout the pages—Silence Equals Death, My Body My Choice, I Believe Anita—a code of resistance you could read only if you knew where to look. Within weeks of arriving on campus freshman year, she'd organized a Take Back the Night march, but when the reaction to it was tepid, she decided she wasn't interested in anything school-sanctioned. So one night that winter, we ran around campus putting tacky bras from Victoria's Secret on every male statue on campus—or, as Debra pointed out, *every* statue on campus. The next day we watched campus security remove them, doubled over with laughter as they fiddled awkwardly with the clasps. Later that year, a group of us plastered campus with stickers that read Womyn Are Everywhere. We stuck them on everything—buildings, lampposts, soda machines, frat house doors. This stunt was more controversial—some of the stickers, including the one we put on the college president's car, couldn't be removed, not easily at least. There was a flurry of pointed op-eds in the school newspaper, talk of vandalism charges, but no one could prove it was us. In the end, I don't know what made people angrier, the vandalism or the word *womyn*.

Sophomore year, Debra swiped the ID of a guy rumored to be groping girls at parties and we taped copies of it on the mirrors of every bathroom on campus. The guy's parents threatened a lawsuit but backed off after a dozen girls came forward to accuse him. (He still graduated with us, became a member of the alumni council, signs his name to cheery annual appeals for donations to the class fund.) It was around that time that we started calling ourselves the "Crushgirls," a name that made us sound more official— and more menacing—than what we really were: a loose affiliation of Debra and me and whoever else we could scare up on a particular night. Crushgirl activity flatlined after Debra founded *bitch slap*, Wilder's first and only feminist journal, but she still talked sometimes about reviving it and pulling off something "big." I'd always gone along with Debra's stunts because they were fun and because she was happy to take whatever consequences they reaped. So far, to my relief—and Debra's chagrin—none had.

All of which is to say, I wasn't surprised when she pulled a can of spray paint out of her backpack when we got to Zev's door. It felt strange to be back there so soon, and I distracted myself by wondering if a universe existed where I was on both sides of Zev's door, like Schrödinger's cat.

Debra shook the can, and the sound was huge in the silent hallway. I didn't know who was still around and who had already left for winter break, so I looked up and down the hall nervously, willing the doors to stay closed.

"Let's keep it simple, shall we?" Debra popped off the top, and I watched as she wrote the word *rapist* in big red letters across Zev's door.

"Holy shit," I whispered.

"Not bad, right?"

After she touched up the letters, wiping off drips of paint with her sleeve, we stood there, basking in the glory of what we had done, what Debra had done. I felt giddy and nervous, my stomach dancing in a way that made it impossible to separate the feelings. The word on Zev's door was bad and bold but, for a moment at least, felt right. Tears pricked at the corners of my eyes as I thought about what Debra had done for me. Debra, my avenging angel. She looked back at me and smiled, and in that instant, she'd never looked more beautiful.

The sound of a doorknob being turned jostled me out of my reverie. The door opened and Zev poked out his head, blinking into the light. His thick glasses were slightly askew, as if he'd just pulled them on.

"Ladies," he said with a smile, his eyes darting from Debra to me. He looked pink, newly hatched. "What's going on? Isabel? Is that you?"

"Let's go," I whispered. But Debra didn't move.

"What the fuck?" Zev said, still smiling as he stepped into the hallway. He rubbed his eyes, pulled at the hem of his boxers. He hadn't yet seen what we had written, and I wanted desperately to leave before he did. I tugged on Debra's sleeve, but she had her feet planted firmly on the worn carpet. I watched as Zev turned his gaze from us to the door, watched as it dawned on him what we had done.

He was quiet for what felt like a long time, and I realized I was holding my breath. I sucked air slowly through my teeth, wishing I could disappear. As if it might help, I imagined myself floating down the hallway like a soap bubble, then dissolving into specks of mist and vapor.

Zev's voice brought me back. "What the fuck?" he said again, louder this time. I yanked on Debra's arm. She ignored me.

"You can read."

Zev's eyes moved in a line from Debra to me. He was fully awake now. Whatever confusion he'd felt was gone, along with whatever certainty I'd felt about the righteousness of our act. In its place was a deep shame that felt familiar and lived in, like a pair of old jeans.

"Is that what you told her?" he said, his voice thick with disbelief. "That I *raped* you?"

"She just told me the truth, asshole," Debra said.

Zev's eyes were wild and shining. He looked hurt and confused, but also scared. "Isabel, you know that isn't what happened. Tell her that. Tell her."

"You don't get to decide what happened," Debra said. "It's her body. She knows exactly what you did."

"What is this, another one of your stupid stunts?" He turned to me. "I can't believe you'd let her use you like this, Isabel. I thought you were smarter than that." And with that, whatever goodwill Zev had ever felt toward me was gone. Something passed between us, a look that encapsulated all the years of our friendship—because I guess that's what it was—all of it, evaporated in a moment. I felt like I'd let him down.

"Debra, come on!" I pulled her so hard she lost her balance. I could hear Zev shouting something, but I was gone, running down the stairs so fast I tumbled on the last few steps, twisting my ankle. I could hear Debra behind me, her tennis shoes slapping the ground, her voice echoing in the stairwell: "You haven't heard the last of us, motherfucker!"

When we got back to our room, I collapsed onto the sofa. My ankle was throbbing. Blood pounded in my ears. Debra sat next to me and lifted my head into her lap. She stroked my forehead, massaged my earlobes, kneaded the muscles on the sides of my neck. It felt so good, I wanted to cry.

"Oh, honey," she said in a voice so sweet I almost didn't recognize it. "Didn't your mother ever warn you about Israeli guys?"

The tears were coming now, fast and hot, soaking the fine hairs at my hairline, collecting in the hollow of my throat. "No," I managed. My mother hadn't warned me about any of this.

2

THE next day, I went home for winter break.

Back to Rosen's Appetizing and the Lower East Side. Back
to my father, Abraham Rosen, whom everybody called Abe,
even me. Back to Orchard Street, Essex Street, Rivington,
Delancey, streets where Jewish immigrants had settled at
the turn of the century, dragging their history and sadness
behind them. Zev was right: most of them were gone. We
had stayed.

Kelsey was from New York too, and people sometimes
assumed we knew each other from the city. During the
early days of our friendship, she used to ask if I knew this
place or that place, this person or that person. I never did. I
could see her struggling to understand how there could be
a New York she didn't know, but even from her lofty perch
on Park Avenue, she couldn't see down into the dark and
twisted streets where I'd grown up. We'd never met before

coming to Wilder—of course we hadn't. We might as well have been from different countries.

I spent most of break working at Rosen's. The holidays were always busy. Never mind that Jews didn't celebrate Christmas, they still came in to stock up on herring and smoked fish, buying food, Abe always said, as though they'd never eat again. This year seemed busier than usual, which was good. The neighborhood was changing, trading junkies for artists. There was a high-rise going up on the corner, pushing out the homeless who'd called the empty lot home for as long as I could remember. So in addition to our usual customers, there were downtown hipsters stopping by for a schmear, along with tourists who didn't know a bagel from a bialy.

When I wasn't busy running the cash register or sweeping the floors or stocking the shelves, I worried about what might be waiting for me when I got back to campus. I wanted to talk to Debra, but she was in Boca with her grandparents and too busy to come to the phone. The one time I did speak to her, she assured me everything would be okay. "Please. Isabel, he thinks he got away with raping you. You think he's going to make a big deal about a little paint?" I could hear her crunching ice cubes between her teeth. "Believe me, he's freaking out a lot more than you are." Her words consoled me, but only temporarily. I started knitting, something I did when I was anxious; in the two weeks I was home I made a scarf for Kelsey and a pair of mittens for Debra.

Whatever high school friends I still had were spending the holidays with their families, so on Christmas Eve, I made Abe close the store early and dragged him to see *Titanic*, which I loved, he less so: "I knew how it ended." He spent most of Christmas Day hunched over a stack of bills at the kitchen table until I made him go out for Chinese food. On New Year's Eve, we marched arm in arm to the mailbox on the corner and mailed off my final tuition payment. In less than six months, I would be a college graduate. Abe had done it, somehow. Wilder hadn't offered me as much financial aid as other schools, but Abe had insisted he could manage. "This is what we planned for, your mother and me, so you could go anywhere," he said when he mailed off the first deposit, and I decided to believe him. Then later, as the bills started coming in, not just tuition but room and board and computers and books: "I'll figure out a way to pay for it." And finally, when things were even less certain and he was robbing Peter to pay Paul—and Martin and Joe and whoever else came along: "They can't take the education away from you, can they?"

On the calendar, 1997 turned into 1998, but everything felt the same to me. Princess Diana was still dead, Mother Teresa too. Bill Clinton was in the White House doing whatever it was presidents did on New Year's Eve. Monica Lewinsky was enjoying her last few moments of obscurity: in less than three weeks, the Drudge Report would publish a story accusing the president of having an affair with the intern. That night, after Dick Clark, I watched Abe wrap his tea bag around a spoon, then set it aside so he could use it again, and listened to him enumerate the many opportunities I would have once I graduated. Doctor, lawyer, Indian chief. I sipped my champagne and wondered what he would think if he knew what I was actually doing at Wilder, messing around with boys and vandalizing school property and worrying that no one would ever love me.

I took the bus back to New Hampshire on the first Sunday in January. As we pulled onto campus, I thought about how much I'd been looking forward to my final semester, to finishing my thesis and finding a job and taking Joanna Maxwell's senior fiction seminar. Everything had been coming together, until that night with Zev and Debra's stupid stunt. I clung to her promise that everything would be okay, forgetting that she was the one who'd gotten me into this mess in the first place. Or maybe, as usual, it was me.

WHEN I GOT back from class on Monday, there was a message waiting for me, written on the whiteboard in Kelsey's careful hand.

"I told you this would happen," I said to Debra when she got back from the gym.

She wedged a granola bar in her mouth and considered the message: *Call Dean Hansen.*

"Yeah, he called me, too."

"He did? When? Why didn't you tell me?"

"I'm telling you now." She finished the bar in four quick bites. "Isabel, think about this rationally. What exactly does Zev have on us?"

"Debra, he *saw* us with the spray paint. You had the can in your hand."

"Circumstantial." Debra unzipped her hoodie, then tossed it on her desk where it landed next to a copy of Katie

Roiphe's latest book, which she was reviewing for *bitch slap*. "Remember why we were there. Because of what *he* did, right? The dean probably wants to talk to you about that."

"That doesn't make me feel any better." I fell back on the sofa. "Debra, I don't even know what happened anymore. Maybe I overreacted."

"Stop that," she snapped. "You know damn well what he did. We'll just tell the dean what happened, what *really* happened. Honestly, what can he even do to us at this point? We're out of here in less than six months. Zev's the one who should be worried. When this is all over, he'll be sorry he ever laid eyes on us."

I picked up Roiphe's book and flipped through the pages while Debra took a shower. The bruise on the back of my head was nearly healed, but if I pressed on it, I could coax out the ache. I did that now, to remind myself I had skin, bones, a boundary that defined where I ended and someone else began. Then I tossed the book aside and grabbed my coat so I would be gone before Debra got out.

The library's wood-paneled reading room was quiet, just a handful of people preparing for the semester. Afternoon tea, which they served every day at four o'clock, had just ended, and the smell of Earl Grey filled the warm and cozy space. People looked up as I passed to see if I was someone they might waste time with, as if that was the real work of college, friends and lovers and intrigues, all the rest merely an interruption. The phone booths outside the reading room were empty; as the semester wore on they'd almost always be occupied by students calling home to cry about a breakup or a bad grade. I passed a group of girls from my

French class. "*Salut*, Isabel," one of them said, pronouncing my name the way our professor did, the *s* sharp and sibilant. I swept up the stairs, my long gray coat trailing behind me as if I were a Russian princess. The heaters clanked and moaned, working hard against the New Hampshire winter. Then I pushed through the turnstile and into the stacks.

I loved everything about the stacks, the musty smell of glue and paper, the way you were only permitted to enter after showing your student ID, as though the collection of books were an important dignitary to be protected at all costs. I weaved my way slowly through the shelves, running my fingers along the spines until my fingertips were black with dust, pulling out books at random, stopping here and there to read a few pages about World War II or electrical engineering or Willa Cather. Books in Chinese and Yiddish and Russian and French. Books about classical music and film, the history of civilizations ancient and modern. I loved the push and pull of the big and small, the way each writer burrowed deep into his or her subject matter, no matter how obscure, and yet, taken together, the books here felt larger than the world.

I wandered until my stomach growled, reminding me I hadn't eaten. I thought about leaving and finding Kelsey and Jason, who'd invited me to join them for dinner, but instead found myself standing in front of Andy Dubinski's carrel. The library was quiet, but I knew I'd find him there. He took his time coming to the door, like he always did.

"Isabel?" He looked as if I had woken him. Andy's dedication to his work was part of his mystique, that and his honey-colored Jesus hair, which today he had pulled back with an office-supply rubber band, the kind that ripped your hair. Andy was a construct, a type I'd meet again and again in the literary world I eventually became a part of. The kind of guy who wanted you to think it was so hard to do what he did that you wouldn't try to do it, too.

"*C'est moi*," I said. "Can I come in?"

"*Oui, oui. Entrez, s'il vous plaît.*"

Andy's carrel was small, not much bigger than a shower stall. There was a desk pushed up against one wall, a sliver of window, and a long metal heating pipe that ran from floor to ceiling. Andy's computer was off; he rarely used it, preferring to write his poems on index cards with pencils no longer than his thumb. There were scraps of paper pinned to the bulletin board above his desk, some with only one word: *pomegranate*, *chasm*, *dun*. I wondered if Andy was disappointed to see me. I wasn't the only girl who visited him in his carrel, but maybe the only one he wasn't currently sleeping with.

I sat down on the floor next to the heating pipe and tucked my knees under my chin. "Are you ready for Professor Maxwell's seminar?"

"Getting ready," Andy said, lowering himself into his chair.

"Do you know who else got in?"

"The usual suspects. Holly and Alec, Kara Jiang, Linus Harrison. Ginny."

"Ginny McDougall? Seriously?"

"Apparently, she wrote a really good story about a girl who loses her virginity the day her King Charles spaniel dies. Very effective description of cunnilingus."

Professor Joanna Maxwell's senior seminar was the class

everyone in the English department worked toward. It was intense and exclusive, admission based on a set of criteria no one could rationally discern, and not for lack of trying. I was thrilled when I found out I'd been accepted, but that feeling had since turned to dread because, despite her soft voice and beatific smile, Joanna Maxwell, award-winning novelist, department head, and campus legend, scared the shit out of me.

"Did you hear about Jason?" he asked.

"Yeah." I'd been shocked that Jason, Kelsey's boyfriend, had been rejected. He was what I thought of as a "real" English major: he memorized poetry, annotated short stories in the *New Yorker*, and was writing an incomprehensible thesis on James Joyce. All I did was write stories about "girls with feelings," as Andy put it once in a workshop. According to Kelsey, Jason was devastated.

"Well, *c'est la vie*." Andy turned back to his desk. His shoulder blades jutted through his T-shirt like wings. Debra joked you could grab onto them if you were ever caught in a gust of wind. In another life, Andy might have been an athlete, but in this one, his lean muscles were zipped under the thin skin of a poet, pale and blue-veined like the cheeses behind the glass display at Rosen's.

Andy and I had slept together exactly twice, the last time after a St. Patrick's Day party sophomore year. He'd had shamrocks painted on his face; as we fucked, the green paint had dripped down his cheeks, collecting in the cleft of his chin. There wasn't much more to say about it except that we decided never to do it again and had somehow managed to stay friends.

"Actually," he said, turning around in his chair. "I have something to tell you, but you can't tell anyone. I mean, I guess everyone will find out on Wednesday, but . . ."

"Oh, come on. What?"

"Joanna isn't teaching this semester."

"What? She always teaches English 76! Are you serious?"

"I'm serious."

"Why not?"

"It isn't public knowledge so you can't say anything." I crossed my heart. "She's telling people her publisher moved up her deadline, but the truth is"—his voice dropped—"she and Tom Fisher are getting a divorce."

"She's not teaching because she's getting a divorce? I had a high school teacher whose husband got hit by a bus and she didn't even miss a day."

"I gather it's a bit of a shit show. Tom is . . . complicated, and they have the kid . . ." I had the feeling he wanted to say more. Andy and Joanna had been close ever since he'd been the first freshman admitted to her advanced poetry seminar. Since then, he'd worked for her as a research assistant and TA. Last summer, he'd lived with her and her husband in their house on June Bridge Road, doing yard work and helping take care of their daughter, Igraine. He had been working all year with Joanna on his senior thesis, a collection of poems about masculinity, technology, and parental control; there was talk he'd be listed on the acknowledgments page of her next novel. If anyone knew what was going on with Joanna and Tom, it was Andy, but he wasn't saying.

"Hey," he said, "isn't Professor Fisher your thesis adviser?"

"Yeah."

"Good luck with that."

Before I had a chance to ask what he meant, Andy turned and jotted something down on an index card, and I could tell that whatever window of time he'd allotted to me was coming to an end.

"Oh, hey," I said, reaching into my backpack. "I made you something."

"*Pour moi?*" he said, opening the package I'd wrapped in the front page of the *New York Times* Arts and Leisure section. "*Mon dieu*, Isabel! Did you *make* this?" He held up a navy blue woolen cap.

"Yeah. Over break. I didn't have that much else to do."

Andy pulled on the hat and turned his head from side to side. "How do I look?"

"*Très joli*," I said. "Now, you better wear it or else."

"Or else what?" he said. "You'll spray-paint ASSHOLE on my door?"

It took me a second to understand what he meant. Of course Andy knew what had happened with Zev. And if he knew, soon everyone else would too, if they didn't already. Andy was smiling, as if waiting for me to get the joke. I wanted to rip the hat off his head and light it on fire, or maybe light it on fire while it was on his head.

"Fuck you, Andy."

"Oh, Isabel. I'm kidding," he said as I stood up and reached for the door. In my haste, I tripped over my coat and my hand landed on the long heating pipe. The foam used to insulate it had worn away long ago, and the heat seared my palm.

"Shit, are you okay?" Andy asked, but I didn't answer him. I ran back down the stairs and out of the stacks, pushing my way outside, where an icy rain had started to fall. I stopped under a streetlamp and waited a minute before looking at my hand. The skin was pink and shiny, but not broken or blistered. I watched as the color slowly faded, then squatted down and held it against the snow. The cold felt good, the heat rising from my hand with a sizzle. I held it there until it hurt, then held it there a little longer.

3

WEDNESDAY morning, I sat on a tufted green settee outside Dean Hansen's office. Debra had had her meeting with him the day before.

"Honestly, it wasn't a big deal," she'd told me the night before, climbing into the top bunk with me. "He didn't even ask about the rape. He was mainly concerned about the spray paint. Like *that's* the biggest problem here. Then he was all, 'I'm going to have to put a note in your file.' And I was like, 'I'm about to graduate, *fucker*. What do I care about some note in my file?'" She took my hand and rested it on top of hers. Our hands were practically the same size, except hers was mostly palm and mine was mostly fingers. "You'll be fine," she whispered. "I promise."

I stood up and studied a picture on the wall across from the settee, a black-and-white photograph of the Wilder green taken in 1897. If you looked out the window now, you'd see almost exactly the same scene. Wilder lived for continuity and tradition; any change, no matter how small, like updating the font on the school stationery, was endlessly debated to be sure to preserve Wilder's "character." Debra hated what she thought of as Wilder's inherent conservatism, but I found it comforting to know things here would always stay the same.

"Honey? He's ready for you now." Dean Hansen's receptionist, a small woman in a Fair Isle sweater, nodded toward a heavy wooden door.

Dean Hansen's office looked like a hotel room, albeit the nicest hotel room I'd ever been in. Floor-length green-and-gold curtains, leather sofa, an oriental rug so plush I wanted to curl up on it and take a nap. Dean Hansen was sitting behind a wide embossed desk, empty except for a folder, a set of matching leather accessories, a Rolodex file, and a photo of his blond weak-chinned family standing on top of a snow-covered mountain.

"Still windy out there?" Dean Hansen said as he held out a hand. It was dry and papery. "Please," he said. "Have a seat."

Bill Hansen, Wilder's dean of students, was a small man with thinning blond hair and watery blue eyes. He appeared around campus at various ceremonial events, and his signature was on the letter informing each student of their acceptance to Wilder College. Other than that, he was a shadowy figure, rarely seen except for when he handled disciplinary matters. He was best known for the bow ties he wore every day. Today, it was a yellow one with whales.

"Have you made it up to the ski mountain yet?" he asked.

"Me? Um, no."

"Back when I was a student, we used to schedule all our winter classes for Tuesdays and Thursdays so we could spend long weekends skiing." I smiled, not wanting to tell him I didn't ski, never had, and that I'd come to Wilder not knowing it had its own ski mountain.

"Let's see what you've been doing instead of skiing." He opened the folder in front of him with one finger. His nails were pink and shiny, the cuffs of his sleeves monogrammed, like the labels my mother used to sew on my mittens.

"Well, well," he whistled. "You've done very well here. No wonder we haven't met before. English major, French minor. Member of Young Democrats, writer for *The Lamplighter* and *bitch slap*. You even played percussion in the marching band."

"For one semester," I said. "They needed someone to play the triangle."

He closed the folder. "So tell me a little bit about yourself, Isabel. Where are you from? What do your parents do?"

"I'm from New York. My father owns an appetizing store. My mom was a painter."

"An appetizing store? What's that?"

"It's like a deli, except delis serve meat and appetizing stores serve fish and dairy—cream cheese, smoked fish, herring. The kind of stuff you'd put on a bagel. Observant Jews don't mix meat and dairy, so the stores are sort of, you know, separate."

Dean Hansen nodded. I wasn't sure why I'd gotten so

specific. Most of the time, I said my father owned a deli and left it at that. No one here ever knew what an appetizing store was, and Dean Hansen didn't seem like someone who spent a lot of time around smoked fish.

"Any plans after graduation?"

"I'm not sure," I said. "I want to be a writer."

"Tough business." He leaned back in his chair. "I was a bit of a scribe myself when I was younger. Had my own column in the *Wilder Voice*." He talked for a while about what Wilder was like when he was a student in the early 1960s. It was the kind of conversation I would often find myself in later, when I was a writer, and someone, usually an older man, would corner me at a cocktail party or wedding and tell me the story of his life in case I might want to write about it, as if coming up with ideas was the hard part. And every time I found myself in that situation, I would think of Dean Hansen, by that point long dead of a rare cancer of the pituitary gland, and the morning I'd spent in his office.

"Isabel," he said, adjusting his face into a suitably grave expression. I tried to match it. "Just smile and nod and get out as fast as you can," Debra had said. "Admit nothing." She'd promised to buy me cheese fries when it was over.

"I'm sorry to say your name has come up with regard to an incident in the residence halls last month. You and another student have been accused of vandalizing a dorm room?" His voice rose to a question as if the whole idea was so ludicrous, how could it possibly be true?

"I spoke with your friend," he went on, checking his notes, "Debra Moscowitz, yesterday." He looked as if he were going to say something about Debra, but thought better of it. "She said it was a misunderstanding, that the three of you were friends, and this was some sort of a joke? Is that true?"

A joke? Is that what Debra had called it? "It wasn't really a joke," I said. "I mean, not exactly." I looked down at my lap. There was a white circle of skin peeking through a hole in my jeans. I covered it with my thumb.

"When I spoke to Mr. Neman, he told me your friend had a habit of doing things like this, but that you weren't the sort of person who would." As he spoke, saliva collected in the corners of his mouth. "Mr. Neman seemed to think you may have been under her influence. Or something to that effect."

I held my breath, thinking of Zev—Mr. Neman—sitting in this chair defending me.

"Can I ask," said Dean Hansen, "how long you and Zev have known each other?"

"Since freshman year."

"And were you friends?"

"Not exactly. I always thought he hated me."

"Well now, why would he hate you?"

"No—more like, he hates the *idea* of me." I shook my head. Why was I telling him this? In what universe would Dean Hansen understand the kind of Jew Zev thought I was—weak and self-hating and content to let other people carry machine guns to protect the Jewish state, which had taken his family in after the shah was overthrown and Khomeini came to power? "Where would we be without Israel?" he used to say. "Look at what happened to our people in every other country in the world, Isabel. You think your family left Russia because they wanted to sell smoked fish on the Lower East Side? They left because they were being slaughtered."

Dean Hansen was waiting for me to say something, but I had no idea what. I locked eyes with the girl in the photo on his desk—his daughter, I supposed. She was wearing ski goggles and a pale-pink parka and looked like the kind of girl about whom my mother would say, "Why can't you be friends with a nice girl like that?"

"I guess we were friends," I said finally. "The way you're friends with people here."

"In any event," Dean Hansen said, "Mr. Neman said he didn't want to get you into any trouble. And in light of your academic record, I'm going to let the vandalism charge go." And with that, he slid the folder to the side.

"Oh, that's great. Thank you so much."

"There's just one thing I'd like to discuss with you, if you don't mind. Mr. Neman said the two of you had had a consensual encounter that same night. And," he cleared his throat, "if that is the case, it is the nature of the vandalism more than the vandalism itself that concerns me." He raised an eyebrow as if to say, do you get my drift?

Dean Hansen looked uncomfortable, and I could tell this wasn't the conversation he wanted to be having, not today, not ever. "Isabel, forgive me if this sounds indelicate, but did some kind of assault take place? Because the word you wrote, even if it was a joke . . . That is to say, if something *did* happen, of that nature, that's something we would need to address above and beyond a simple vandalism charge. We take this sort of thing very seriously, you know."

"Nothing happened," I said, louder than I meant to.

"Are you certain?"

Admit nothing.

"Yes. I'm certain."

"Because I understand this might be hard to talk about."

"It's not."

He sat back in his chair and exhaled sharply. "Perhaps you'd be more comfortable talking about this with someone else. Dr. Cushman, for example, has more experience with this sort of thing." He flipped through his Rolodex, freed a card from its slot, and handed it to me. I knew Dr. Cushman, knew of her at least. Her office, in the basement of Potter Hall, was where girls were sent to talk about their bad sexual experiences and eating disorders—the full menu of women's psychological issues. I wondered if Dean Hansen remembered the letter Debra had written him the year before, saying that the placement of Dr. Cushman's office was "symbolic of how Wilder treats women: it tucks us away in the basement where our messy female problems can be hidden from view."

"Of course," Dean Hansen went on, "I have no reason to challenge your interpretation of events, but something made you go back to Mr. Neman's room and write that word on his door. And if that is not what happened . . . I'm sure you understand we need to take these things seriously. Because they are serious." He folded his hands and smiled, a grandfatherly sort of smile that was stern and condescending at the same time.

"Dean Hansen," I said, looking down at the card in my

hands. I could feel tears pressing on the back of my eyelids. I willed them not to fall.

"Yes, Isabel?"

"Do you have to tell my father about this?"

"Your father?"

"I really don't want him to know . . ." My voice cracked, and I tried to imagine what I looked like to Dean Hansen, how desperate and sad. I wondered if he'd felt as desperate about anything in his whole life. It was hard to imagine.

He pursed his lips. "I don't see why he needs to know about this. You just be sure to take care of yourself. Go and see Dr. Cushman. Or try the ski mountain! Nothing like a day on the slopes to cure what ails you."

"I will. I promise." At that point, I would have promised him anything.

"Stay warm out there," he said as I pulled on my coat. "These are the days when it feels like spring will never come."

I stumbled out of his office and into the bright winter morning. It had snowed overnight, a thick layer that covered everything, blotting out every imperfection. I wished it could do the same for me. I pictured Debra walking out of this same meeting, the one she'd assured me was no big deal. Of course *she* thought it was no big deal. Nothing was a big deal to Debra, who barreled through life with little thought to how her actions affected other people. Everything landed more heavily on me.

It was nearly ten. I'd have to hurry to not be late for Professor Maxwell's class, or what used to be her class, but my heart was beating so fast I had to stop and sit down on the nearest bench. It was one of those memorial benches, the kind you saw around campus dedicated to the memory of someone who had died—in this case, according to the plaque, Walter "Binky" Ballard, Class of 1979. Abe and I hadn't done anything to commemorate my mother, gone now almost four years. She'd been cremated, even though Jews didn't believe in cremation, and her ashes were still in the box they'd come in, which was stashed in the back of Abe's closet last I'd checked. "We look forward, not back," Abe said, and so that is what we did. But sometimes the feeling backed up on me, the way it did now. Would I feel better, I wondered, if my mother had a bench like Binky Ballard?

After a few minutes, I stood up and started walking to class. I stopped when I heard someone yell, "Look out!"

Joanna Maxwell was crouched down on the snow a few feet in front of me. She had her arm around a small girl. "I'm sorry I yelled," she said. "I didn't want you to step in it." She pointed at a puddle of vomit by my feet.

"Oh, that's all right," I said. "Are you okay?"

The little girl looked up at me, then back at her boots. This was Igraine, Joanna Maxwell and Tom Fisher's daughter. She shared her name with the mother of King Arthur, and it seemed a heavy mantle for such a little person. Igraine was around four—I didn't know anything about children, but remembered she'd been a baby when I first came to Wilder. Tiny and delicate like her mother, Igraine's coloring was all Tom: fair skin, green eyes, strawberry-blond hair. Igraine was quiet and serious. She wasn't one of those kids who worked for your attention or approval, and I admired that about her.

"You're okay, aren't you darling?" Joanna said, wiping her daughter's face with a tissue. "You just drank your hot chocolate too fast."

Joanna had on a long down coat that looked like a sleeping bag and a thick plaid scarf. Her worn tennis shoes were wet with snow, her gray eyes framed with eyelashes so pale they were almost invisible. My Aunt Fanny had eyelashes like that, which she coated with thick layers of mascara that always ran down her face. "What a shame to be fair like Fanny," my mother used to say, as if she had an incurable disease.

"Professor Maxwell," I said as she fumbled in her bag. "I wanted to tell you, I reread *Birdbrain* over break. I think I've read it half a dozen times now."

"Thank you, dear," she said. "That's so kind."

"I read somewhere you'd thought about telling the story again, from the grandmother's point of view? Is that true?"

Igraine was tugging on her mother's sleeve. "I'm looking for it, sweetheart. Oh, people used to ask me that and I think I said that once, to be nice. I did consider it, but not anymore. Other stories got in the way. Ah, here it is!" She held up a pacifier triumphantly, then cleaned it with her own mouth before handing it to Igraine. The child relaxed instantly, her eyes drooping as she leaned against her mother.

"Oh well," I said. "Then I guess it's perfect the way it is."

Joanna rested her knees on the ground and loosened her scarf. When she did, I saw a dark bruise at the base of her neck.

The clock on the bell tower began its ten o'clock descant.

"I have to go," I said. "Or I'll be late for class. I'm so sorry you won't be teaching this semester."

"Yes," she said, and I thought I heard a catch in her voice. "Have a lovely day," she called after me, and I promised her I would.

4

I'D wanted to get to class early, but my meeting with Dean Hansen and the encounter with Professor Maxwell had slowed me down so I ran in just as the professor started taking attendance. I slid into an empty seat at the far end of the seminar table, pulled out a spiral notebook, and wrote my name and the date at the top: "Isabel Rosen. January 7, 1998." It was the same way I'd been heading papers since the first grade. It occurred to me briefly that this might be the last first day of school I'd ever have.

"Isabel, how the heck are ya?" Whitney Shaw clapped me on the back. Whitney was a field hockey player from Southern California. She had a long straight nose and ruddy complexion. She looked as if she'd spent a lot of time at sea.

"You know, living the dream," I said, lifting my hand as the professor called my name.

"Did you have a good Christmas? Wait—do you guys even celebrate Christmas?"

"I mean, no—"

"God! Sorry. My bad." Whitney's voice was raspy, like she'd grown up breathing in too much fresh air. Stacks of paper made their way around the table as Whitney told me about her winter break: two weeks on Jupiter Island, golfing with her dad, lunches at the club with her grandmother. "She's an epic bitch, but she bankrolls everything. The only price is fealty." She pressed her palms together and bowed her head. "Oh, hey, I meant to ask: Is everything okay with you?"

"Yeah. Why?"

"I heard something happened between you and Zev Neman."

I'd forgotten Whitney lived in Zev's dorm.

"It was nothing," I said, taking a copy of the syllabus and passing the pile to Whitney. "We're cool now."

English 76: The Art of Writing Fiction. Professor R. H. Connelly. I looked up at the man sitting at the head of the table. Joanna's replacement, I supposed. Andy hadn't known who was taking her place, and this wasn't anyone I recognized. He seemed to be around forty, but I wasn't sure: anyone older than me but younger than my father occupied a stratum I could not see. His thick dark hair was flecked with gray, and his face held the shadow of a beard. He was tall and broad-shouldered, big but not heavy. His body had a solidity that, although I'd never thought about it before, came only with age.

Whitney started to say something else, but the professor started talking.

"You're probably wondering if you're in the right room," he said. "This *is* English 76, but as you can see, I am *not* Professor Maxwell. I'm Professor Connelly, and I'll be filling in for Joanna this semester."

A quick scan of the room revealed who had heard the news about Professor Maxwell and who hadn't.

Professor Connelly leaned back in his chair and folded his hands across his chest. His hands were big, like he could easily palm a basketball or the top of your skull. On the back of his right hand, a thick ropy scar snaked from index finger to wrist. On his left, he wore a simple gold wedding band.

"Joanna and I have known each other for years," the professor said. "She's a damn good writer and a helluva teacher. I'm truly sorry you won't have the opportunity to study with her." As he talked, he rubbed his thumb back and forth across his leather watchband. It looked weathered, like he wore it all the time, even in the shower. "So who am I, other than a pale comparison? I'm best known as a poet, but I've written all sorts of things, short stories, essays, a couple of novels still in the proverbial drawer. Now I work as a reporter at the *Daily Citizen*. Best job I've ever had, by the way. You write every day, you're always on deadline. No sitting around waiting for your 'muse.' Journalism is utilitarian, it's purposeful. There's nothing precious about it. How many of you read newspapers?" A couple of us raised our hands. "Good," he said, his eyes resting briefly on me. "People like to value art for art's sake, but the way I see it, literature is all around us. It's real life. It's school board meetings and droughts. Missing kids and corrupt politicians. Conflict. Resolution. Man against nature. If you can't make people care about the community they live in, how can you get them to care about anything?" He reached for his water bottle, took a noisy sip. I had the feeling he wasn't used to talking this much. "I'm a lot happier than I used to be, I'll tell you that. It also pays the bills, which I know none of you care about yet, but you will."

He was quiet for a minute. His dark eyes shone like a bottle of Goldschläger held up to the light, and he had the kind of eyelashes my mother would have said were wasted on a man. There was something familiar about him, the way he touched himself as he spoke, running a hand through his hair, rubbing his chin, tracing the scar on the back of his hand with one finger, as if he were testing the boundaries of himself, to make sure he still existed.

He turned his face to the window. "But that's not why you're here. You're writers. You want to write. So." He slapped his hands on the table. "Can I teach you how to write? Joanna would say yes. She believes anyone who wants to write can, as long as you have the right tools." He picked up a copy of the syllabus. "If she were teaching, this whole thing would be full of workshops. We'd pull your stories apart and put them back together again. Tools, craft, feedback, critique. Follow X to get to Y, and Z will follow. As for me," he tossed the paper down, "I have no clue. All I know about writing is you sit down and write, and sometimes, if you're lucky, the words come. All I know is some people are talented and some aren't, and some stick with it no matter what. Others give up. The truth is, most of you won't become writers. You're here at this fancy school and, let's be honest, I don't think your parents sent you here hoping you'd become writers. They sent you here so you could learn to make money, to become doctors and lawyers and investment bankers and consultants, whatever the fuck those are." I giggled into my hand. I'd never heard a professor talk like this before, not just the profanity but the acknowledgment that he didn't have all the answers. That he was as lost as we were.

"So," Professor Connelly said, looking around the room. Everyone was waiting, their pens poised above their notebooks, unsure what, if anything, we should be writing down. "What *can* I teach you? I can teach you to be honest, to tell the truth, to look at the things you're afraid to see. To not be afraid of what your friends will think or what your parents will think, to peel away the bullshit and see things for what they are. To find moral clarity in your work and in your life."

Whitney poked me with her pen. In the margin of her notebook, she'd written "Hot for Teacher???" in big letters. I scribbled over it, felt my face get hot. I had noticed as Professor Connelly was speaking that he was handsome, very handsome. He might in fact have been the most handsome man I'd ever seen at Wilder, maybe anywhere. There was a whiff of scandal about him, although maybe I filled in that part later. When I was older, I would find men like him too handsome for their own good, striding into bars and conference rooms like mortal gods. But back then, I still believed beauty conferred a kind of moral superiority and so, as I watched him walk over to the window, traced the line of his shirt with my eyes to where it disappeared down the back of his pants, I would have followed him anywhere.

"Let's begin," he said, and so we did.

"I want you to write about something you've lost. It can be anything—an object, a person, an illusion. Your virginity." Ramona Diaz, the only junior in the class, laughed a short, nervous laugh. Whitney raised her hand, but Professor Connelly ignored her. "Now close your eyes and picture it." I looked around the room. Only Ginny McDougall had her eyes closed, but she might have been asleep.

"Come on. Close them." I waited until everyone had closed their eyes, then closed mine. "Write about the first thing that comes to mind, the thing that scares you, the thing you *don't* want to write about. The thing you don't want your mother to know about, or your best friend. Or your lover." I could hear him walking around the table, the soft slap of his boots, the jingle of something in his pocket. "What's it like to lose something you can never get back? What does your life look like—what does it *feel* like—without it? Maybe you've grown used to its absence. Maybe you haven't." He stopped behind me and rested his hands on the back of my chair; if I leaned back, my shoulder blades would have touched his fingers. "Whatever it is, start writing. Keep your pen moving no matter what. You'll think it's shit, and a lot of it will be. But I'm here to tell you, it isn't all shit." I could hear him breathing, could smell him. Woodsmoke and peppermint. I held my breath, felt it swell in my chest until

I couldn't hold it anymore. Professor Connelly whispered, "Now go."

The first thing that came to my mind was Binky Ballard—lost to his family and friends, lost to time, to the world—and so I wrote about Binky, imagining the life he'd had at Wilder and beyond. I kept my pen moving, as Professor Connelly had instructed, and before I knew it Binky and the family he'd left behind dissolved into a story about my mother, shuffling around our kitchen in her cornflower-blue bathrobe, boiling coffee on the stove in a silver espresso pot someone had brought her from Italy, one of many places she had never been and would never go. I wrote about my mother, Vivian, sitting at the kitchen table, turning the pages of the *New York Times*, half listening as I told her about my day, thinking instead about the painting she was working on, the one she would turn her attention to as soon as I left, the painting I would run home to see at the end of the day. Everything fell away and I was back in that kitchen overlooking the alleyway, alone with my mother, a cork-screw curl brushing her cheek as she cradled her coffee cup in her hands. I could hear her breathing, the quick rasp on the inhale, coffee breath on the exhale, the smell of paint thinner and perfume so strong I was sure Whitney could smell it. "My mother will never be an old woman," I wrote once, twice, three times in a row. I mouthed the words silently and felt weak.

I closed my eyes, dizzy with remembering, but my pen kept moving, as if it were no longer connected to my hand. The memory shifted again, and I was back in our kitchen the night she died, coffeepot still on the stove, bathrobe hanging behind the bathroom door. Everything there but her. There was a knock on the door. It was the man from the crematorium holding a pair of her earrings. The hospital had forgotten to remove them, he said, and he'd come from Brooklyn to bring them to us. "I thought the girl might want them," he said to Abe, with a pitying glance my way. Abe thanked him, too effusively I thought. When he was gone, Abe dropped the earrings on the table and poured himself a drink, then poured one for me. In the morning, the earrings were still there, some cheap shitty pair like every cheap shitty thing in our apartment. Like her cheap shitty life. I picked up the earrings and tossed them out the window. They landed in the alleyway behind our building where, as far as I knew, they were still.

"Stop writing." Professor Connelly was back in his seat. I had no idea how much time had passed. My palm was wet; I had sweat through my bra. I'd written almost eight pages in my notebook. Across from me, Holly Crane and Alec Collier, who looked like brother and sister and went everywhere holding hands, were each giggling at what the other had written. Linus Harrison, who told anyone who would listen that his grandfather invented the paper shredder, was copying the details of the syllabus into his PalmPilot. Only Andy was still writing; from where I was sitting, I could see he had barely a page.

Professor Connelly was looking right at me. "How was that?" he asked. Before I could answer, he licked his thumb and used it to turn over a paper in front of him. "Now, as for the syllabus, we'll start with Matthiessen . . ."

When class was over, I picked up my things and headed for the door. "Do you think Professor Maxwell is pregnant again?" I heard Ramona ask Kara Jiang, whose eyes I couldn't see well enough beneath her thick bangs to gauge a response. Professor Connelly was sliding papers into his briefcase; his long legs were stretched out under the table, crossed at the ankles. He looked up as I passed, his gaze moving slowly from my eyes to my chin, down the length of my body, coming to rest at the tips of my boots. I felt blood rush to places I'd forgotten about: my pinky toe, earlobes, the backs of my knees. Then he flicked his eyes to mine again and released me. Andy stopped to talk to him, reached out a hand. "Pleasure to meet you," I heard him say as I ducked into the hallway and placed a hand on my cheek. My skin felt hot and alive, as if the membrane that protected me from the world had thinned just a little.

Andy caught up with me outside.

"Isabel! Wait." His army-green jacket hung open over his T-shirt, and he was wearing the hat I'd made him. "I'm sorry," he said, trotting over. "Really, I am. Look. I'm wearing your hat." He touched his head, then held up a peace sign.

"Fine."

He tapped a pack of cigarettes against his hand and offered me one.

"So, who is that guy?" I asked.

Andy lit my cigarette with his scuffed silver Zippo. "The professor? That's R. H. Connelly."

"Yeah, I know. But who *is* he?"

"God, okay! Don't get mad! He's a poet. Wrote a couple

of books back in the eighties. Domain-changing stuff. Sold, too. There might have been a novel, not very good." He reached under the hat and scratched his head. "I think he was on the cover of *Time* magazine or something. Then he totally disappeared. I always wondered what happened to him."

"He's covering school board meetings in White River Junction."

"I know! What the hell. Seriously, his stuff was good." He took a long drag. "How does a guy like that end up working at some small-town paper?"

"Writers have to make a living. Isn't that what he said?"

Andy shrugged. "Anyway, turns out he's good friends with Joanna and Tom. Not sure how I missed that. Oh, and he's married to Roxanne Stevenson."

"Huh." Roxanne Stevenson was a professor in the history department. British historian. I'd never taken a class with her, but my mother and I used to see her on TV in documentaries about the royal family. I'd just seen her on a *20/20* I watched over break, one of the zillion retrospectives about the life of Princess Di.

"I saw Zev Neman last night at Agora," Andy said, and the sudden shift in topic made me dizzy. "I swear I didn't say anything, but he brought you up."

"Andy, I don't want to talk about this."

"No one in his dorm will talk to him. Everyone heard what you and Debra did and he's, like, a pariah now. I felt kinda bad for the guy, actually."

"Andy—"

"He said he's really confused about what happened and just

wants to talk. Honestly Isabel, I think he might be obsessed with you."

"Goodbye, Andy," I said, flicking my cigarette into the snow and turning on my heel. The wind picked up, and I tightened my coat around my waist. I could hear Andy calling after me, but I didn't turn back.

5

WHEN I was young and my mother was well, she used to host dinner parties in our apartment. She'd set a long table diagonally across our living room, cover it with a thick ivory tablecloth, drape pieces of fabric over the furniture, and dim the lights so the shabby paint job wasn't as noticeable. She'd set the table with our "fine" china—I don't know how fine it was, but something other than the plates we used every day—chunky crystal goblets and cloth napkins, everything a bit mismatched because pieces had broken over the years, or maybe we'd never had a matching set to begin with. I don't remember what she cooked or who came or what they talked about. All I remember is the way my mother could transform our home into something beautiful, at least for one night. Come morning, the spell would be broken.

Most businesses like Rosen's were family businesses, but my mother made it clear that the store belonged to Abe and she wanted nothing to do with it. My parents' marriage had always been a mystery to me, but this part wasn't. Later, I would realize the toll this took on Abe, and on me, when I stepped in to help the way a wife might have, but back then, it made sense. My mother was an artist, and her art always came first.

When I came home from school, I would often find her standing by the easel, still in her bathrobe, hair unwashed, breakfast dishes on the table, having worried over the same corner of canvas all day. When I was little, she would set up a small easel for me next to hers, and I would try to see the world the way she did, in colors and shapes and touches of light. But no matter how hard I tried, I never could. Later, when I started writing, I hid my work from her, certain that what I created wasn't art, at least not the way she defined it. It was neither tortuous nor difficult. It didn't bring me pain.

There was a poster I passed every day on my way in and out of my dorm, tacked to a bulletin board, a message of hope for those considering taking their own lives: "Don't make permanent decisions to cope with temporary feelings." The words floated above a picture of a tree that reminded me of a series my mother had painted then sold to my dentist in exchange for some bill or other. She often painted that tree, the only one we could see from our living room window. It was a sad little thing, scraggly and wan, surrounded by empty beer cans and piles of dog shit. But in my mother's paintings, she always placed it somewhere else, in a field surrounded by wildflowers or next to a mountain stream. She seemed to be searching for something in her work, a life beyond Rosen's Appetizing and the Lower East

Side. Escape. She wouldn't have been the first artist looking for that.

KELSEY AND JASON were in our room when I got back on Friday afternoon. Kelsey was at her desk, her fingers flying across the keyboard of her turquoise iMac. Jason was stretched out across the couch reading *Rabbit, Run.* Sarah McLachlan played quietly on the boom box.

Jason sat up to make room for me. "Where have you been?" Kelsey asked, still facing her computer. She had one foot tucked underneath her and, from where I was sitting, it looked like it was growing out of the crack in her ass.

"At the information desk."

"Really?" she said, turning around. "I didn't know you were working today."

"They needed me to take an extra shift. Ramona had cramps." Kelsey turned back to her computer, and I took out my cigarettes. Jason handed me the peanut butter lid I used as an ashtray. He hated when I smoked, something about a grandmother who had lung cancer, but he didn't say anything because that was Jason, sweet and rosy. Perennially agreeable. My mother would have called him a marzipan man.

"I never asked you how Maxwell's seminar was," he asked. Kelsey stopped typing.

"It was okay," I said. "Do you know she isn't teaching?"

"I think everyone knows."

"Knows what?" Kelsey asked, turning around again.

"Professor Maxwell isn't teaching this semester," Jason said. "She and Professor Fisher are getting a divorce."

"Is that the couple with the cute little girl and the house on June Bridge Road?" Kelsey asked. Jason nodded. "Aww, that's so sad!" She turned back to her typing.

"Do you know the guy who's subbing for her?" I asked Jason.

"R. H. Connelly? Yeah. I've read some of his stuff. The poems are amazing, and he wrote this one crazy novel everyone hated but I kind of liked. I always wondered what happened to him. Actually, I thought he killed himself." I thought about the scar on Professor Connelly's hand. "How's Andy doing?"

Kelsey groaned.

"What?" asked Jason.

"She hates Andy," I said.

"Babe, you don't hate anyone."

Kelsey turned around again. "Well, I don't like Andy. He's pretentious, and he treats you like shit."

"He does not," Jason said. "Not all the time." Jason and Andy were coeditors of the *Lamplighter*, Wilder's literary magazine. Theirs was a cordial rivalry, although lately Andy had been giving Jason a hard time about applying to law school. Jason's parents tolerated his English major—a gentleman should be well read—but the expectation was that he would become a lawyer like his father, and Jason was too nice to object.

"He has great hair though," I said. "You gotta give him that."

"Yeah," Kelsey said sadly, twirling a strand of her thin blond hair. "He does. Hey, are you coming to Gamma Nu tonight?"

I looked at her blankly.

"Their winter beach party. Remember? They have it every year."

"Right," I said. Every January, Jason's fraternity Gamma Nu Alpha filled the first floor of their house with sand and blasted space heaters until everyone was sweating and girls were forced to strip down to their bras. A lot of straw hats and Jimmy Buffett. Last year, the floor had nearly collapsed under the weight of the sand but, I'd been told, it had since been reinforced. I wasn't a fan of fraternities and found Jason's devotion to Gamma Nu off-putting and out of character, but they threw good parties and in tiny Wilder, New Hampshire, a town with only one bar, that was no small thing.

"Bo Benson will be there," Kelsey said.

"Kelsey."

"What?"

"Stop trying to make Bo Benson happen."

"Why? He likes you—doesn't he, J? Plus he's cute. And really nice."

"That is all true," I said. "But let me ask you something: Does that sound like someone I would go out with?"

Jason looked at his watch. "Babe, I gotta go." He stood up and put his hands on Kelsey's shoulders. She turned and gave him a quick kiss. I looked away, not wanting to get caught admiring their easy, unstudied intimacy. Kelsey and Jason had been together forever—or what felt like forever, since the first week of freshman year—so I was used to sharing her. I'd always known she didn't need me as much as I needed her.

Debra walked in as Jason was leaving. "Don't everybody

leave on my account. Ugh, do we have to listen to this sad-girl music *all* the time?"

I pulled her into the bedroom while Kelsey walked Jason downstairs.

"I had the meeting with Dean Hansen," I said. "Where have you been?"

"Oh, right," she said, flopping onto the bed. "I forgot about that. How was it?"

"It absolutely sucked. But he said he would let it go."

"See? I told you."

"He gave me Dr. Cushman's card, in case I 'need some-one to talk to.'" I pulled the card out of my pocket and handed it to Debra.

"Fucking Dr. Cushman." She studied the card briefly, then tossed it back at me. "I wonder how many girls he's sent down there. A lot of good she does. Remember Elizabeth McIntosh?"

I nodded. Elizabeth McIntosh was a senior when we were sophomores, one of those tall, thin, prep-school types; Kelsey knew her from summers in Quogue. For more than a year, we'd watched Elizabeth climbing the stairs from Dr. Cushman's office two or three times a week. It was clear she had a pretty serious eating disorder, but back then I found that sort of thing glamorous. Then one day, a week before she graduated, she was taken away in an ambulance, an outrageously dramatic event on our tiny campus and one people still talked about nearly two years later. According to Kelsey, Elizabeth was doing better, but one could hardly call her a shining endorsement of Dr. Cushman's clinical prowess.

I lay down next to Debra. "How's Reinhard?" Debra had spent the last couple of nights with Reinhard, a German grad student who'd delivered pizza to our room before break.

"He's a pain in my ass. Now I know why my mother warned me about German guys."

Kelsey popped her head in and asked Debra if she was going to Gamma Nu's beach party.

"No," Debra scoffed, and I knew where the conversation was heading. I folded Dr. Cushman's card into a tiny square as I listened to them argue, first about the Greek system and what Debra called its corrosive influence on campus life, then about whose turn it was to clean the bathroom. At some point, I would intervene, remind Debra that she'd had fun the last time we went to Gamma Nu—we'd convinced the DJ to play Björk all night—and tell Kelsey that Debra was the one who'd cleaned the bathroom last time, even though it was also true she made the biggest mess. But for now, I sat there listening. I found the sound of their bickering comforting.

My eyes rested on a picture of us on the dresser. It was taken in the fall of freshman year, not long after we met. We made an unlikely trio: Kelsey, tall and blond in a Patagonia fleece and round tortoiseshell glasses; Debra, broad and busty, her thick dark hair cut chin-length so her head floated atop her neck like a triangle; and me, the smallest, standing between them, swallowed up by my long skirt and oversized sweater. I was always cold that year, my body adjusting to the northern weather, the way the cold creeped into your skin like a sickness. Debra said when she first met me, she thought I was Orthodox.

My mother used to warn me about threesomes, but I'd never had friends like Debra and Kelsey. My high school friends were harder and meaner, a desperation born out of their hardscrabble lives. Debra and Kelsey had love and security to spare, and they shared it with me freely. They brought me soup when I was sick, held my hair back when I puked. Last year, we'd gone to Jamaica together over spring break and they'd helped pay my way—it wasn't a big deal to them, they said, and they wouldn't have dreamed of going without me.

"You guys," I said, as their bickering reached a crescendo. "Isn't it chili night?"

"Is it Friday?" Kelsey asked. Debra nodded. "Then it is indeed chili night."

I stood up and tossed Dr. Cushman's card in the trash. "Well, let's go." And so we did.

6

THE door to Professor Fisher's office was open when I arrived, but I knocked anyway.

He waved for me to come in. "Isabel. Sit, sit. I'm almost finished with your pages. Want one?" He held out a bag of Starburst.

I took a handful, then sat down on the faded plaid sofa next to a tower of manila folders. There were similar stacks all over Tom Fisher's office—on the floor, on a broken chair in the corner, on the two overstuffed bookshelves by the door. I'd run here, worried I was late, but saw I needn't have. Professor Fisher—or Tom, as he insisted I call him—didn't seem to know what time it was. I unwrapped a Starburst and waited for him to finish reading the pages I'd left him last week.

Tom's office on the second floor of Stringer Hall was a few doors down from Joanna Maxwell's. Igraine usually sat somewhere in the hallway between them, coloring or writing in a black composition notebook, but she wasn't there today. The large window behind Tom's desk overlooked the campus green; the half dozen plants on the windowsill were lush and overgrown, making it look like he was working in a tiny jungle. There was a poster of Cesar Chavez on the wall next to a sign promoting the now-defunct Wilder Grape Policy Action Committee. The whole room reeked of cigarettes—Tom rolled his own, a ritual he repeated several times during our weekly meetings to discuss my thesis, a literary examination of domestic spaces in Edith Wharton's *The Age of Innocence.*

"Well, hot damn!" Tom said when he finished reading. His voice was loud, foghorn loud. It was one of the many things I liked about him, along with his tattered sweaters, potbelly, and slightly lazy left eye. "This is really shaping up into something! Don't you think?"

"Oh, I don't know."

"I have to admit, I was worried for a while, but here, the way you bring in Darwinism. 'Wharton's society is a tightly constructed ecosystem and Countess Olenska the contagion that must be cast out.'" His face broke into a lopsided smile, and I couldn't help but smile, too. I had no idea if my thesis was shaping up into something or not. I just stuck five pages into Tom's mailbox every week and waited for him to pass judgment. "So, what's next?"

I told him about the section I was working on about the iconoclastic Mrs. Mingott, Ellen Olenska's grandmother and fiercest defender, who shocks New York society by living above Thirty-Fourth Street and placing her bedroom on the ground floor. It was an arrangement old New York found shocking because from the sitting room, one might catch "the unexpected vista of a bedroom." Such arrangements, Wharton wrote, "recalled scenes in French fiction" by providing "the stage-setting of adultery."

"Okay," Tom said, reaching for his rolling papers. "But when are you going to write about money? Money's the engine for everything in this world, even if no one wants to talk about it. It's one of those 'unpleasant' topics they avoid at all costs. They hate the nouveaux riches, but they need them to survive. The joke is New York was always a commercial society. Its aristocracy was never based on birth—it was based on *money*. They just liked to pretend otherwise." He drizzled tobacco into the trough he'd created and licked the cigarette shut.

Tom hadn't been a fan of Wharton when we started working together. He'd largely dismissed her work because of her social conservatism and wealth and had only reluctantly agreed to be my adviser. But he'd warmed to her since then, which I took as a compliment. I'd learned a lot from him, too. I'd always loved Wharton's novel about doomed love in old New York, but Tom had pushed me to examine the social forces that roiled beneath the surface. "We think our stories are personal," he told me, "but we're all products of our time."

He handed my pages back to me. "Keep going, Isabel. You can do it. I know you can." He lit his cigarette, took a puff. "How's the fiction seminar going?"

"Good so far."

"Connelly's an old friend of mine. I'll put in a word." He smiled again, and I remembered what Andy had said about the divorce, the way he'd hinted at something ominous. But Tom seemed to be his normal, gregarious self, and I was happy to think Andy might be wrong.

"Thanks a lot," I said. "So I'll see you next week?"

"Actually, Isabel, do you have a minute? I wanted to talk to you about something—something other than Wharton." Tom rested his cigarette on his ashtray as a gust of wind rattled the window. "I don't think we need to meet every week anymore. You're in pretty good shape and, well, I'm going through a bit of a rough patch at home. I don't know if you've heard, but Joanna and I are getting a divorce."

I wasn't sure how to respond. I assumed professors knew we gossiped about them, but I didn't know if I was supposed to acknowledge it.

"I could get the department to assign you to a different adviser," he continued, "but I don't think that's necessary. I'll still sign off on your pages, so it shouldn't affect your progress. And, as charming as these meetings are, I'm not sure they're entirely necessary."

I nodded, although I found them vital. But I understood why Tom didn't want to ask the department to find me a different adviser because asking the department meant asking Joanna.

"I'm sorry about all this," he went on. "None of it is your fault. What do they call it? Collateral damage?" He laughed. "Joanna and I have been together for more than twenty years, so I guess you could say we've had a good run. Twenty years. God, I feel old saying that. And the whole time, we were always able to talk to each other, you know? Like, really talk. Some couples lose that. Not us, despite *everything*." He stressed the word so intensely, I could feel the weight of it across the room.

Tom turned his face toward the window. I unwrapped another candy. Outside, a few students were walking across the green, hunched over to protect themselves from the wind.

"It got hard when Joanna's career took off. She was constantly on the road. But I was so proud of her! And when she wanted to move to New Hampshire, I said fine, even though it was a detour for my career. My career. What a joke." He looked down at his hands. I noticed he was still wearing his wedding ring. "Are your parents divorced, Isabel?"

"Mine? No."

"That's good. Because I think all of this is hardest on Igraine. Poor thing. Joanna was the one who wanted a kid," he said, as though I'd suggested otherwise. "People said things change after you have a child. I thought, well, they don't know Joanna. They don't know *us*." His cigarette was still resting on the ashtray, gradually turning to ash. He picked it up and took a shaky drag. "We went through a lot to have her, but I wouldn't trade any of it. Igraine is the light of my life! More than that—she's *everything* to me." There was that word again. "Does your mother work?"

"My mother? I mean, not really. She was an artist."

"Oh! So you know what it's like! Being married to an artist, all the time and focus needed for creation." His already loud voice was getting louder. "I understood that going in, but then you have a child and everything changes. The time you once had for each other disappears. The work always comes first. And you know that, sure, but in the meantime, you have this little person and someone has to raise her and take her to the pediatrician and make sure she has boots. Someone has to wake up with her when she has a nightmare and bake cupcakes for her birthday. People say, 'Oh, that's what mothers do. *Fathers* don't get involved with *that*.'" His voice was loud, mocking, singsong. "You know what I mean, don't you?"

I nodded, but what did I know? I'd never thought of myself as a burden to my parents, any more than a houseplant might be, or a goldfish. But then again, Abe would never have imagined a burden that didn't fall on him. Maybe I was just another part of what he was willing to bear.

Tom was still talking. "'Tom, can you bring her to your sister's for the weekend? I have to finish this chapter. Tom, can you take her to the playground? I need time to prepare for my lecture.'" He was practically shouting. I wondered if people could hear him down the hall. "I'm the one who gave it to her, the awards and novels—*my* career be damned. And now *she* wants to take it away?" He slammed his hand on the desk, sending a flurry of candy wrappers to the floor. The plants behind him swayed, rustled by the force of his anger. And then, just as quickly as it had started, it was over.

The bells on the clock tower started to ring. It was twelve o'clock. If I didn't leave soon, I would be late for my next class. Tom picked up his cigarette, now just a column of ash, and took one last drag before grinding it out. "Why don't we plan to meet in, say, a month? In the meantime, you can continue leaving pages in my mailbox. Oh, and Isabel? Would you let Amos Jackson know about my situation? I think he's still up north." Amos was Tom's other advisee, but I didn't know him well and couldn't imagine how I would convey all of this to him.

I stepped into the hallway feeling shaky and unsettled. It wasn't the first time I'd seen a man lash out in this way, nor would it be the last. But it was the first time I felt myself on the receiving end of it, although, of course, I wasn't. Tom would have had his tantrum—because that's what it was—whether I'd been there or not. There were a few students milling around in the hall. Holly and Alec were sitting together on the floor, their heads bent over a copy of *Vanity Fair*. They called my name as I passed. If they'd heard Tom's outburst, they didn't seem bothered by it. I slowed down in front of Joanna Maxwell's office, her name stenciled in gold on the milky glass door. Taped to it was a schedule of her classes from last semester, a black-and-white postcard of Virginia Woolf, a couple of *New Yorker* cartoons. In the corner under her name, a small index card read "On Leave Winter 1998. Please direct all inquiries to Mary Pat Grimaldi."

THE LIBRARY WAS busier the second week of the semester. The reading room was filling up, but still not full. I spotted Whitney barricaded behind a stack of books, dragging a yellow highlighter lazily across the pages of an article. She waved me over, but I pointed to my watch and kept moving.

I stopped in front of the card catalog, pulled open one of the long skinny drawers and flipped through the cards until I found the one I was looking for: Connelly, R. H. 1958–. Over the weekend, I'd read the *Time* magazine article Andy had told me about. Professor Connelly wasn't on the cover, but he had been prominently featured in a story about contemporary writers who were "reshaping the landscape of American poetry." He was one of several poets they profiled, mostly white, good-looking men in their twenties and thirties who had turned their backs on the 1980s ethos of get rich at any cost and chosen to write poetry instead. "And readers," the article went on, "mostly young women, are responding." One of the poets was a Princeton grad, former ROTC, photographed riding a tractor on his Montana ranch. Another, with long black hair to his shoulders, was sitting behind the wheel of a '67 Mustang parked in a graffiti-covered alley. Professor Connelly was photographed standing barefoot in front of a cabin in the woods. He was wearing a flannel shirt and jeans; behind him was a pile of firewood and an axe leaning against a tree stump.

According to the article, R. H. Connelly was born into an Irish Catholic family in New Jersey. His love of literature alienated him from his working-class parents—his father was an airline mechanic, his mother a cafeteria worker (one of his poems, "Lunch Lady," was about her). He left home early, worked as a construction worker, train conductor, waiter, all the while writing poetry. He eventually published two books; the second, *I'm Sorry I Can't Stay Long*, about the death of his father, garnered rave reviews and an important prize. According to the article, he'd received countless love letters, even marriage proposals, from enthusiastic readers. One young woman had driven up to his cabin, where he retreated when he needed peace and inspiration, to profess her love. "She was a sweet girl," he said, "a poetry lover and an old soul." But he was a gentleman and wouldn't say more.

Card in hand, I headed into the stacks, up to the fourth floor where poetry was shelved. At the end of our last class, Professor Connelly had said, "When you write, you have to take people to the closet. Not to the living room or the kitchen, not even to your bedroom. No, you take them straight to the goddamn closet, the place you keep your most secret, unmentionable things." I thought about that as I sat down on the floor and opened his first book, *A World of Green*. I did it slowly and carefully, as though I were running my hand through his underwear drawer.

This first collection was quiet, poems about nature mostly, sunsets, seashells, the play of light on a blade of grass. When I told Jason once that I didn't understand poetry, he said, "That's because you're searching for meaning. You have to let the work happen to you. Forget whether you understand it or not—how does it make you *feel*?" As I read Connelly's work, I could feel myself grasping for meaning, looking for a narrative strand that would help me understand the work and, by extension, him. I read all the poems through once, then took a deep breath and read them again—and again— until I felt myself letting go. I let his language wash over me and, after a while, felt it wriggle inside, burrowing in like earthworms.

Connelly's second book, *I'm Sorry I Can't Stay Long*, was shorter than the first, not much thicker than a pamphlet. It seemed funny to me that such a big man would write such slim books. Connelly's relationship with his father had been fraught. He was an angry man, an alcoholic, competitive with his only son in all the worst ways, and yet Connelly wrote about him lovingly. In one poem, he described his father standing on a patch of grass outside his house, beer in hand, watching planes take off. It reminded me of a poem from his first book about a man watching a flock of geese cross the sky overhead. There was something sad about both images, two men yearning for a freedom beyond their reach, and I wondered if Connelly meant for the two poems to mirror each other. I made a mental note to ask him one day. There were more poems about his father, only the one about his mother, a few that hinted at his own complicated relationship with alcohol and the many ways he'd turned his anger at his father back onto himself, summed up by the phrase "blood, booze and women."

The poems in this collection were short and terse except for the last one, about his father's death, which spanned nearly seven pages. I read it quickly, my eyes tripping over the page, gulping it down so fast it stuck in my throat. When I finished, I read it again, slowly, trying to see how he had done it, captured something so ineffable, that moment when you pass from one state to another. But also how he had managed to describe the terror and ugliness of death so beautifully. It seemed impossible and yet he had done it. His words brought me back to my mother's last moments, the hospital room, the incessant beeping of machines, the smells appalling and vile. My mother terrified and desperate and out of her mind with pain. "This isn't supposed to happen," Abe kept saying as though he had a say in things, as though the world made sense.

Toward the end of the poem, Connelly wondered if his father would have wanted his son to witness his body making its final, horrifying turn against itself and if it would be wrong to leave. He wrote about wanting so desperately for it all to be over and then, when it was, his shame at having wished it. It was exactly how I had felt when my mother died, but I'd never told anyone because it felt wrong. How could you not want to spend every last second you could with someone you loved? But here Connelly was, not just talking about it but writing it. It was true what he told us in class: you could write anything, say anything. There were no rules. This poem was proof. I'd once read that writing is a conversation you have with an invisible reader and that is exactly how it felt to read his poem. It was as if he had written it so I might read it one day, sitting on the floor of a library in New Hampshire, as if he had moved across time and space and spoken directly to me.

I closed the book and studied the author photo. Connelly looked straight at the camera, as if daring it to take his picture. His hair was darker, his face fuller, but otherwise he looked the same. He may even have been more handsome now. Below the photo in tiny letters was the name of the photographer: Roxanne Stevenson. I looked around before peeling back the plastic cover and tearing the photo from the dust jacket. I placed it deep in the pocket of my coat and headed downstairs.

Roxanne Stevenson was a Wilder alum, a member of the first class to graduate women. She had written seven books, all published by academic presses, at a healthy clip of one every two years. Her area of expertise was the Tudor court;

she was best known for a feminist reimagining of Anne Boleyn, portraying her not as a crafty temptress but as a victim of Henry and his court, which systematically dismantled her reputation. On the acknowledgments page of her most recent book, she thanked R. H. Connelly for "his necessary and unstinting support."

I gathered all of Roxanne's books together and studied the author photo on each one, charting her transformation from fresh-faced young academic to middle-aged woman. In early photos, she had a chin-length bob that traced the line of her jaw; in the latest one, she'd cut her hair short. Her eyes were the same, steady and focused, a little too small for her face, her dark eyebrows cutting across her forehead like a slash of permanent marker. She wore sensible monochromatic clothing, blazers, turtleneck sweaters, a white button-down shirt with the collar popped.

"Look at her," I remembered my mother saying one night as we watched the small television at the foot of her bed. I was eleven, maybe twelve years old. "She's going to be on television for God's sake. You'd think someone would tell her to put on a little lipstick. And that blazer," she said, pointing at the television with her cigarette. "Some cheap polyester blend. You see that, right?" I nodded as my mother brought the cigarette to her lips and took a long, slow puff.

I walked closer to the television and watched Roxanne as she flickered across the screen, no longer listening to what she was saying but studying the slope of her nose and the way it turned down at the end, the dark skin under her eyes, the open pores on her cheeks. I could feel my mother watching me. She was training me to search for beauty, and while I'd never be an expert like she was, even then I could see that Roxanne wasn't beautiful. I curled up next to my mother, studied her long neck, deep-set eyes, and delicate bone structure while she stroked my cheek, checking for beauty, as if it might be something subterranean, buried beneath the surface like a winter bulb.

I took Connelly's picture out of my pocket and held it next to Roxanne's. Kelsey always said couples were "attractive in the same way," and Connelly and Roxanne certainly were not. I didn't yet understand what drew men to women besides beauty, and I could see that Roxanne wasn't beautiful and Connelly was—beautiful, yes, something I'd never known a man to be. I tried to picture the two of them together, Roxanne's hair against his face, his hands spreading her legs open like a book. The light above me shut off and I rose, leaving the books in a pile on the floor.

7

I stepped over the coats and backpacks strewn across the floor of Room 203 and slid into my spot across from the windows. Professor Connelly was in his seat already, writing something on a yellow legal pad. He had a black fleece vest over his button-down shirt, and it looked like he'd gotten a haircut. I liked these in-between times, when I could sit back and study him, soak in every detail as if I might be quizzed later. I watched him stroke the space above his upper lip and wondered if it was bigger or smaller than the tip of my index finger.

"Okay, everyone," he said as Ginny ran in. "Welcome, Ginny. First up is Isabel's story. Remember, we start with what we like about a piece before letting the writer know what could be improved. And please, folks, starting your comments with 'no offense' does not give you license to say whatever you want." He looked right at Alec, who shrugged as if to say, "Who me?"

We all laughed, including Connelly. We had an easy rapport now, three weeks into the semester. I liked the way he talked to us, as if we were peers. When he laughed at something one of us said—once, something I had said—it felt sincere.

There was a shuffling of paper around the table as people took out copies of my story. Some were crumpled and scribbled on, others completely blank; Ginny's copy was so crisp and clean, I could tell she hadn't read it. I wiped my hands on my skirt and tried to breathe. I was eager to hear what people thought. I'd tried to write the way Connelly told us to, uninhibited, without editing or filtering. To write like no one was looking over my shoulder. The only person I'd imagined looking over my shoulder was him, smiling at something I had written, maybe even moved. I imagined his face, serious and thoughtful, his hands brushing the pages, licking a finger as he turned them.

My story took place in the 1950s in a bungalow community in the Catskills. The main character was Miriam, a twelve-year-old girl from Brooklyn. Her parents were Jews who'd escaped Poland during the war. Despite these historical particulars, the story was really about me and a trip I'd taken with my parents when I was twelve to visit Abe's brother Leon and his family at their lake house. We never traveled as a family—Abe's work made it impossible—and I don't know how he managed to get away that week or why my mother agreed to go. She couldn't stand Leon's wife, my

Aunt Fanny, and Fanny didn't like my mother either. Also, both of my parents hated the Catskills. My mother found it shabby and depressing. "Too many Jews," said Abe. What I remembered most about the trip was the very fact of it, seven days when we'd behaved like a normal family, doing the sorts of things I imagined normal families did.

I learned to swim that week in the lake that abutted the property. All day long, I raced my cousins Celia and Benji to the dock that marked the end of the swimming area. When we got there, we'd climb up and wave at our mothers back on shore. From a distance, my mother looked almost like she belonged with the other mothers on the beach, wiping noses, passing out sandwiches, pouring lemonade into Dixie cups. Like the Polish refugee I'd turned her into, my mother had always been a kind of outsider, but that week, she looked happy, and I saw what she might have been had her life taken a different direction.

The reason my mother was so happy that week, the reason she'd agreed to go to Leon and Fanny's in the first place, I found out later, was because she was planning on leaving my father when we got home. But right after we returned, she learned she had cancer and "What was the point?" She told me this later, much later, in her hospital room, while Abe was downstairs feeding the meter, when she was dying and telling me things, things I didn't want to know. I think that was why I gave the story the historical context that I did, not only because I feared it wouldn't hold up on its own but because I wanted my characters to be haunted by something. For Miriam and her parents, the haunting was the war;

for my family, it was cancer. Even though we didn't know about it yet, whenever I thought about that week, I thought about my mother's illness. So many of my happy memories were like this, it seemed, blotted out by the shadow of disease and decay.

In the final scene, Miriam spends the last night at the lake sleeping on the screened-in porch with her cousins. Her aunt tucks her in and brings out a plate of cookies, then strokes Miriam's hair while she reads them all a story. When Miriam looks up and sees her mother standing in the doorway, she feels guilty for liking it all so much—the cousins and the cookies and the lake and the feel of her aunt's hand, for wanting to give in to it, to love a place that is nothing like home. That's what I'd wanted to convey, at least; whether or not I'd succeeded, I was about to find out.

"I like the description of the mother on the beach," said Kara from beneath her bangs. "In her hat and caftan, she reminds me of a flower."

"And it's like she's been transplanted to a different pot," Linus offered, but no one ever listened to Linus.

"The bond between the mother and daughter is really strong," said Ginny, one of several vague comments she made that confirmed she hadn't read my story.

"She reminded me a lot of my mother," Holly said, and then she launched into a story about a trip she took with her mother to Johannesburg. Connelly usually stopped us when we made self-referential comments, but he didn't stop Holly. He'd been quiet all morning, slouched in his chair sucking on the end of his pen like a cigarette. He liked to let us sort things out before saying anything. I wanted so badly to know what he thought about my story, if he loved it or hated it. Worst of all would be indifference.

Alec raised his hand, even though Connelly always told us we didn't have to. "How old is Miriam supposed to be?"

"Twelve," said Holly.

Alec screwed up his face. "She feels way older than that." He looked like he was about to say something else when Connelly interrupted him.

"I agree, it is a mature voice." He took the pen out of his mouth. "It's hard to believe this is the voice of a twelve-year-old." I wanted to say something to defend myself, but the writer wasn't allowed to say anything while their story was being discussed.

"But," Connelly continued, sitting up in a leisurely way, like a cat getting up from a nap, "I think that's deliberate. It is the voice of someone looking back on an experience, rather than writing from inside the experience. It's a choice the writer has made, and I believe it was a good one. Let's see how she does that, on page five, for example." As the class turned to page five, Connelly looked over at me and winked. It was so quick, I almost missed it. I looked down at my lap, at the whites of my knees shining through my tights.

I sat and listened as Connelly discussed voice and narrative distance, shocked at what he was able to find in my writing—themes, imagery, allusions, things I hadn't intended and didn't know were there. It wasn't a great story. Miriam's motivations were murky. The historical context was thin. But Connelly ignored the weaknesses and pointed instead to the places where my writing sang. I'd successfully "charted the emotional landscape of the story," he said and, the way he described it, that was all I was interested in as a writer or a reader anyway: what people said and did and what they thought about when they weren't saying or doing anything. Girls with feelings. If it had felt like a poverty before, now it felt like a gift.

"You've been quiet, Andy," Connelly said when he was finished. "Anything you'd like to add?"

Andy was sitting across from me, writing something in his notebook. Before Connelly called on him, he had leaned over and whispered something in Kara's ear and she smiled, like she was laughing at an inside joke. I'd seen them together a few times outside of class, standing in line at the dining hall, once walking down Main Street sharing an umbrella. Andy hadn't said anything all morning, even though I could see he'd read my story; his copy was marked up.

"There's something unfinished about it," Andy said, thumbing through the pages. "Some of the writing is nice, a little sentimental maybe, but I think the real problem is that it felt too close to the truth."

"What do you mean by that?" Connelly asked.

I looked down at my hands. Andy knew the broad outlines of my life, and I'd talked to him perhaps more than anyone, besides Kelsey, about my mother. "I don't know," he said. "It feels autobiographical to me. I think if the writer had left more to the imagination, the story might have been successful."

"So you don't think she pushed it far enough?" Connelly asked.

"Exactly. It feels more like a fragment than a complete story. A memory." Andy pushed the pages aside. "Oh, and you should never start a story by describing the weather. Sorry, that's just a pet peeve."

The room tittered. I felt something turn in the pit of my stomach. Kara looked over at me and smiled wanly.

"Fair enough," Connelly said. "It's possible the author didn't take it as far as she could have. There are things I'm left wanting to know as well. For example, what is the life Miriam has left behind, and what makes it so different from the one she finds at the lake? There's also the curious absence of the father, although he feels like a benevolent figure to me. And certainly, the historical details could be fleshed out better." He spoke slowly and deliberately, like he were backing a truck onto a busy street. "As for the weather, I'm not sure I agree that you should *never* start that way, but there might be a more effective opening. Do you have a suggestion, Andy?"

"Me? Oh, I'd have to think about it."

"Okay then." Connelly folded his hands. "What I would say is that this character feels richly drawn, perhaps because of what you call the autobiographical piece. As for the fragmentary quality—I would argue that that is part of its strength. We may not know everything about this narrator, but we know enough. She doesn't need to tell the reader everything. She respects us enough to let us figure it out for ourselves. Listen, for example, to what she does at the end:

"One afternoon," Connelly read, "I swam out too far, way past the buoys. When I looked back, the people on the beach were impossibly small. My mother was turned away from me, her face hidden by the brim of her hat. The water below me was dark and cold, and I wondered if I could make it back to shore. For a brief moment, I was afraid. But then I focused on the echo of my breath and my mother's hat and I made my way back to her, stroke by stroke, kick by kick. When I got there, I lay my head in her lap. She jumped up, surprised by the feel of my wet hair on her thigh. She hadn't even noticed I was gone."

Connelly put the paper down. "Do you see how she does that? This short piece of writing, a fragment," he looked at Andy, "tells us all we need to know about this girl. She's strong. She loves her mother, who she feels is somehow out of reach. She can get herself out of a tough situation." He pinched his bottom lip with his fingers. "She knows how to save herself.

"I guess for me," he said, studying my pages as though there were something hidden there, "what resonates is the question of what we owe our parents and what it means to step fully into our own lives, to decide what we want beyond what they have offered us. So despite the story's flaws, at its heart is a question that is meaningful and true, and what else do we want out of literature anyway?"

The classroom was quiet. I sat there, stunned. The sound of my words in his mouth had moved me deeply. Connelly turned toward the window, and it looked like he was about to say something else, but then he inhaled sharply and said, "Okay, then. Let's move on."

When class was over, I gathered my things. When I pulled my coat off the back of my chair, I heard something rip.

"Isabel, wait up a second," Professor Connelly said.

While I waited for him to finishing talking to Holly, I inspected my coat. There was a tear in the lining, nothing that couldn't be fixed, but I felt disproportionately sad about it. Someone had left behind a four-color pen, and I slipped it in my pocket as Andy walked by with Kara. I refused to meet his eye.

"Have a seat," Connelly said when the room was empty. "I won't bite." I hugged my coat to my chest and took the seat closest to the door. Up close, the scar on his hand was jagged and long, hinting at some great violence. I thought about what Jason had said, about an R. H. Connelly who had killed himself, and wondered if there was any truth to it.

"I wanted to make sure you were okay," he said. "It's not easy to get criticism on something you've worked hard on, and I can tell you worked hard on this."

I nodded, and my eyes filled with tears. It surprised me, and I tried to blink them back, but that only made them come faster.

"Shit," I said. "I don't know why I'm crying. I'm not even that upset."

Connelly pulled a handkerchief out of his pocket and handed it to me. "My wife says women cry when they're angry."

"I'm not angry." I held the handkerchief to my nose. It smelled like him, peppermint and woodsmoke, mixed with laundry detergent.

"Let me ask you something," he said. "Did Andy's comments make you want to go back and work on your story, to make it better?"

I thought for a moment, then shook my head.

"No, of course not. It made you doubt yourself and everything you instinctively know about storytelling—and you know a lot. People want to tear apart your work because they've been taught that critique is how you learn and grow. But if Andy had his way, you'd never work on that story again. You'd never work on any story. That's what critique does, shuts us down so only the strong survive. Thins out the competition." He smiled and whatever anger I had felt—because it was anger after all—dissolved like ice in water.

"So tell me," he said, resting his chin in the L of his fingers. "Where are you from, Isabel?"

"New York? The Lower East Side?" My voice kept rising at the end of each sentence, which Debra said revealed insecurity. I hated when she pointed it out, probably because she was right.

"Ah, so that's why you were so enamored with the Catskills. Miriam, I mean," he added with a smile. "I lived in the city for a while—well, Brooklyn. I'm not sure real New Yorkers consider that the city."

"Yeah, probably not," I said, laughing. "I have family in Brooklyn. Borough Park? The religious side of my dad's family. We don't see them much. We're not religious—I mean, my dad's not. He says he doesn't have time for religion. Because he's always working? They think all we care about is money, which is weird since we don't have that much." The words were tumbling out. I held my hand over my mouth to stop them.

"Then I guess we're both a long way from home."

Connelly handed back my story and I held out his hand-kerchief. "Keep it," he said. I shoved it in my pocket and stood up, lifting one hand when I got to the door in a kind of awkward wave. Then I hurried out, nearly bumping into the doorframe.

The lights were off in our bedroom when I got back. I turned them on and heard a groan from the bottom bunk.

"Debra?" I looked at the clock. It was after two.

Debra rolled onto her side and pulled the blanket over her head. The room smelled like cloves and sweat. "Bitch, turn out the light."

I did as she asked. "Why are you in bed?"

"Because I'm tired."

"Is that all?"

"Yes," she snapped. "That's all. I had a paper and I was up all night. Could you let me fucking sleep?"

I closed the door gently and sat down at my desk. I took out my story and turned to the last page, where Connelly had written a note.

Lovely story about childhood experiences and the ways they shape us, about discovering there are many ways to live. You elo-quently and effortlessly capture the voice of an outsider wanting to get in. But something is holding her back. I want to know what.

On the second to last page, Connelly had written some-thing else, at the part of the story where Miriam sees her mother standing in the doorway. I had to turn the page sideways to read it: *I feel like something is stalking this woman. A part of me wonders if she will die.*

I held the pages close to my chest, forgetting about

Debra and the fact that she was sleeping in the middle of the day. The room was warm, but I was shivering, a tremor that started somewhere deep inside of me. I thought about the way Connelly had looked at me, like he could see something I didn't know was there, the way he said my name, curling it around his tongue. I took the handkerchief out of my pocket and held it to my face, remembering the way his hand looked when he gave it to me: rough and wind-chapped, his wedding band digging into his flesh like a vise.

8

MY parents met at Rosen's. "Where else would I have found him?" my mother, Vivian, said whenever I asked her to tell me the story. She'd wandered in one winter day with a friend, looking for a place to get a cup of coffee, and Abe was smitten. Tall and slim with long brown hair ironed straight like Ali MacGraw's in *Love Story*, my mother didn't look like most of the women who shopped there. "Movie-star pretty" my grandmother Yetta, Abe's mother, called her, but it wasn't clear she meant it as a compliment.

Abe was already forty, a bachelor who ate dinner with his mother almost every night. On the day she walked into Rosen's Appetizing, Vivian was twenty-five and new to the city. She'd spent her childhood in and around Rockland County, moving from house to house and town to town, each smaller and more run-down than the one before; she liked to say the most elegant thing about her was her name.

She'd gone to work straight out of high school, eventually saved enough money to move to New York with the hope of going to art school. The details of my parents' courtship were hazy, but a year after they met, they were married. Soon after that, I was born.

Abe wasn't supposed to marry Vivian. He was supposed to marry Barbara Horowitz, whose family owned the upholstery store down the street. It wasn't an arranged marriage, more of an understanding that they would marry when the time came, but when the time came, they didn't. Barbara married Stanley Fishman instead and moved to Great Neck. Her parents eventually sold the store, which was a shame, Abe said: "Pillows is a good business."

One day when I was eight, Barbara Fishman née Horowitz came into the store with her family. I don't know if Abe knew she was coming. All I remember is standing behind the counter with him when the door opened and a woman walked in. Barbara was not beautiful like my mother, but pretty, with a bobbed nose, French manicure, and long fur coat. When she leaned in and clasped my hand, she smelled like tea rose.

Barbara had a daughter my age named Lauren, and my father told me to let her pick out something from the candy counter. As Barbara and Abe talked, I showed Lauren how I liked to eat the chocolate jelly rings off my fingers.

"Do you have any brothers or sisters?" Lauren asked. She had two brothers, twins. They were sitting together in a large stroller Stanley was pushing back and forth with one hand.

"No."

"Lucky," Lauren said, but I didn't feel lucky. I'd just started asking my mother why I didn't have a brother or sister. "Isabel, please," she said. "One child is plenty."

"Where do you play?" Lauren asked, glancing around the cramped, dusty store. From outside, you could hear the sound of honking horns and music blasting from a parked car on the corner.

"There's a playground at school," I said, but it wasn't really a playground, just a courtyard where we played Chinese jump rope and bounced balls against a graffiti-covered wall. I hoped we'd change the subject before Lauren asked if I knew how to ride a bike, which I didn't.

Abe walked outside with Stanley to admire his Mercedes. Barbara kneeled down to wipe something off one of the twins' faces. Lauren kept asking questions about my house and school, what I liked to do, where I played. It made me uncomfortable, like she was trying to poke holes in the facade of normalcy I had started to construct for myself. Even then, I had the feeling that the way we lived wasn't normal. I had friends who went to summer camp and church, who had brothers and sisters and grandparents who gave them five-dollar bills and kissed their cheeks. My own family, in comparison, was small and strange—Abe in his apron, my mother and her paints, Yetta with her glowering stares. Even the way we ate, at a small table pushed up against the wall in our kitchen, surrounded by ashtrays and paint cans and greasy packages of smoked fish.

"We have a swing set in our backyard," Lauren said, nibbling the ring around her pointer finger. Her teeth were small, like a squirrel's. "It has monkey bars and a tire swing."

"You have a tire swing?" I loved the tire swing at the

playground where my mother sometimes took me, but I always had to wait my turn, and if the teenagers were on it, they never got off.

"Ask your dad if you can come visit," Lauren said.

"Really?"

"Yes. But he can't smoke in our house. My mother hates it." I looked outside where Abe was leaning against Stanley's car, a cigarette dangling from his hand. "Where's your mother?" Lauren asked but before I had a chance to answer, Barbara called her name and they were gone.

After Barbara left, I asked Abe if we could visit them. "We'll see," he said. Over the next few weeks, our apartment became intolerable, especially compared to Lauren's house, which I pictured as something out of a sitcom with a patch of green lawn, an upstairs and downstairs, and, of course, that tire swing. I watched my parents sitting silently at dinner, both of them smoking, my mother's fingernails caked with paint as she turned the pages of her magazine. Later, Abe would wash the dishes, then soak his feet in a basin while watching the Yankees game, and my mother would fall asleep on the sofa in her bathrobe. What would my life be like if Abe had married Barbara instead? Would I live in Great Neck in a house with wall-to-wall carpeting? Would I have baby brothers and a tire swing, a long yellow Slip 'N Slide stretched across the grass?

"Daddy?" It was a few weeks after Barbara's visit. My mother was asleep but Abe was still awake, his face illuminated by the game on TV. "Where would we live if you married Barbara? Here or in Great Neck?"

"*Bubeleh*," Abe said, smoke from his cigarette swirling under the reading lamp. "If I'd married Barbara, you wouldn't exist!" And he laughed and walked me back to bed. But I didn't think it was funny, how quickly I'd been erased. I never asked about Barbara or Lauren again.

I WAS SEWING the tear in the lining of my coat when the phone rang.

"Isabel?" My father always sounded confused on the phone, as though he were unfamiliar with this new technology.

"Hi, Dad. How are you? How's your toe?"

"Nothing a little aspirin can't help. How are things up there?"

"Still in business. You?"

"Still in business." Unlike Kelsey who told her mother everything, I rarely got into specifics with Abe about how I spent my time. "Still in business" was shorthand for everything was okay, I was managing. It was the same thing he said when people asked how the store was doing. Still in business was as good as it got.

I brought the phone over to the sofa and flipped through a magazine—"Everything You Wanted to Know about Ally McBeal!"—while Abe talked about the weather, where he'd parked the car, and the latest news about President Clinton and his supposed affair. "The Republicans have been trying to get this guy for years," he said. "Looks like they finally did."

"Looks like it."

"Some say he'll resign by the end of the week. The guy's his own worst enemy, I'll say that much."

A car stopped short outside. I looked out the window and saw a guy and a girl walking quickly down the path in front of our dorm. At first glance, it looked like she was running away from him.

"Did I tell you about Lenny Hurwitz's daughter?" Abe asked. "What was her name?"

"Casey?"

"Casey, right. Lenny told me she got into a graduate program at Johns Hopkins where they train you to be in the CIA."

"Wow." I tried to picture Casey Hurwitz in the CIA. The last time I'd seen her, she was standing in front of the Mercury Lounge in a bikini top, a live snake coiled around her neck.

"You always said she wasn't that smart," Abe said.

"Maybe being smart doesn't matter."

"Oh Isabel, of course it matters."

Outside, the guy said something to the girl that made her spin around on her heel. It was clear they were arguing about something. The girl's hands were fluttering around her face and even with the window closed, I could hear the rise and fall of their voices. I squinted but couldn't make out who they were. He had on a heavy green parka with the hood cinched over his face. She had a hat pulled over her long hair.

"Did you, Isabel?" Abe asked.

"Sorry. Did I what?"

"Did you make an appointment at Career Services?"

"No, not yet."

"You said you would do that as soon as you got back. It's important. That's why you're there, so you can get a good job when you're done."

"Oh, is that why I'm here," I mumbled.

Abe sighed, and I felt bad about being snarky. I heard him take a sip of something. Dr. Brown's Cel-Ray Tonic. He usually called around this time, late afternoon, when he was getting ready to close for the day. I wondered if the store had been busy or if it had been another slow Sunday. I wondered what he was having for dinner, if he would eat it alone at the table or in front of the TV. I wondered if he had anybody to talk to.

"I'll call tomorrow. I promise."

After we hung up, I turned my attention back to the couple outside. I opened the window a crack to try to hear what they were saying, got up on my knees to see better. I noticed the car stopped on the street behind them. It was still running, the passenger door hanging open as if one of them had run out to grab something. There was someone inside. As I watched, whoever it was crawled from the back seat into the front.

The sun was almost gone. With the window open, the room was freezing. I was about to close it when I heard the guy yell "Goddamnit, Joanna!" loud enough for me to hear it four flights up, loud enough for the words to ricochet against the buildings and fly off into the dome of night. I gasped as I saw Tom Fisher grab Joanna Maxwell by the arm and pull her back to the car, her heels dragging through the snow. Then he pushed her inside and slammed the door. Before he peeled away, I saw Igraine's small face through the window contorted with sobs.

I spun around on my knees and ducked under the windowsill. I could feel the blood pulsing in my temples and armpits. Later, I would convince myself that what I had seen hadn't been that serious, but right then, in the immediate aftermath, there was no denying the violence of the scene I'd witnessed—the way Tom had grabbed his wife, how desperately she'd tried to get away from him. I shivered, remembering the bruise I'd seen on Joanna's neck that day outside Dean Hansen's office, Tom's outburst during our meeting, the way he'd slammed the desk. I thought about calling Abe back, but he'd probably already left his office to head upstairs and soak his feet. I didn't want to bother him, and, besides, what would I tell him and what would he say? And how did any of it involve me anyway?

I closed the window and listened to Joan Armatrading sing about mixing water with the wine as I finished sewing the lining of my coat. The sun was gone now, the room nearly dark. I broke the thread with my teeth the way my mother used to, then headed into town to meet Kelsey and Jason at the movies. I thought about telling them about Joanna and Tom, but then the lights went down and I fell into the dream of the image on the screen. As we passed a bucket of greasy popcorn back and forth, I wondered why I'd been so shocked. Married couples fought, didn't they? Sometimes in public, sometimes in front of their children. It was unfortunate but not unusual and, in any case, it wasn't my problem. So I tucked it away and, as the promo commanded, sat back and enjoyed the show.

TOM HAD SUGGESTED I reread *The Custom of the Country*, Wharton's 1913 novel about the social-climbing Undine Spragg. Unlike Ellen Olenska, whose decision to divorce nearly ruins her, Undine uses divorces, several of them, as a way to get ahead. What did it mean for a woman to control her own destiny, Tom asked me? And why did we find Undine so distasteful? Did we prefer heroines who suffered?

I grabbed a bag of M&M's from the vending machine and ate them slowly as I wandered through the stacks, sucking off the sweet coating then letting the chocolate melt on my tongue. The light was on in the stacks where Wharton was shelved. There was a man standing there. He had his head cocked to one side, his arms crossed high on his chest. It took me a second to recognize Professor Connelly.

"Isabel," he said. "My God. You startled me."

"I'm sorry." I took a step back.

"That's okay. I was lost in my thoughts. I get a little spacey in the stacks." He was wearing a gray sweatshirt that said RUTGERS and a black wool hat. With his hair pulled off his face, he looked young, like someone I might find in a frat basement or dorm laundry room.

"I was just getting a book."

He looked around. "I figured."

"No. I mean, here." I pointed at the shelf in front of him.

"Oh." The stacks were narrow, but there was enough

room for me to grab the book without touching him. "Wharton. One of my favorites."

"Mine, too." I pressed my knuckles to my cheeks to hide my blush. He asked what I was working on, and I told him about my thesis.

"Sounds interesting," he said, like he meant it. "Hey, I meant to tell you. I read a story you wrote, in that feminist journal." He tapped his forehead. "Something bitch?"

"*Bitch slap*," I said. "How'd you read that?"

"Roxanne—my wife—she was interviewed for one of the issues, so we had it lying around."

"Oh, right." Debra had interviewed Roxanne last year about her experience at Wilder. The piece was called "Better Dead Than Coed," which was one of the rallying cries against coeducation. I'd forgotten I had a story in that issue too, about a frat party gone wrong. I'd interspersed the action with entries from the Wilder glossary, a booklet they sent to incoming freshmen so they'd be familiar with Wilder vernacular.

"Is there really Wilder slang?" Connelly asked.

"Sure," I said. "Boot, rager, mung."

"God, what are those things? Wait—do I want to know?"

I pretended to think about it. "I think you can handle it. Boot means vomit, a rager is a party, and—my personal favorite—mung: the layer of spit, piss, beer, and puke that coats the floor of every frat basement."

He laughed. "Good Lord. What a place. My wife has some stories. Before the school went coed, they used to bus in women for parties. They called it, if I remember correctly, the 'fuck truck.'"

"Jesus," I said, laughing with him. "I can't believe you read my story. It was kind of dumb."

"No," he said, suddenly serious. "It wasn't dumb at all. It was chilling. By using the glossary, you showed how this behavior is condoned by the culture at large, which goes so far as to write it down."

"Is that what I was doing? Wow. You're good."

He looked down at his tennis shoes. "It's what I do. Kind of my superpower. The only one I have. Is that what it's really like here?"

I opened my mouth, then closed it before saying, "Yeah."

"Shit."

I laughed again. The light above us buzzed, a drone like a bee trapped in a window frame. I thought about the story in *Time* magazine and the girl who'd driven up to his cabin. I wanted to ask him about it, the poems, the cabin, the girl, but then the light turned off. Connelly's eyes glowed in the sudden darkness, like an animal caught in headlights. There was something so intimate about it, the laughter, the darkness. I wanted it to last forever but knew it couldn't. I spoke first, not wanting him to be the one to break the spell.

"I should get going," I said.

"Bye, Isabel. Nice talking to you. Enjoy the Wharton." He cranked the timer that operated the light and turned back to the stacks. I realized as I walked away that I hadn't asked him what he was looking for. I hadn't asked him lots of things. I wondered when I might get another chance.

I moved quickly through the stacks, clutching the book to my chest. I ran past Andy's carrel, not checking to see if the light was on. I didn't know where I was going, but I needed to be alone. I slipped into the single bathroom under the stairs and locked the door. I was breathing hard, my chest heaving. I caught a glimpse of myself in the mirror above the sink. My face was flushed, a spiderweb of red that ran down my neck. I placed a hand on my breastbone, felt a tingle in my palm, a tangle of energy that traveled down my body, collecting at the root of me.

I closed my eyes and pictured Connelly watching me in the dark, the slice of his cheekbone, the thumbprint-shaped space above his lip, remembered the warmth of his body as I squeezed past him. The feeling came over me so fast, I didn't recognize it at first. I slipped my hand under my sweater as images from my story flashed through my mind: sweaty frat basements, bodies pressed against bodies, hands probing soft, secret places. The smell of sweat, beer, puke, desire. The book fell to the floor as I reached my hand into my pants, pictured the fuck truck pulling up outside, its windows steamy with sex, heard Connelly's voice, soft and low, lapping against me like water. Then I dove beneath that wave and swam toward the light.

9

I'D been keeping an eye on Debra ever since finding her in bed in the middle of the day. She went to these dark places sometimes—depression, I'd call it now, but back then it was just part of what made Debra Debra. Scintillating highs and harrowing lows. I saw it for the first time freshman year, a few weeks after a Crushgirls stunt. We weren't roommates yet, barely even friends, but we had a class together. After she didn't show up for a few days, I stopped by to check on her.

Debra lived with Kelsey that year, in a double on the first floor of Sagebrook Hall. They fought constantly, mostly about cleaning. I knocked a few times before letting myself in. As my eyes adjusted to the darkness, I understood why Kelsey was always complaining. The room was a disaster, clothes and papers all over the floor, an empty Doritos bag, a half-full bottle of Sprite. The garbage can in the corner was full, and I could see unfolded maxi pads smeared with blood. The room smelled bad, like body odor and what I can only call decay.

I walked over to the window and opened the blinds. Debra poked her head out of a pile of dirty blankets. She looked as bad as the room. She was thin, which probably pleased her, and her hair was ratty, her skin drawn and blotchy. Scariest of all were her eyes: usually so glittering and quick, they looked flat and opaque. Dead.

Before I could ask her what was wrong, the phone rang. Neither of us moved to answer it. It rang four times before the machine picked up.

"Debra?" It was Debra's mother, Marilyn Moscowitz. "Honey, pick up if you're there." She waited a minute, cleared her throat. "I hope you're not answering because you've gotten yourself up and out. That's a good sign. Listen, Patel called in a prescription for you. You can pick it up at the Health Center tomorrow. And I talked to Dean Hansen. He said since there are only a few weeks left in the semester—"

Debra crawled out from under the covers and pushed stop on the answering machine. She moved slowly, like the bones in her feet were broken.

"What's the matter with you?" I asked. "Are you sick?"

"Not really," she said as she climbed back into bed. "I get into these moods. Something with my wiring." The answering machine beeped and whirred. "She's just worried I won't finish the semester. I have that internship in New York this summer. Wouldn't want to miss that." She rubbed her eyes and looked at me. "Why are you here?"

"I didn't know where you were. I missed you." Before saying it, I hadn't known it was true.

I stayed with her for the rest of the day. While she slept, I took out the trash, ran a load of laundry, put away her clothes. The sun set. Debra woke up, and I helped her get out of bed; while she showered, I changed her sheets. We walked over to the dining hall and, over bowls of frozen yogurt, she told me everything that had happened over the years—the moods, doctors, medications. I told her about my mom, how she sometimes didn't get out of bed for days, didn't wash her hair or change her clothes. I'd always said, even to myself, it was because she was consumed with her work, but that wasn't the whole truth. Debra nodded. "I think I'm going to get some more," she said, lifting her bowl. She had four helpings of yogurt that day.

Debra slowly came back to herself after that. She caught up on her schoolwork, finished the semester, took the internship at a law firm in New York. Something changed between us that day. I'd seen Debra at her worst, and I've found that is often what binds women together. Men admire each other when they are at their best, but women enjoy meeting each other in pits of despair. Debra had never had another breakdown, not that I knew of, but any time I suspected she was slipping, I became vigilant, as if by sheer force of will I could keep her up on shore with us.

Now I was worried again. Debra had been moodier than usual, her behavior more erratic. She was letting the clothes pile up on her bed and hadn't washed her sheets in weeks. There were unanswered messages from Marilyn on our answering machine. Kelsey had been reluctant to live with her again after freshman year, but had relented because of me and because Debra promised she was better. I was never sure how much Kelsey knew, if Debra had ever confided in her the way she'd confided in me. Even if she had, I wasn't sure Kelsey would have understood. I knew she thought of Debra's messes as a character flaw, a sign of her general lack of discipline, something she could control if she just tried hard enough. "You don't have to protect her," Kelsey said whenever I worried about Debra. "It's not your responsibility." But whose was it, I wondered? Who was there to catch us if not our friends?

EVERY FEBRUARY, THE English department hosted a party for seniors called the Senior Mingle. It was always the source of the best department gossip and was always hosted, as far as we knew, by Joanna and Tom. But this year, given the circumstances, it wasn't clear if the Mingle would take place as usual, or if it would happen at all.

When we got to Professor Connelly's class on Wednesday, invitations still hadn't gone out. There was a collective sense of disappointment that we might be denied the chance to dress up and drink alongside our professors as legions of Wilder English majors before us had done. These feelings of injustice outweighed whatever concerns we might have had about Tom who, I'd heard, had called in sick to class last week, or Joanna, whom Ramona had seen at the Grand Union late Saturday night wearing sweatpants and dark glasses and pushing a cart filled with toaster waffles, maxi pads, and Motrin. Or was it Pop-Tarts, diapers, and Excedrin? We giggled, like assholes, at the absurdity of these details. I hadn't told anyone about the fight I'd seen them having, and the more time passed, the more distant the memory became. I'd seen Tom only once since then, standing outside the student center staring into space. I didn't know what to say to him, so I'd taken the long way around to avoid passing too close.

It was a miserable day, rainy and gray, the kind of damp cold that made your bones ache. Room 203 was usually so bright we didn't have to turn on the light, but today we did. Across the table, Linus was reading the newspaper. "Logs at White House Show 3 Dozen Visits by Lewinsky," a headline read.

Whitney sat down and ran her fingers through her wet hair.

"If I'd known it could get so cold my hair would *freeze,*" she said, "I would have listened to my mother and gone to USC."

Connelly walked in a few minutes late. His shirt was buttoned wrong and there was a smear of shaving cream under his chin. I blushed remembering our conversation in the library. I'd had crushes before, but there was something different about this. Debra always said that when it came to guys, "If you feel it, it's there. You don't make that shit up." I agreed. There was something that passed between two people when there was a mutual attraction, a frisson. But Connelly was older, married, my professor—there were rules about these things. Later, I would understand there were not rules about these things and would run from inconvenient attractions, to a colleague or a friend's boyfriend, as quickly as possible. But back then, I didn't know any better. Or maybe I did: when I'd gotten home from the library that night, I'd taken Connelly's handkerchief and author photo out of my underwear drawer and put them both in the trash can at the end of the hall.

"Let's get started." Connelly unbuttoned the cuffs of his sleeves and rolled them up. "Andy, you ready?"

"Yup." Andy sniffed loudly. He had a box of tissues next to him and an insulated mug from which he took slow, careful sips. His nose was red, his cheeks flushed like someone had slapped him. With his coat on and wine-red scarf wrapped around his neck, he looked like a consumptive nineteenth-century poet. All that was missing was his garret.

"Did she just unwrap a Halls for him?" Whitney whispered. I looked over as Kara slid something to Andy, her smooth, hairless forearm barely brushing his.

Andy's story was short, only three pages. I appreciated the brevity; last week, Linus had submitted a thirty-page excerpt from his work in progress, something about a serial killer stalking prostitutes. I'd barely read it. Andy's story was about a woman suffering from dementia. Her name was Agnes, and she appeared to be in a hospital or nursing home. A couple of characters floated in and out—a nurse maybe, and a granddaughter, or maybe it was her son. The overall effect was one of wispiness, reflecting, perhaps, Agnes's tenuous hold on life. It was beautifully written—Andy's work always was—but something about it felt forced. Cold. I'd always found Andy's work hard to understand, which I'd blamed on my deficiencies as a reader. But Connelly had been telling us, "You write *for* your readers. It's your job to make sure they understand." Also, there wasn't anything about Agnes, aside from her name, that made it clear she was a woman and, despite it being a story about someone close to death, I was surprisingly unmoved by it. This is what I would have said about the story if asked, but I'd already decided I wasn't going to say anything.

Professor Connelly opened the discussion the way he always did, asking for our "thoughts, impressions, biases, and confessions." Holly was the first to raise her hand.

"You can totally tell a poet wrote this." Holly sat up straight with her shoulders pulled back. I could never tell if she had a big chest or if it just looked that way. My mother would have liked Holly, would have said she made the most of what she had.

Connelly had one leg crossed over the other, like a figure four, his foot vibrating like a hummingbird's wing. "Tell me why you think that, Holly."

Holly pointed out phrases that were signature Andy, where you could see the work on the page, the effort it took. It reminded me of my mother and the way she'd made being an artist look—difficult and painful. It wasn't like that for me. Stories and words flowed out easily. I was starting to think that maybe that wasn't a bad thing.

"The language you're describing is poetic." Connelly broke the word into syllables, as if he were biting it. "But I would argue that the language functions as a mask in this work. A way to hide from the truth. This is a woman at the end of her life. Maybe beautiful language isn't what's called for."

The room shifted nervously. Holly's mouth hung open, as if she were waiting for someone to pop something into it. Kara unwrapped another cough drop and passed it to Andy. It lay on the table between them, untouched.

"What is this story about?" Connelly asked, waving Andy's story in front of him. "I mean, what is it *really* about? Is it about a woman at the end of her life, or is Agnes a sig-nifier for something else? Either way, before she can be a signifier, she has to be an actual woman." He tossed the story down. The room was so quiet you could hear the pages land on the table. "Does she feel like a real woman to you?" His eyes rested briefly on me, and my heart seized, but then they moved onto someone else, and it became clear he wasn't asking anyone in particular. "A woman's voice isn't easy to capture, and I'm not sure this writer has done it."

Whitney whistled under her breath. Linus's eyes grew wide. The only person who didn't react was Ginny, who appeared to be asleep again. We'd never heard Andy's work criticized in this way, in any way. Of all the writers who slipped their work hopefully under Joanna Maxwell's door, Andy was the one who had been anointed. But Connelly had hit on something that felt right to me. I wondered if the rest of the class thought so, too.

Andy dabbed at his nose with a tissue. He looked so mis-erable and feverish, I couldn't help but feel sorry for him. It was a harsh assessment, and Connelly was never harsh. But he seemed distracted today. He kept glancing at his watch and the door as if he had someplace else to be.

Andy raised a finger tentatively, and Connelly nodded for him to speak, breaking his usual rule.

"I don't think I'm hiding from the truth," Andy said. "I think it's just—well, I'm not a fiction writer. I'm used to working in a more minimal form."

"I'm a poet too, remember?" Connelly said. "But poets have to tell stories. Even the shortest poems contain multitudes." He folded his hands. "Let me ask you something: Have you ever been present when a person died?"

"No."

"I can tell. Listen, Andy, there's a lot that's strong in here. Let me show you." Something shifted and Connelly became gentler, as though having said what he needed to say, he could relax. For the rest of class, he walked us through Andy's story, showing him where he could expand it by exploring the emotion behind the descriptions. I tried to write down everything he said, as if he were giving directions for something I'd need to know later. I was writing so quickly, I almost didn't notice when he said my name.

"Do you remember what you said about Isabel's story? You said it was a fragment, unfinished. But her story was *about* something. It had an honesty that allowed you to enter it. The language didn't soar, but it was real. It was true. That's the kind of story I want to read, one I can't stop thinking about, one that crawls inside me. Takes up residence."

I found it hard to take a full breath, like my lungs had become too small for my body. I could feel Whitney's eyes on me, but I wanted to stay in the moment a little longer. Because once it was over, I knew I'd start doubting what Connelly had said. Andy was the better writer—everybody

knew that—and for Connelly to say different made me wonder if he could be trusted. But for the moment at least, it
felt good.

"Looks like somebody's teacher's pet," Whitney said as I
gathered my things at the end of class. I shook my head in
response and hurried out the door.

I practically bumped into Tom Fisher in the hallway.

"Professor Fisher!" I said. "Hi—I've been meaning to call
you. Did you get the pages I left?"

Tom startled and took a step back. "Isabel. Yes. Your
pages." He had one eye fixed on the door to Room 203,
the other zagged off to the side. Despite the weather, he
was wearing cargo shorts and a pair of shower shoes; a cigarette dangled precipitously between his fingers. "I, I—I just
picked them up from my mailbox."

"Oh, great. Do you have time to talk this week? I reread
The Custom of the Country like you suggested—"

Just then, Professor Connelly stepped out.

"Randy!" Tom cried.

"Tom." Connelly nodded at Tom, then at me. "You know
Isabel?"

"Isabel? Yes, of course." Tom turned his face toward me,
struggling to focus. "Why don't you talk to Mary Pat about
scheduling a meeting? I don't have my schedule right now."

Connelly placed a hand on Tom's shoulder. "Come. Let's
talk upstairs. Isabel, I'll see you next week?"

On my way out of the building, I passed the mail room
where I saw my pages sitting in Tom's box, exactly where I'd
left them three days before.

Later that day, when we checked our mailboxes in the

student center, we each found a small ecru card tucked inside a matching envelope. With apologies for the delay, the English department was happy to announce that the Senior Mingle would take place next Saturday night at the home of Joanna Maxwell and Tom Fisher. Despite the short notice, we were all able to attend.

10

THE student center, where I worked ten hours a week, was the hub of campus life. Everyone passed through the large modern building at least once a day to meet a friend or check their mailbox or grab something to eat on their way to class. They were usually moving too quickly to notice me sitting behind the information desk, where I became invisible, another part of the hidden machinery that made this place run.

It was snowing when I arrived for my Thursday morning shift, and the linoleum floor was already smudged with salt and slush. Someone cleaned these floors—they were always shiny when I arrived—but I'd never seen anybody do it. My responsibilities at the desk were few: answer the phone, direct visitors, sell tokens for the video games downstairs. Not much happened at the information desk, except for one time junior year, when someone forgot to log off the public computer and someone else used that account to send an email that said "I'm going to rape you after winter break." The girl who received the email notified campus police and, since I'd been working that day, the officers asked me if I'd seen anyone who might have sent it. I couldn't remember seeing anyone who would have sent an email like that— and at the same time, I'd seen so many people who might have sent it. In the end, I wasn't any help, and that, as far as I knew, was the end of that.

Things quieted down after the breakfast rush. I picked at a corn muffin and took out my knitting. I'd started making a scarf using leftover yarn, something my mother used to do. It was a peculiar, patchwork-looking thing, but it had a strange charm. Debra had called dibs on it, but I thought I might keep it for myself. Outside, a small band of students had gathered on the green to work on the ice sculpture in preparation for Winter Carnival. A few people were up on the scaffolding that had been erected around the ten-foot-tall sculpture of Jack Frost; the rest were down on the ground, spraying it with cold water from a hose. The process took weeks, and there was always a concern that it would rain or get warm and they'd have to start all over again. Lucky for them, it had been a cold winter.

The giant laser printer behind me hummed. I rose from my seat with a bounce. This was my favorite part of the job, filing the documents that came off the public printer. Confidentiality was assumed, but I read everything—essays, stories, medical records, angry letters to mom and dad. Recently, people had started printing their résumés, which revealed GPAs, internships, awards, accomplishments, and ambitions.

The one I held in my hand was impressive: 3.89 GPA, women's studies major, sociology minor. Internship with NARAL, founder and editor in chief of *bitch slap*. It belonged to Debra Sadie Moscowitz of Scarsdale, New York, and before I could place it in the alphabetical hanging file that sat at the corner of the desk, the door opened and Debra walked in.

"Anything good come through?" Debra pointed at the printer. She had on a long paisley skirt and a bright purple ski jacket. Her dark hair was covered with a dusting of snow, making her look like she was dressed up to play Golde in a high school production of *Fiddler on the Roof*.

I thumbed through the files. "Let's see. Hannah Lamb has a 4.0."

Debra yawned, unimpressed by Hannah Lamb. "What else?"

"Marcus Wainwright is looking for a job in marketing."

"Let me see that," she said, grabbing the letter. "'I believe my dedication to excellence and strong interpersonal skills make me a prime candidate for this position.' Please— Marcus Wainwright wouldn't know strong interpersonal skills if they fucked him in the ass. I can't believe these frat guys are going to run the world." She handed the letter back to me, then rested her head on the desk.

"What's wrong?" I asked, curling a strand of her hair between my fingers.

"Nothing," she sighed. "Just that *everyone's* pissed at me."

"Who's pissed at you, *bubeleh*?"

"Where do I begin?" she said dramatically. "Gamma Nu's

mad because I sent Crashy and Maureen undercover to write an exposé of their rush party. And now the conservative douchebags at the *Wilder Review* are trying to get our advertisers to pull out because I published those vagina pictures in *bitch slap*. God, it's like they never saw a clit before. Oh, right! They haven't." She tore open a bag of sunflower seeds. "And don't get me started on Kelsey, Miss Junior League. I swear, if she does my laundry one more time." She held up a fist. "You know I only agreed to live with her so I could live with you."

"I know. Who else is pissed at you?"

She cracked a seed between her teeth. "Well, you are."

"Me? I'm not pissed at you."

"It feels like you are. You know, after the whole Zev thing."

"Oh, honey, I'm not. I promise." I gripped her hand. "A little worried maybe."

"Worried? About me? What, you think I'm going to pull an Elizabeth McIntosh and get carted off in an ambulance right before graduation? Please, have you seen how much I eat? Hey, did you see this?" She pulled out a copy of the *New York Observer*. "I'm trying to get the same kind of round table together for *bitch slap*, asking women, 'Would you fuck Bill Clinton?'"

"I don't think they even fucked."

"Whatever. Fucking Puritans. The guy should *not* resign. She said it was all consensual." Debra tossed a handful of shells in the trash, then pointed at my scarf. "I want that by the way."

"I know," I said as she came around the desk to give me a hug. Debra hugged with her whole body, pressing herself so close I imagined no daylight escaping.

I watched her walk off and wondered again if she was okay. Kelsey had told me what her "reporters" had done at Gamma Nu, pretending to be hostesses at their rush party, then writing a scathing hit piece about the whole house. According to Kelsey, everyone at Gamma Nu was furious—even Jason, who never got mad at anyone. And even I thought her decision to print detailed anatomical sketches of vaginas was crude. I'd also heard every frat house on campus had a copy taped to the wall. I wondered why Debra couldn't leave well enough alone. We had so little time left here, why not enjoy it?

I turned back to my knitting and remembered the night Debra and I met, freshman year, at a meeting of *The Lamplighter*. I was sitting next to Jason when Debra walked in, wearing combat boots and a "Keep Abortion Legal" pin. Halfway through the meeting, she turned to me and said, "Let's get out of here," and even though I didn't know her, had never even talked to her, I followed her out of the room. Eventually, she convinced me to stop writing for *The Lamplighter* and write for *bitch slap* instead, which I didn't regret, but still. How many times had I done something because Debra told me to or believed something because she said it was true? Look where it had gotten me. Maybe she was right, I thought as I started a new ball of yarn. Maybe I was mad at her.

The rest of my shift passed slowly. Debra had left her newspaper behind, and I read the article she'd been talking about: "New York Supergals Love That Naughty Prez," the headline read. "What do women really want? A boyish chief executive who's alive below the waist." Holly stopped to see if anyone had found a cashmere sweater. Around eleven, Sally Steinberg ran by, eating a blueberry scone as big as her fist. Twenty minutes later, a pack of Zeta Psi brothers dressed identically in khaki pants and puffer jackets bought fifty dollars of video game tokens. They had just disappeared down the stairs when the door opened again and Zev walked in.

I hadn't seen him much that semester. It was hard to completely avoid people on a campus as small as Wilder's, but since we didn't have any classes together and I knew he mostly studied in his room, I found I could go days without seeing him. But now here he was, walking toward me. I looked around the student center, which was, suddenly and unprecedentedly, deserted. I reached for the newspaper again, fiddled with my knitting, then pretended to look for something in my backpack, hoping when I looked up he'd be gone. He wasn't.

"My document isn't here," he said, gesturing toward the hanging file. His dark hair was wet with snow, and he had a black scarf tied in a knot around his neck.

I looked back at the printer, but I knew there was nothing there; I would have remembered seeing something from Zev. "I filed everything that came through. Are you sure you sent it to this printer? Sometimes people—"

"You know, you made a lot of problems for me."

It took me a second to realize he wasn't talking about the printer.

"Everyone's talking about what you did. I had to go see Dean Hansen. My parents think I should come home, but

I'll be damned if you and your friend are going to run me off my own campus."

What was he talking about—*he'd* had to go see Dean Hansen? I thought he was the one who'd contacted him in the first place. I wanted to ask what he meant but was afraid to open my mouth, afraid if I did some sort of apology would tumble out. *I'm sorry we wrote* rapist *on your door. I'm sorry you have no friends. I'm sorry you were such a shitty lay and it all had to come to this.*

Zev was staring at me like I was something he'd scraped off the bottom of his shoe. I looked around hoping someone— anyone—would walk by. Didn't the Zeta Psi guys need more tokens by now? Outside by the ice sculpture, a guy was teasing a girl with the hose, threatening to spray her with it. The girl covered herself with her hands; in her eyes, glee mixed with terror.

"Your friend's a real cunt, you know, always getting involved in things that do not concern her." He rested a fist against the desk. "I think it was a cultural misunderstanding, what happened between us." He spoke slowly, as if he'd been considering his theory for some time. "I don't think American women understand the sexual aggressiveness of Israeli men. But then again, you also kind of like it, so." He smiled and bile rose in my throat. I wanted to say something, but the words were stuck inside my head, my connection to them fuzzy, like a wire had been cut. I was off the hook, bleating out nothing but an incessant busy signal.

Just then, the front door blew open, bringing with it a gust of cold air.

"Oh, my God! Isabel! I'm so glad you're here. Have you

seen my wallet?" Sally Steinberg rushed over, breathless. She launched into a story about how she'd stopped by earlier to pick up her mail—her grandmother had sent her a birthday gift and she'd come by to get it before the mail room closed. She'd gotten the package—hadn't opened it yet, who knows *what* she sent?—but now she couldn't find her wallet *anywhere* and it wasn't at the mail counter so had anyone turned it in to me at the desk?

Zev slithered away while Sally was talking, but before he did, he knocked the hanging file to the ground, sending the papers flying. "What's up with *that*?" Sally said, watching Zev's retreating form. As the two of us bent down to pick the papers off the dirty linoleum, I thought about something he had said to me the night we met, at that long-ago dinner at Hillel House. "Are you real?" he'd asked, right before the girl dropped the plates, before he grabbed my arm. *Are you real?* The words repeated in my head—*are you real are you real are you real*—and I pressed my knees hard against the cold tile to remind myself I was.

11

IT was mild the night of the Senior Mingle. There was a hint of spring in the air, soft and fragrant like a promise. The Winter Carnival folks were worried Jack Frost wouldn't make it through the weekend. Kelsey and I passed him on our way to dinner. He looked soggy, his face dripping as if he'd been out for a run. Kelsey thought it looked like he was crying. "Who hurt you, Jack Frost?" she shouted as we walked by.

Jason and I headed over to Joanna and Tom's a little past eight, early for a Saturday night. Kelsey wasn't coming—the Mingle had a strict guest list: no plus-ones. June Bridge Road was the prettiest street in town. Houses there overlooked Corness Pond. Back when I gave campus tours, they told us to always finish up at the pond because it looked pretty year-round, even in winter when it froze over and people skated on it. That morning, as part of Winter Carnival

festivities, the Outing Club folks had cut a hole in the ice
and set up platforms for the Polar Bear Plunge.

There were houses on June Bridge Road that were newer
and grander than Joanna and Tom's, but I would have chosen their ramshackle Victorian every time. Set at the end of
a winding stone pathway, it had a wide front porch, window
boxes, and dormer windows; that it needed a paint job only
added to its charm. Jason and I walked up the front steps and
into the living room. Light, tinkling music you might hear
in a restaurant during brunch service was playing. All the
furnishings—flowered sofas, worn wingback chairs, thread-
bare oriental carpets—were shabby and mismatched, as if
everything had been acquired at different places and times.
I imagined you could chart the entire course of Joanna and
Tom's life together through each chair, rug, and piece of art.
There were books everywhere, spilling out of the floor-to-
ceiling bookshelves, stacked on end tables and in towers on
the floor. Near the front door, a small winter coat hung on
a hook next to a leather satchel; an umbrella stand shaped
like a Labrador retriever sat gathering dust. Looking around
the warm and cozy room, I wondered how Joanna and Tom
would even begin to unravel the many threads that bound
them.

Jason and I dumped our coats in a bedroom then headed
over to the makeshift bar. I poured myself a glass of wine,
grabbed a couple of crackers, and walked over to talk to Whitney, who was waving at me from a sofa near the fireplace.

"Shit, girl," she said as I squeezed in next to her. "What is
happening with that dress? Seriously, you look hot."

"Shut up," I said. I was self-conscious about the dress, which I'd borrowed from Kelsey. It was pretty, navy blue with a scoop neck and bell sleeves, fancier than anything I owned; it even had a matching slip. But it was too big for me in the chest. Kelsey and I had tried to pin it, but still it gaped awkwardly. Also, I had no shoes to go with it, so I had to wear my duck boots.

"I can't believe they still had this party," Whitney said. "When my parents were getting divorced, my mother could barely get out of bed. Have you seen Professor Maxwell? She looks exhausted. Poor thing. My mother says divorce is hardest on the wife."

"I wonder who'll keep the house," I asked.

"This dump? I'd be glad to get rid of it."

Joanna Maxwell walked by clasping a long silvery cardigan at her neck. She was tiny, barely more than five feet, and with a slightly hunched back that made her appear smaller. Delicate embroidered slippers peeked out from under her long lavender dress. I looked down at my boots and regretted them even more. We watched as she stopped to talk to Amos Jackson.

"He's sort of cute, don't you think?" Whitney asked. I did not think. Amos wasn't around much; he spent most of his time in northern New Hampshire working on his thesis, an annotated collection of unpublished stories written by his great-grandfather, which had been discovered in an attic a few summers back. It was exactly the sort of thing I knew Tom loved—folksy, rural, unvarnished—and I always had the sense that Amos was on the cusp of something great. Joanna said goodbye to him and crossed the room toward us, Igraine behind her, clinging to her skirt like a bur.

"Hello, girls," Joanna said, alighting on the coffee table, Igraine nestled into her side. Whitney was right: she did look exhausted.

"Professor Maxwell," Whitney said. "Thank you so much for having us."

"Oh, it's our pleasure. Tom and I love hosting this party. Gives us a chance to soak up all this youthful energy." Her voice was high and melodious. "I know we've met," she said to me, "but, I'm so sorry, I can't remember your name."

I held out my hand. "I'm Isabel Rosen."

"Isabel!" she cried, pulling my hand to her chest. "You're the one Randy's been telling me about!"

"Who?"

"Randy Connelly, honey! He told me you've been writing some wonderful pieces for him."

"Oh, I don't know about that."

"No, no," she said. "None of that. I've known Randy a long time, and he isn't one to offer empty praise. You should choose to believe him." She squeezed my hand. "I, for one, was thrilled to hear it. We need young women with voices to lead the way."

"*Randy!*" Whitney cooed after Joanna walked away. "Speaking of whom . . ."

Professor Connelly was standing in the doorway talking to an older couple. He had a bottle of beer hanging loosely between his fingers; as I watched, he brought it slowly to his lips. The hump of his Adam's apple rose and fell as he swallowed.

"Wait, is that his wife?" Whitney asked.

I'd never seen Roxanne in person and was surprised how tall she was. Her hair was short and mostly gray, and she wore no makeup. She was dressed simply and without fuss but had chunky silver rings on each of her long, knobby fingers, a collection of studs running up and down the length of each ear. She held herself straight like a dancer, or as if she had a steel rod embedded in her spine. There was something elegant about her, graceful and feline, as if her intelligence had been transmuted into a physical attribute.

"You know, I heard from someone who knew someone in her seminar last year that she was pregnant," Whitney said. "Then one day, she just didn't show up for the rest of the semester. When we saw her that summer, no baby." She swiped her hands together.

At that, Roxanne turned her head and I saw she had a birthmark on her cheek near her jawline. It was red, about the size of a quarter, and it stood out against her skin like a drop of wine on a tablecloth. That she made no effort to hide it, either by wearing her hair long or with makeup, struck me, and I wondered what kind of woman would be so unselfconscious about the way she looked.

Just then, Connelly turned and saw us looking at him. He raised a hand in greeting, and I waved back, blushing furiously, as Whitney giggled.

"Shut up." I stood up and wiggled my empty wineglass. "You want anything?"

Whitney shook her head. "Have fun with your boyfriend!"

I headed back to the bar, past Ginny and Linus, who were

sitting together on a window seat. Ginny had a flower in her hair; Linus was wearing a bolo tie. Everyone looked nice, the girls in dresses and makeup, the boys, mostly, in button-down shirts and khaki pants. As I looked around the room, I could see a hint of the grown-ups they would become—the same way I would, when I was older, be able to see the young person inside their middle-aged avatar. I still hadn't seen Tom, but there were signs of him: the leather satchel by the front door, a pair of men's slippers near the kitchen. Joanna was still making her rounds, Igraine trailing her. The little girl looked pale and stricken; I wanted to scoop her up and put her to bed.

I refilled my glass and wandered down the narrow hall-way that led to the back of the house. The wall there was covered with family photos. I'd seen similar collections at friends' houses; Kelsey had one lining the stairwell in her apartment. But unlike hers, which included photographs of extended family going back generations—Granny and Poppy on their wedding day, a gaggle of cousins gathered on a wide green lawn—the photos here were only of Joanna, Tom, and Igraine. There was one of Tom standing alone on a beach, his long hair blowing in the wind; another of Joanna cradling her round belly. But other than that, every photo was of the three of them, as though nothing and no one else existed.

There was one photo at the end of the hall, of Tom and Joanna sitting with another couple on Adirondack chairs. I leaned in closer and saw it was Connelly and Roxanne. In the background was Connelly's cabin, the one I'd seen in *Time* magazine. It hadn't occurred to me that it was somewhere he brought people. I'd imagined it as austere, holy, the kind of place my mother always said she wanted, where she could go for peace and quiet, to hear herself think. The kind of retreat I sensed even then belonged only to men. I thought again about the girl I'd read about, the one who'd driven up there to profess her love. I wondered how she'd known she would find him alone.

There was a bustle at the front door. Andy and Kara had arrived, their tardiness intentional. Andy had his hand on the small of Kara's back and was steering her across the living room like a shopping cart. Kara was wearing a knee-length dress and fishnet stockings. Her dark hair hung down her back like a beaded curtain. As they headed toward the bar, I noticed Andy was wearing my hat.

Andy and I hadn't spoken much lately, not since Connelly had criticized his story and praised mine. Last week, he'd printed some financial aid documents at the information desk, but I'd been on the phone when he came to pick them up and he hadn't waited to say hello. And just last night I'd stopped by his carrel, thinking he might be amused by a French assignment I was working on, but he didn't invite me in. "Deadline," he grunted, before closing the door in my face. Maybe it had something to do with Kara, whom he was most definitely dating now. Maybe she was being weird about our friendship, or whatever it was, although she didn't strike me as the jealous type. But I didn't know what else it could be; he couldn't be mad about the story.

I saw Kara give him a kiss on the cheek before slipping into the bathroom. I sidled up and knocked him playfully with my elbow. "Nice hat."

"Is this the one you made me?" He pulled it off. "It's nice. Itchy, but nice."

Andy had his hair in a smooth ponytail, and he was wearing a checkered shirt with deep creases, as though he'd just unwrapped it.

"Did you finish your grad school applications?" I asked.

"Yup."

"Have your parents finally come around?"

"I mean, they still don't understand why I can't be a teacher who writes over the summers." Andy's parents were gym teachers in upstate New York. They didn't know what to do with a son who wanted to be a poet, and they worried about how he would support himself through grad school and beyond. One of the things Andy and I had in common was that we were both poor. In fact, he might have been even poorer than I was.

Andy turned to face the bathroom door, waiting, it seemed, for Kara to come out. Whatever had been between us lately was definitely still there, and it annoyed me that he wouldn't tell me what it was. He was still holding the hat in his hands, stroking it absentmindedly, and I thought about all the time I'd spent making it. Maybe it had been too much, I thought, had given him the wrong idea. My mother always told me never to knit something for a boyfriend because the affair would be over before you finished, but Andy wasn't my boyfriend, so I thought I'd be okay.

"How's Agnes?" I asked.

"Who?"

"The old lady from your story. I just—I was wondering how your story was going, if you were still working on it."

Andy narrowed his eyes. "Are you serious right now?"

"What do you mean? I liked that story. You should keep working on it. Has Joanna seen it?" I hadn't liked his story. I wasn't sure why I was lying.

Kara stepped out of the bathroom and placed a hand on Andy's arm. "Hi, Isabel," she said. "I like your dress."

"Thanks." I turned to Andy. "I'm sorry—did I say something wrong?"

He shook his head and started to walk away.

"Wait," I said, grabbing his sleeve. "Are you mad at me?"

He turned to face me. "Please. Stop pretending you aren't loving all of this."

"All of what?"

"Being teacher's pet."

"Is that why you're mad? Because Connelly liked my story?"

"Give me a break," he said. "I don't give a fuck what that guy thinks, some washed-up has-been who hasn't published anything in fifteen years. What pisses me off is how much you enjoyed it."

"Me? I didn't—"

"Yes," Andy said. "You did."

Later, I would understand that I didn't owe Andy an apology or anything else. He had a right to be mad at me, and I didn't have to care or try to fix it—I couldn't fix it. He was mad for reasons that had far more to do with him than with me. But I didn't know that yet, so I kept trying to explain myself.

"I'm sorry, Andy. I didn't mean to offend you."

Throughout our conversation, Kara didn't say a word.

She just stood there, a smile frozen on her pockmarked face. Years later, we'd bump into each other in a bar in New York and she'd hug me, warmly, as though none of this had ever happened.

"Forget it." He thrust the hat at me and walked away, Kara eager to join his retreat.

I stood there for a few minutes, perilously close to tears. Someone had turned up the music, so everyone had to shout over the tinny drone of electric guitars. The party was quickly devolving, like every cocktail party I'd ever go to, the result of too much alcohol and too little food. *Nice dress*, Holly mouthed from across the room, and Alec gave me a sly thumbs-up. Amos had joined Whitney on the couch—from where I was sitting, I could see him looking straight down her blouse. Ginny was slow dancing by the bar with no one in particular, punching the air and moving her arms in a way that made it look like she was doing a drum solo. After a few minutes, I saw her run outside; I heard later she'd thrown up in the pachysandra. Everywhere I looked people were talking and talking, working their mouths like cows chewing their cuds, but absolutely no one was listening.

I walked back to the bar, picked up a bottle of wine. If Kelsey were here, she would tell me to stop drinking or, better yet, to go home, but she wasn't, so I filled my glass. Roxanne walked by like a woman on a mission, her back straight, her steps quick and efficient. I remembered the documentaries I'd watched over winter break about Princess Diana, Roxanne there to place her in historical context. My mother had always felt a kinship with Diana, a young woman married too soon to a man who didn't understand her. Diana's death would have devastated her, and I was glad she hadn't lived to see it. I'd watched everything I could about her death, absorbing the news in my mother's place, crying so much I burst a blood vessel in my eye. Of the many things I wished I could tell my mother, I wished I could tell her she had been wrong about Roxanne, that she was beautiful, the way a mountain is beautiful: remote, craggy, forbidding.

My head was spinning, my mouth cottony and sour. I clutched Andy's hat as I watched him and Kara standing by the fireplace talking to Joanna, Joanna nodding as if what Andy was saying was important and significant. Kara had her fingers interlaced with his, her head resting gently against his shoulder. After a minute, I saw Andy lean down and whisper something in Igraine's ear, and the little girl laughed.

I set my glass down and ran into the bedroom. I wanted to go home, take off this dress, climb under the covers, and forget about tonight. Maybe Kelsey and Debra would be there and we could heat up ramen and watch bad TV in the common room, or stay up late talking, the way we used to. The night had begun with such promise, and now I couldn't wait for it to end.

I was rummaging through the dark mountain of coats when I heard someone say my name. I turned and saw Connelly standing in the doorway, his body outlined in shadow.

"Oh, my gosh," I said, holding a hand to my chest.

"Guess it's my turn to startle you."

"Guess so." Tears slid down my cheeks unprompted. I plopped onto the pile of coats and covered my face with my hands.

"Hey, hey, what's the matter?" Connelly came and sat next to me, letting the door close behind him.

"God," I said, wiping at my eyes. "I feel like I'm always crying around you. What was it you said? That women cry because they're angry?"

"That's what my wife says."

"Maybe I am angry this time." I explained, briefly, what had happened, about Andy and my story. I even told him about knitting the hat, and my mother's warning.

"I forgot how complicated this all is," he said. "All I see when I look at you is how young you are, and talented. What can I say that isn't completely clichéd—this, too, my dear, shall pass?" I laughed through my tears, and it sounded strange, like trying to sing through milk. "Listen, I've met a million Andys in my life. Hell, I've *been* Andy. Let him sulk all he wants. It won't be the first time someone's jealous of how good you are."

I was about to say something self-deprecating, but then I remembered what Joanna had said, about choosing to believe him, so I just said, "Thanks. But I'm not sure that's all it is."

"Oh. Are you and Andy . . ."

"No." I looked down at the hat in my hands. "I mean we were—we *did*. But that was a long time ago. We decided to be friends—or, I guess, *I* decided."

"That's never easy."

"I thought it was. But with guys—even when they say they forgive you, they never really forget."

"I could say the same about women."

"Touché." I touched my forehead. "I can't believe I just said, 'Touché.' I really should go home."

I started to look for my coat again. "Is this it?" Connelly asked, freeing it from the pile. "Every day, you come in wearing this coat, and . . . How could you not be curious about a girl with a coat like this?"

"It was my mother's. After she died, my father got rid of everything that belonged to her, couldn't stand having any of it around. I grabbed it before he could throw it away." I paused. "I never told anyone that before."

"Why not?"

"I thought it sounded morbid, wearing a dead woman's coat."

He looked down at the coat, reverently. "Well, it is something."

He lay the coat across his lap and stroked the heavy gray wool, the hood, the toggle buttons. In the dim light of the bedroom, his face glowed above his white shirt. Muffled party sounds traveled through the closed door: footsteps, the rush of voices. That we were alone in a dark bedroom, sitting so close I could see the place on his throat where he'd cut himself shaving, his wife somewhere nearby—all of this should have felt strange, but it didn't. It felt so good to be near him, like slipping into a hot bath. He moved closer to me, and I felt his shoulder press against mine. I looked down and saw the edge of my bra peeking out of my dress. Connelly saw it, too. And then, without saying a word, he reached out and held my wrist, circled it with his fingers like a cuff. I was surprised at how easily the barrier between us was breached, that the lines I thought existed were really nothing at all. I reached out and traced the scar that ran up the back of his hand. The skin there was smooth and hairless, like a run in a stocking.

"What happened?"

"I punched a window," he said. "Back when I was a poet."

I wanted to ask him more but found I couldn't speak. Connelly's hand moved slowly around my wrist, his fingertips resting on the flutter of my pulse. Warmth flooded me. My breath became shallow, the sound loud and echoey in my ears. With his other hand, he reached out and touched my cheek. "You look so beautiful when you cry," he said. And then he leaned over and kissed me.

He kissed me slowly at first, as if I might break, and I forgot all about Andy and his hat, which fell out of my hand and disappeared somewhere in the mountain of coats, never to be seen again. Anyone might have walked in and seen us, but I didn't think about that. He kissed me and I forgot about Roxanne and Joanna and Tom, Andy and Kara, Debra, Zev. I forgot about Abe and his expectations, my mother and her coat and her broken, ravaged body, dead now, dust. Later, we would learn to be careful, secrecy part of the story we told about ourselves, but that night, the first night, we were bold. Everything distilled to the feel of his lips on mine, his hands on my face, the smell of him—woodsmoke and peppermint, and a hint of gin. He kissed me and I went liquid. The room was cold and dark, but inside I was fire, heat, blue, blue flame. He kissed me and I was awake. He kissed me and I was alive.

Suddenly, there was a crash, the sound of people running, gasps, raised voices. Connelly stood up and opened the door a crack. I could see everyone moving in the same direction, as if the house had been picked up and turned on its side.

"Shit," he said. "I should go out there. Wait a minute before coming out." I nodded. He smiled, then ducked outside. I counted to a hundred before standing up. I'd never been scuba diving, but I imagined this was how it felt to rise from the deep.

I nearly bumped into Whitney in the hallway. "What happened?" I asked.

"Something with Professor Fisher!" she said with glee she didn't try to hide.

I pushed to the front of the crowd. Tom Fisher was standing in the middle of the kitchen, water dripping from his hair and onto the floor. His wool sweater hung down over his hips, revealing the edge of his boxer shorts. It took me a second to understand that he wasn't wearing pants. There was a towel wrapped around his left hand, dark with what looked like blood.

"Tom." Joanna was standing a few feet away from him. Roxanne stood behind her, one hand outstretched, ready to pounce. Andy and Kara were crouched down on the floor, picking up shards of glass and placing them carefully into a dish towel. The whole room reeked of gin.

"Tom. Darling." Joanna spoke softly, as if she were trying to lure a dog out of the street.

"Leave me alone!" Tom's voice was ragged. He'd been crying. He was also, I could see, terribly drunk.

"My love. Please. Let's not do this here."

"Why not? Why not do it here?" Tom wailed. Blood was dripping from the towel, collecting in a puddle at his feet. "Let them see what we really are. Let them see what becomes of people." He shook his head, sending a spray of water around the room. Roxanne took a step forward, but Joanna waved her back.

I looked around, wondering what we were supposed to do. Andy and Kara had finished clearing the glass. They stood together by the counter, Andy holding the dish towel, Kara biting her lip. Igraine stood behind her mother, her face twisted up like a rag.

"Hey, buddy." Connelly stepped forward with the calm authority of a paramedic. He whispered something to Roxanne, and she nodded, an almost imperceptible movement. Then he put his hand on Tom's shoulder.

Tom startled, then blinked. "Randy," he said, as if awakened from a trance.

"I'm here, man," Connelly said. "I'm right here." He pointed at Tom's arm. "Why don't we get that cleaned up?"

"None of this is mine anymore," Tom said, his voice thick with tears. "It's never been mine, any of it. Why are you doing this to me, Joanna? Why?" He lunged for her, and the room let out a collective gasp as he reached for his wife with a bloody hand.

Connelly pulled Tom back and Roxanne stepped forward decisively, wrapping one arm around Joanna and grabbing Igraine with the other. Joanna buried her face in her hands as Roxanne peeled Igraine's fingers from her mother's skirt. The girl's silent sobs turned into wails as Roxanne hurried her out of the room. Joanna collapsed onto a chair Andy held out for her as Tom fell to his knees. The leg of his boxer shorts puckered open, and I could see the pale skin of his upper thigh. For the first time since I'd stepped into the kitchen, I had to look away.

"Okay, guys," Connelly said. "Show's over." He held my eyes for a moment, then looked away. Joanna gave us all a weak smile as we began to depart. The last thing I saw before I left was Connelly putting an arm around Tom's shoulders, helping him to stand.

We took our things and staggered quietly down June Bridge Road. We'd seen too much, the world of adults revealed in all its glory and despair. I was reminded of the needlepoint designs my mother used to make that looked so perfect from the front, but when you turned them over, you could see every knot and string.

The crowd broke up around Frat Row, people searching for late-night parties, wanting to blot out the memory with cold beer and loud music. Jason and I walked slowly together past Jack Frost. He was a sad, soggy mess, the bulk of him disintegrating before our eyes. It would rain all night; by Monday, he'd be little more than a puddle.

"Poor Jack," Jason said, before turning down the street that led to his dorm.

No one was there when I got home. I peeled off my dress and climbed into bed without brushing my teeth. I was exhausted but knew I'd never sleep. Images from the night played over and over again in my mind like frames in a film-strip: Igraine's tiny fingers, Tom's waterlogged sweater, the plume of blood on the towel. I don't know why it shocked me but it did, how quickly violence descended upon us.

Moonlight streaked the room, and before long the bloody scene in the kitchen faded, replaced by memories of the coatroom and Connelly's kiss. Because what did I care about Joanna and Tom and their sad, pathetic decline? Nothing; as small and unimportant as I mostly felt, the egotism of youth hadn't left me, and I placed myself firmly and squarely at the center of the universe.

I held my arm above my face, cold marble in the moonlight, traced the crisscross of veins through the skin. I remembered the feel of Connelly's lips on mine, the scratch of his cheek, felt everything inside me straining toward the surface. Then I closed my eyes and slept a hard, dreamless sleep.

12

IT turned out Tom had jumped into Corness Pond, off one of the platforms set up earlier that day for the Polar Bear Plunge. A neighbor, watching from her kitchen window, saw him take off his coat, boots, and pants, lay them neatly at the water's edge, then jump into the icy water.

I heard it all the next day from Whitney, who'd stayed behind to help Roxanne clean up after Connelly took Tom to the emergency room and they'd finally gotten Joanna to bed. They were still there when the neighbor, an elderly woman in curlers, knocked on the door to make sure everything was okay. Roxanne poured them all some Scotch, and they sat at the kitchen table listening as the woman told them how it had taken her several desperate minutes to coax Tom out of the water and up onto the platform. When Roxanne asked why she hadn't called the police, the woman said, "I didn't think there was time."

Within twenty-four hours, everyone knew what had happened, even people who hadn't been at the Mingle. In the dining hall Sunday night, a group of us sat and examined the evening from every angle, piecing our stories together like a puzzle, fitting and refitting the pieces to be sure we had the whole. Holly and Alec had been outside smoking when they saw Tom stumble up the back steps. Jason was talking to Amos and Whitney in the living room when they'd heard the crash, which turned out to be Tom knocking over a chair, then smashing a bottle of gin against the kitchen counter, cutting his hand badly enough that he'd needed thirty-four stitches, according to Whitney—forty-four, according to Holly.

Had he really meant to kill himself, we wondered, or was it a cry for help? There were certainly more efficient ways to kill oneself, we agreed, less wet, less public. "The guy wanted an audience," said Holly, popping a cherry tomato in her mouth. "Like the kids who slit their wrists to get attention. Horizontal's always the giveaway. Everyone knows straight down means business." According to Holly, if Tom had really wanted to die, he wouldn't have jumped into the pond during a party when there were so many people around to stop him; the fact that none of us had did not dissuade her. Holly was convincing, but I wasn't convinced. I'd seen something in Tom's eyes that night, something unhinged, as if whatever tethered him to reality had come loose, like a screen door flapping in the wind. Andy might have had more insight, but we weren't speaking.

While everyone was talking about Joanna and Tom, I couldn't stop thinking about Connelly. I was cagey about where I'd been when I heard the crash—getting something

out of my coat, I said when people asked. I hadn't told anyone about the kiss, not even Debra. In the absence of having
anyone to talk to, I kept having to remind myself it had really
happened, and then, once I did, I wondered what it meant.

By the time I walked into Room 203 on Wednesday
morning, I'd replayed the scene in the bedroom so many
times, it threatened to crumble in my hands like an old love
letter. Connelly wasn't there yet, and for a moment I imagined it had all been a dream, that Joanna had never stopped
teaching, that I'd never met Connelly. Then suddenly there
he was, unzipping his parka with his big hands, the same
hands that had held my wrist and touched my hair.

We were discussing Ramona's story that day. Connelly
seemed more animated than usual, offering praise to Ramona,
complimenting Ginny on her careful reading of a passage.
He barely glanced my way. I'd wondered what he might say
when we were finally alone, if he would kiss me again or
tell me it had all been a mistake; now I worried he wouldn't
say anything at all. The thought threw me into despair, and
I counted the minutes until I could run back to my room,
never to emerge again.

When class was over, I hurried for the door, but Connelly stopped me, holding up two fingers as if he were hailing a taxi. I waited by the door while he said something to
Ramona. When he laughed at something she said, I imagined him leaning over to kiss her, too.

"All right," he said when she left. "Let's go up to my
office."

I followed him silently up the stairs, dragging my feet the

way my mother hated: "You look like you're being led to the executioner." That's how I felt as Connelly led me down a long, dark hallway on the fourth floor, lined with mostly empty offices.

"Why is your office up here?" I asked. Most English professors had their offices on the second floor.

"They always stick me up here. Whenever I fill in for someone, it's usually at the last minute." He fumbled for his keys. "I like it up here though. Nice and quiet."

Connelly's office was small with a slanted ceiling that made it feel smaller. Unlike Tom's office, which faced the campus green, Connelly's office was in the back of the building and had a view of the parking lot. It was sparsely furnished—desk, chair, a couple of mismatched bookcases; a brown leather sofa was the only thing that looked new. No photos or framed diplomas, plants or kitschy mugs. Nothing to indicate he was here to stay.

"You've taught here before?" I asked as he gestured for me to have a seat on the sofa.

"A couple of times. I filled in for Joanna after Igraine was born, and once when she was on book tour. Tom, too, when he was ill." The heater in the corner clanked loudly. "God, that thing never shuts up. Aren't you hot?" He pointed at me still in my coat. I had it buttoned nearly to the top.

"I'm okay."

Connelly walked over to the window. "Nice to have some sunshine for a change. Although they say it's supposed to snow this weekend."

"It's February, what do you expect? I mean, everyone

makes such a big deal about the weather. At least in February, there are no surprises. It's February: it's cold, it snows. March on the other hand—I hate March."

"Oh yeah?" he said, the hint of a smile on his face. "Why do you hate March?"

"It's inconsistent—sunny one day, freezing the next. It offers the promise of spring, but never delivers. Nope. Give me January or June."

"Got it." Connelly was unwinding a paper clip with his fingers, twisting it into a long spiral. I'd read an article once that said the way you bent a paper clip revealed something about your personality, but I couldn't remember anything else it said.

"So," I said, "did you want to talk about the weather?"

"No. I did not want to talk about the weather." He placed the paper clip on the windowsill and sat down at his desk. "I wanted to talk about what happened the other night. At Joanna and Tom's," he added, as if I needed clarification. "That's not something I usually do, kiss young women in coatrooms."

"I'm sure it isn't."

"I'd had quite a bit to drink, and I think it clouded my judgment. I hope you didn't take it the wrong way."

"I didn't. Take it the wrong way—or any way." My face burned. This apology, or whatever it was, was humiliating. He was drunk? It sounded like the kind of thing a frat guy would say. I expected better from him. I stood up, glad I'd kept my coat on so I could leave quickly.

"Isabel, please. Don't leave." He held out his hand. "God,

I'm sorry. I really botched this. I just wanted—I don't know what I wanted." He took a deep breath. "Please. Don't leave." I waited a moment, then sat back down and unbuttoned my coat.

"Thank you," he said. He picked up another paper clip, unwound it into a shape resembling a poker and used it to scratch at his desk. "Let's try this again. Some party, huh?"

"Yeah," I said. "Some party."

"Are they always like that?"

"I don't know. I've never been to one before."

"Right."

He tossed the paper clip in the trash and picked up another one. He seemed nervous. I still didn't know why he'd invited me here or why he hadn't let me leave. I wondered what he was waiting for.

"Can I ask you something?" I said.

"Shoot."

"Do you know why Tom did it? Jumped in the pond, I mean?"

If Connelly was surprised or offended by my question, he didn't show it. "It was unfortunate, what happened. I imagine everyone's talking about it?" I nodded. "No surprise there. It was rather dramatic. I don't know exactly why he did it. I know he's having a hard time with the divorce. And now Joanna's fighting him for custody. Men usually get the short end of the stick in these sorts of things." He was quiet, perhaps deciding what more he should say. "The guy's seeing everything he ever worked for get taken away. That's hard. Don't believe men's posturing, Isabel. We need women.

Somewhere along the way the balance shifts and all these boys you pine for now become men who are very afraid of being alone."

Outside, the bell tower started playing the alma mater, which it did every day at noon, a clunky, out-of-tune rendition. Connelly was still twisting the paper clip, and I realized I could leave now and what happened between us would stay a small indiscretion that never came to anything. Or I could push him to acknowledge what he'd done, what he'd wanted to do, and not because he was drunk. I felt a strange power coursing through my veins as I realized I was the one who would decide whether we were done with each other.

I looked down at my boots, their tips dusty like a chalkboard. "I think with everything that went on that night, no one noticed us."

"Really?" he said. "That's a relief."

"And I didn't tell anyone. Did you?"

"Of course not."

"So then, I guess we're good."

I stood up and walked toward the door. I could feel his eyes following me. I placed my hand on the doorknob, then turned back to face him. "Can I just say something?"

"Go ahead."

"You didn't seem that drunk."

"What?" he laughed.

"I said, you didn't seem that drunk. When you kissed me. I mean, it's fine if you want to forget about it, but I don't think you did it because you were drunk."

The heater clanked again. The bell tower was still playing,

verse after verse, noisy and insistent. "Maybe you're right. But can I ask *you* something?"

"Shoot."

"Why'd you kiss me back?"

I took my hand off the doorknob, let it hang at my side. I could feel my heart beating hard in my chest, like the slap of a dog's tail against a hardwood floor. "Because I wanted to."

A flash of color rose to his cheeks. "So what do you think we should do?"

"I think you should kiss me again. Then we can decide."

"Lock the door," he said, and I did.

Connelly walked over to the sofa. I met him there. It felt like we were performing a carefully choreographed ritual, each of us nailing our part. We sat together, shoulder to shoulder, the same way we had in Joanna and Tom's bedroom.

"We should probably talk about discretion," he said. "This can't become part of the," he twirled a finger in the air, "rumor mill."

"What about your wife?"

"That's the thing," he said, reaching for my hand. "This could get messy, if we're not careful."

It wasn't really an answer, but I let it go. We seemed to be inching toward an agreement of some kind, but I was having a hard time focusing. I just wanted him to kiss me. I placed my index finger on the space above his lip. The skin there was damp and softer than I'd imagined.

"This is going to change everything," he said.

"Promise?" And then, before he could say anything else, I kissed him. I kissed his mouth, his cheeks, his eyelids, the soft skin behind his ears, the tip of his chin. I heard his breath catch as I kissed the base of his throat. He tasted like menthol and something else, something earthy, salty. Desire moved through me, pushing everything else to the side. We kissed until the clock tower was quiet, then he put his hands on my shoulders and pushed me away.

"We should stop," he said. "Before we can't."

I sat back. Everything looked different, clearer, like I'd never worn glasses and someone had handed me a pair. Connelly looked different, too. I realized I hadn't under-stood his purpose—why I'd met him, why he was here—but now it all fell into place. Of course I'd met him. Of course he'd kissed me. Of course, of course, of course.

"If anyone asks," Connelly said as I stood up and smoothed my hair, "tell them you came to talk to me about your job search, that I had some leads for you."

I nodded.

"And that you might need to come back to show me things, résumés, cover letters. Do you understand?"

"Yes."

"And Isabel?" He pulled me onto his lap. "I might need to see those things pretty soon." He wrapped his arms around my waist and kissed me again, harder, deeper; I thought he might swallow me whole. Before I left, he held a finger to his lips, the annunciation of a secret.

I WAITED FOR him every day, a folder filled with copies of my résumé and cover letters I'd never send tucked under one arm. Sometimes he walked past without making eye contact, or tossed a curt "Hello, Isabel" my way before head-ing upstairs with a colleague or another student. On those days, I learned to hold my face in an expression of detached disinterest. On those days, I became a master of waiting. But on the days he walked by alone, the days his eyes met mine as he brushed past, I would wait until he reached the second landing before following him upstairs. I took my time walk-ing down the hallway, feeling the tickle of my hair against my shoulders, the rub of denim on my thighs, the nub of my tongue behind my teeth. I'd knock on his door three times and wait for him to open it, the sound of my breath hot and hollow in my ears, anticipation rising in me like a cobra. Then he'd pull me toward him, wrap his hands around my rib cage, press his lips against my ear, and tell me what he liked. Good student that I was, I learned quickly.

February deepened. Snow lay heavy across the ground. In Washington, DC, Monica Lewinksy sought immunity in exchange for testimony against her former lover. In New Hampshire, I disappeared behind the locked door of Con-nelly's office.

We kissed on his leather sofa until I was slippery with desire. I was desperate for him, but he wouldn't have sex with me until he was sure I understood the rules.

"We have to be careful," he said. I had his fingers in my mouth and was nibbling on them, delicately, like I was suck-ing the meat off an olive stone. "I'm serious." He pulled his hand back. "This isn't a joke. Do you understand?"

"I understand."

"No gossip. No telling your friends."

"I won't. I promise." I reached for him, but he pushed me away.

"I want to be sure you want it."

"I do."

"Soon," he whispered.

Tom was still technically my thesis adviser, although I hadn't met with him in weeks; the pages I left sat in his mailbox, untouched. Jason thought I should talk to someone about getting a different adviser, but the only person I could think to talk to was Joanna, who was still head of the department despite being on leave. I saw her sometimes, floating in and out of Stringer Hall, Igraine in tow. She looked thin and distracted, her pale skin even paler, the hollows beneath her eyes deep and bruise blue.

Besides, Connelly had been reading my pages instead. He wasn't an expert on Wharton, but he read my work carefully, asked penetrating questions, and found connections I didn't even know I had made.

"This," he said one afternoon, jabbing at my pages with his finger. "This is the kind of writer you should be. One who writes what everyone is thinking but is afraid to say." He reached for my cigarette and took a drag. "Everyone here is so fucking self-conscious. Sometimes I want to grab them and say, 'The world will not fall apart if you tell the truth.'"

I lay back on the sofa, feeling his praise reverberate in my chest. He'd moved a few more things into his office—a brass lamp, a spidery-looking plant, a couple of paisley throw pillows. It didn't look homey per se, just a little less temporary, which comforted me.

"Has no one ever told you this?" he said, passing back my cigarette. "How good you are?"

I shook my head.

He stroked my cheek with his knuckle. "Well, that's a goddamn shame."

We didn't talk much about him or his work or the time in his life when he'd been, briefly, famous. I imagined it would be painful for him to be reminded of what he'd lost, but maybe I was projecting, as Debra would have said.

"Do you ever go up to your cabin anymore?" I asked once, tentatively.

"No. I only needed that kind of solitude when I was writing poetry. It wasn't a very happy place in the end. That's where this happened." He pointed at the scar on his hand. "Too much time alone isn't good for me, it turns out."

I brought his hand to my mouth, traced the ridge of the scar with my lips. "Do you miss it?"

"The cabin?"

"The writing."

"I still write, Isabel."

"I know. I mean, writing poetry."

"No. I'm lucky to have had the success I had. Most people don't get it even once. And I don't punch windows anymore, so that's good. Plus, I like what I'm doing now—writing for the *Citizen* and teaching. Passing the torch on to worthier successors."

He never talked about the novel, the one Jason had told me about. It had been published a few years after *I'm Sorry I Can't Stay Long*, soon after he and Roxanne were married.

According to the few mentions of it I could find, it had been widely panned. "A crass attempt at mass market fiction from one of our finest poets," said one review. "I think this is called, in common parlance, a 'money grab,'" read another. It was the last thing he'd ever published; two years later, he started writing for the *Citizen*.

Some people didn't like him. Alec thought he was moody. Holly thought he played favorites. Linus wondered what class might have been like if Joanna was teaching instead. I said nothing when they criticized him. When they talked about favorites, I suspected they were talking about me, but I didn't care. I'd never been anyone's favorite.

Only one question gnawed at me.

"Have you done this before?" I'd skipped calculus again and was lying on the sofa, my feet pressed against the soft pooch of his stomach. He'd hinted that students had come on to him in the past. Nothing happened, but he had to be careful; at times, dodging their advances could be harder than teaching.

He ran a finger along the arch of my foot. We still hadn't slept together. "Do you mean, am I a virgin?"

I gave him a kick. "You know what I mean."

"Ohhh," he said. "This? No."

"Really?"

"Really, Isabel. You're the only one."

The thrum of a word vibrated through me like a neon sign. Special. I sat up and buried my face in his chest. Did I believe him? We'd just heard Bill Clinton swear he hadn't had an affair with Monica Lewinsky. Did we believe *him*? We believed what we chose to believe, what was in our best interest. Lies weren't as bad as we'd been taught when we were children and besides, we weren't children anymore.

"You have your answer," he whispered, reaching a hand under my shirt. "Are you happy now?"

Was I happy? It was something close.

MARCH ARRIVED, AND all around, people started waking up to the fact that we would soon leave this place. Debra was making plans to move to San Francisco. Jason was waiting to hear from law schools. Kelsey hoped to find a job at an art gallery in New York. I had no interest in their plans or in making any of my own. Because I'd finally found what I'd been looking for, my purpose revealed on the leather sofa under the eaves. This is why I'd come here, I thought, as Connelly placed his big hands on me, as I peeled off layers of myself and fed them to him. This had always been the reason.

I told him everything, about Rosen's and growing up in New York, how I loved it, how I feared it. I told him about the first time I'd seen Wilder, junior year, the requisite college tour. My mother had been too sick to come, so I'd taken pictures of everything I thought might please her—the wood-paneled dining hall, stone fireplaces, sculpture garden. When I got home, I had them developed at a one-hour photo shop. The chemo had given her terrible mouth sores, so she didn't say much as she examined each photo, slowly and carefully, as if she were memorizing them. Later, I noticed she had them propped on her nightstand so she could see them from bed. Sometimes when I walked through those spaces, the ones I'd photographed, I imagined she could see me, even though I didn't believe in things like that.

I told him about my mother, how she thought I read too much, while Abe thought I read the wrong things. I told him how she valued beauty above all else and that her favorite painting of me was one she made when I was sick, my cheeks flushed pink with fever. I told him how angry Abe was with her for making me pose when I should have been resting, but she'd believed it was worth it, and I agreed. I told him I'd never thought I could be an artist like her because the ways we perceived the world were fundamentally different: she saw things with her eyes while I felt them through the thin skin of my heart.

"But you are an artist," he told me, and I wrapped myself up in his words.

In exchange, he shared little about himself. Aside from what I'd gleaned from his poems and the magazine article, I knew almost nothing about his childhood or his parents, and we never discussed his marriage, how it came to be, why it endured. I'd dug up the *bitch slap* interview Debra had done with Roxanne. It focused mostly on her time as an undergrad. Stories about the early years of coeducation at Wilder were legendary, the hostility and harassment, the alumni who openly questioned whether the presence of women would change Wilder's "character." The women who'd paved the way for us were largely considered heroes, but Roxanne had a different take.

"I'm not saying we had it easy," she said, "but I would argue that, in some ways, our struggles were easier than yours.

We got you in the door, but you have to fight to belong here. And believe me, that's a much bigger fight."

In the photograph that accompanied the interview, Roxanne sat behind her desk, her hands splayed out in front of her face, midgesture. I looked closely at the lines criss-crossing her face, the dark circles under her eyes. My own beauty had never been accessible or easy to understand, my body all straight angles, my face tinged with a serious-ness men my age found difficult or forbidding. But com-pared to Roxanne, I could see that I was beautiful or, at least, that youth conferred its own kind of beauty. (Later, I would know this implicitly. I would pass young women on the street and see that they were all beautiful, even the ones who weren't.)

I put down the interview and looked at my face in the mirror: smooth cheeks, apple-colored lips, dark hair hanging loose over my shoulders. Pretty—*shayna maidel*, the women who came into Rosen's used to call me. I thought about the story Whitney told me about Roxanne's mysterious—and lost—pregnancy. In comparison, my own body felt full and fertile. I could give him that, I thought, if he wanted it. I could give him everything.

IT WAS THE first weekend in March. Debra was at her cousin's bat mitzvah, and Kelsey and Jason were heading up to Bo Benson's ski condo in Killington.

I started getting ready as soon as they were gone. Rox-anne was at her sister's, so it was a rare Friday night that

Connelly could get away. I'd hoped tonight would be the night, that I'd proved my devotion to him and our secret. I showered and shaved, then put on my prettiest bra and a pair of black pants with no zipper that I imagined him pulling off me with a yank.

Stringer Hall was dark at night. I tiptoed up to the fourth floor, then knocked my secret knock—three short taps.

"Come in."

The lights were out. Connelly was lying on the sofa. His shoes were off, and he had one arm slung over his face.

"Are you okay?"

"Not really," he said. "I'm having a vertigo attack. I'm waiting to see if it passes."

"Should I go?" I asked, my voice heavy with disappointment.

"No," he said, patting the sofa. "Come. Leave the lights off."

I squeezed my hips into the space next to his shoulders. "I thought you got vertigo climbing high things."

"Yeah, me too. But apparently not. Such are the indignities of old age." He took my hand. "Talk to me. Tell me something."

"What?" I wasn't in the mood for talking.

"Anything."

I took a deep breath and told him about the room I shared with Debra and Kelsey, how I slept on the top bunk because Debra was afraid of heights, the result of some sleepaway camp trauma. I told him about the couch we'd inherited from friends who'd graduated, how we'd had to carry it up four flights of stairs. How Kelsey had wanted to ask Jason and his brothers for help but Debra had insisted we do it ourselves.

"Ah, that Debra," Connelly said.

I told him how the three of us used to be close but weren't so much anymore, but that part made me sad so instead I told him how sophomore year, Ginny had gotten drunk and slid down a flight of stairs at Zeta Psi. She'd badly bruised her coccyx and had had to miss the rest of the crew season, and because of that I still got the words coccyx and coxswain mixed up. I told him about the time freshman year when my roommate and I woke up and found a guy peeing in our closet because he thought it was the bathroom. I told him about my job at the information desk and the Crushgirls, and even Bo Benson.

"Bo Benson," he said. "Sounds like the name of a super-hero. Is he a nice boy?"

"He's okay."

"Does he like you?"

"I don't know."

"I bet he does." His eyes were still closed, his long lashes resting on his cheeks. "I bet every boy here is in love with you."

"Hardly."

"Their loss." He ran a hand along my thigh. "Go. Lock the door."

"I thought you were sick."

"I feel better now."

I ran for the door and locked it. As I headed back to the sofa, Connelly held up his hand.

"Stop," he said.

"Yes, sir." I saluted, then started to unbutton my shirt.

"No. I want you to tell me something with that smart mouth of yours."

"I've already told you everything."

"No. You haven't." His face was serious in the moonlight. "You haven't told me what you want."

"I don't know. World peace?" I didn't want to talk anymore. I wanted him to kiss me, to wrap me in his arms and press me into the sofa until I couldn't breathe.

"No," he said. "You're going to stand there and tell me what you want."

"I don't know what I want."

"Then tell me what you want me to do to you."

My knees buckled, my breath came hard out of my mouth. Had any college girl in the history of the world ever been asked what she wanted? I was most certainly the first.

"I want . . ." I undid another button on my shirt.

"Stop," he said, louder this time. He pushed himself up to sit and rested his hands on his knees.

"Come on. I feel dumb."

"There is nothing dumb about you, Isabel." His tone was serious, less playful. "But if you can't tell me what you want, then we can't keep doing this. Do you understand what I'm saying?"

I shook my head.

"Do you remember when you told me about that night, with that boy—what was his name? Zev?"

I'd forgotten I'd told Connelly about Zev, and I couldn't

remember why I did, only that at the time it had made me feel better knowing that he knew. Now, I wished I hadn't.

"You told me you weren't sure that night what you wanted," Connelly continued. "Or maybe you were, but you didn't say. Right?"

"I—I don't know."

"You don't know." He shook his head. "You see, I don't want you telling a story like that about me someday. I know you think you won't. But you don't know what you might think about all of this later, when it's over. What you wanted me to do to you, what you didn't. We need to be clear about it now so there are no misunderstandings. Because the stakes are too high."

My palms were damp. I felt dizzy. My shirt was open, and for the first time since we'd been together, I felt naked, exposed. All this time I had been telling him stories, had he been ferreting them away to use later, as a test of my loyalty? What had started out as a game had become an order because implicit in what he was saying was a threat: do this now, promise me this now, or we cannot continue. Didn't he know I would do anything, promise him anything? I just wanted him to stop talking and kiss me.

"Are we clear, Isabel?"

"Yes," I said. "We're clear."

"Good. Now, stand there and tell me what you want."

"I want . . ."

"Louder."

"I want you to kiss me."

"Where?"

I pointed to the side of my neck.

"Say it."

"My neck. On my neck."

"What else?"

"Your tongue. I want your tongue . . ."

"Where?"

"Here." I lifted my hair and pointed to the patch of skin behind my ear.

He nodded. "Keep going."

"I want your hands here." I slipped off my shirt, cupped my breasts in my hands.

He lay back on the sofa and exhaled. "That's right. What else?"

I stood there, concentrating on the feel of the wooden floor beneath my feet. I pressed against it so I wouldn't float away. Words poured out of me, a string of sounds that became sentences, sentences that became a story, one I'd always been writing but didn't know it until I started telling it to him. By the time I was finished, I was on my knees, crawling across the floor, my body a live wire, an electric-blue flame. Connelly was a gentle lover. He did everything I asked and nothing more. He talked to me, made sure I was okay, that I liked what he was doing; before he came, he asked if he could. When it was over, he kissed me tenderly across my damp brow, along the shelf of my collarbone, on the tip of every finger. Then he helped me dress and walked me downstairs. "Hurry home," he told me. "Do not pass Go."

The room was empty when I got back. I crawled into bed but couldn't sleep. My mind was reeling with thoughts about desire and control—and consent.

Consensual. The word had been rattling around in my

head ever since Dean Hansen used it to describe what had happened with Zev. *He told me the two of you had a consensual encounter.* I didn't disagree with him—what Zev and I had done seemed consensual while it was happening, not wanted perhaps, but not done against my will. But now, comparing that night to what I had just done with Connelly, I realized the two acts were worlds apart, linked only by their most basic biological similarities. I hadn't known what I wanted then because I'd never wanted anything as much as I wanted Connelly.

THIS IS THE time I go back to, those five or six weeks when everything was easy between us. Drowsy afternoons on Connelly's sofa, the smell of him in my hair and on my skin, underneath my fingernails. I go back to March, that season of transition, when the world stops being one thing and starts being another. Outside, the world was waking up into spring, but we kept the shades drawn to block out the light.

It was snowing the day I walked into Joanna Maxwell's office and asked if Professor Connelly could be my thesis adviser now that Professor Fisher had officially taken a leave of absence. Igraine was asleep on a sofa, clutching a tattered blanket to her cheek. She made a soft purring sound as she slept.

"Professor Connelly?" she asked. "Are you sure?"

"Yes," I said. I was sure.

13

MY mother got sick when I was thirteen. It was a familiar story: a lump that led to a series of tests, surgery, chemo, more surgery, a period of remission, and finally a slow, agonizing march toward the end. As my mother descended into illness, slowly at first and then all at once, I started growing. As her body wasted away, mine burst into sickening bloom.

My mother must have noticed I kept wearing the same pair of jeans and oversized hoodie, so one day she sent me shopping with my grandmother. It was the opposite of a shopping spree, Yetta, dour and thin-lipped, swathed in a haze of menthol cigarette smoke, leading me through the aisles of Century 21. I was ashamed of everything, of my grandmother and my body, of poverty and illness and the meagerness of everything. We left with only a few things that day—a pair of jeans, a couple of bras, three T-shirts, and a sweater—even though I needed and wanted much, much more.

Later that year, while my mother was in the hospital, I spent the night at a friend's house. When she left the room to get some snacks, I saw her closet door was open. She had so many clothes—blouses, skirts, dresses, cardigans. I ran my hand over the soft fabrics and then, without thinking, grabbed a sweater off a hanger and shoved it in my bag. When I got home the next day, I tried it on in front of the mirror. It was nicer than anything I owned, a beautiful dusty rose wool blended with cashmere, the neckline delicate and flattering. I didn't know clothing could be so nice. She never noticed the missing sweater, so the next time I was at her house, I took a pair of jeans and a peasant skirt.

After that, I started taking things whenever I had the chance. Clothing mostly, but also earrings, handbags, makeup. Sometimes I wore the stolen item to school, right in front of the person I'd taken it from. I'd see their eyes narrow when they saw it, but no one ever confronted me. I was a good thief but also an unlikely one.

I set strict rules for myself: I didn't steal from anyone whose family was poorer than mine, a complicated metric based on whether their parents were divorced and whether they shared a room. I didn't steal from close friends or from anyone who'd met my parents, but I didn't steal from strangers either. I didn't take anything that couldn't be replaced, and through it all, I reminded myself that what I was doing was wrong and kept making plans to stop. But then something would happen—my mother would have a bad night and I'd find Abe crying over his toast in the morning—and I'd start up again.

Success made me bolder. Junior year, when my mother was in the hospital for a pancreatic infection, I stole cash from a friend's father's wallet. That spring, after the experimental protocol she'd been on all winter stopped working, I stole a pair of diamond earrings from a friend's older sister. By the time I got to Wilder I'd stopped, the impulse largely dormant, which was good because I had ample opportunity. The girls here were so rich and careless, their closets overflowing with cashmere sweaters and corduroy pants, loafers and add-a-pearl necklaces, everything tossed on the floor or piled on their beds, things my years of stealing had taught me they'd never miss. But my days of wanting other people's things were over.

Also, my mother was dead so I had no more excuses.

IT WAS THE last Thursday in March, and an icy rain was falling. On my way to Stringer Hall, Joanna Maxwell ran past me, pushing Igraine in a stroller she looked too big for. The little girl was sleeping; Joanna held an umbrella awkwardly over her with one hand while steering the stroller with the other. There were times Joanna reminded me of my mother, although she was smaller and, in a way that was hard to explain, clearly not Jewish. I hadn't seen her since the day I'd asked to switch advisers, hadn't even thought of her. I was too consumed by my own drama.

Connelly was at his desk, reading through a stack of student papers. There was a set of keys I'd never seen before next to him, hanging off an old-timey ring, the kind a jailer might have dangling from his belt. Connelly hadn't shaved and his face was tantalizingly rough. I wanted to reach out and feel the prickle of him, but I knew not to bother him while he was working; besides, it was always better when he made me wait. I pulled off my boots, draped my socks over the heater, and lay down on the floor, warming my feet against the radiator. There was a blister on the back of my heel. I poked at it absentmindedly.

After several minutes, he looked over at me. "Well, hello there. Don't you look nice?"

"Thank you," I said.

"What do you have on under that sweater?"

I pulled out the neck and looked down. "Tank top. Bra."

"Take it off."

I did as he asked, then started to move toward him, but he stopped me. "No. Stay there. I like the way you look on the floor."

I lay back down, and Connelly stepped over me to lock the door. I could feel his footsteps through the floor, my body vibrating with each step.

"Close your eyes," he said.

He leaned down and nudged open my hand with something. He ran the tip of it across my palm, along the inside of my wrist and up to the crook of my elbow. I shivered as he dragged it up to my shoulder, then across the shelf of my collarbone. It was a key. I kept my eyes closed as he moved it slowly down the other arm, then in between every finger and around the base of my thumb.

Connelly lifted up the key and readjusted his stance. I could hear him breathing as he took off his sweater, then placed the tip of the key between my breasts, the metal cold against my skin. He drew a line with it down my center, my plumb line, traced circles around each nipple.

"Take these off," he said, tugging on my jeans. I wriggled them down, kicked them over my heels, roughly, breaking the skin that protected the blister. I could hear the sleet hitting the roof, like somebody was tossing pebbles against it. Connelly placed the key at the base of my rib cage, let it dip inside my navel, then ran it down the inside of each leg from thigh to ankle and back again. I didn't know how much time had passed, ten minutes, twenty, half a day. I remembered vaguely that I had somewhere to go but didn't know where. My mind was filled with keys. Connelly plucked the elastic of my underwear like a guitar string and I thought about the keys to our apartment that my mother taught me to brandish like a weapon when I walked home late at night. He pulled my underwear down, and I thought about the key to the safe at the back of the store where Abe kept the cash he brought to the bank every Friday. Shabbos. Connelly spread my legs and I remembered Yetta's drawer of keys, ones she could never bring herself to throw away because what if she needed them one day? The rain picked up. I pictured a hallway lined with doors I couldn't open, things I needed trapped behind them: means of rescue, survival, escape. Connelly put himself inside me and unlocked everything I'd ever held there: shame, fear. There was a string of bruises on my spine when I got home, scratches up and down my thighs. He covered my mouth as I cried out, and I no longer knew what was inside me, only that I never again found a door I couldn't open. He held the key to my undoing, and I let him undo everything.

MY NEED TO link sex with secrecy was born that spring. After that, there was nothing more erotic than a furtive kiss behind a closed door, a hurried grope in a coat closet, a man's hand on my knee while his girlfriend sat across from us. I once asked Bo to meet me at a bar and pretend he didn't know me. I had a dress picked out, short and backless, the kind you couldn't wear with a bra. Black eyeliner, red lipstick—the kind of makeup I never wore. I'd leave my wedding ring at home, but he could wear his. I'd go full slut for him, be easy for once. We'd fuck in a bathroom stall. I'd let him pull off my underwear with his teeth.

"Why would I want to do that?" Bo said, laughing. "I thought the whole point of getting married was so I didn't have to pick up strangers in bars anymore." I laughed too but knew it was the beginning of the end of us. I needed something from him, something I didn't know how to ask for or explain. When we made love that night, at home, in bed with the lights off, I thought about Connelly, imagined myself back in his office at the end of the hall, winter light filling the room, the leather sticky on the backs of my thighs, the feel of cold metal against my skin. Sometimes when Connelly came, he'd bite my lip, hard enough to draw blood. "What happened?" Bo asked when we were finished. He pointed at my face. I reached up, wiped my mouth with my hand and tasted blood, rusty like a key.

14

IN April, I went home for Passover. Abe asked me to, which surprised me: we didn't put much stock in holidays, Jewish holidays in particular, but because he asked for so little, I told him I would come.

"Tell me about Passover again?" Connelly asked when I stopped by to see him before I left. He didn't know much about Judaism—he'd been raised Catholic—but I always thought he would, or should, that because he knew me so well, he would know this part, too. It didn't make sense but still, the disconnect felt strange.

He was on the sofa so I sat at his desk, put my feet up and told him everything I could remember about Passover: the Jews in slavery, Moses in the bulrushes, the parting of the Red Sea. Connelly listened intently, his fingers steepled beneath his chin.

"And we only eat matzah for eight days," I said. "No bread."

"That sounds awful."

"It's hard at first, but then I kind of like it. Something about pushing through the wanting and coming out the other side." Connelly was looking at me with a funny expression. "What?"

"Nothing," he said. "I just like to listen to you talk."

I blushed. It felt like the nicest thing anyone had ever said to me.

I usually rode home with Debra, but she was skipping the holiday this year, so I took the bus.

"Wow," the guy sitting next to me said as I pulled out my knitting. Nearly three feet long, the scarf spilled across my lap. "You making that for your boyfriend?"

I shook my head but, despite my mother's warning, I was thinking of giving it to Connelly.

"Lucky guy," he said, inching closer. He smelled like garlic and patchouli oil. As the bus lumbered down the interstate, he talked, mostly about Clinton and the political theater playing out in Washington. According to him, what a man did behind closed doors was his own damn problem, and the only people he had to answer to were his wife and his God, in that order. "So a guy cheated on his wife," he said. "So what? Happens every day, every goddamned day."

Every time I came home, the neighborhood had changed a little more. On my walk from the subway station, I passed a gourmet dumpling shop and a boutique hotel where a rival appetizing store had once been. On the corner was a hole in the ground where Litkowski's bakery used to be. Growing up, I went there every weekend with my mother to get a seeded rye and a Linzer tart. Mr. Litkowski was a stout, unsmiling man; when I was little, I called him "the white man" because he was always covered in flour. Abe liked to say that New York was a city allergic to nostalgia, buildings always rising and falling, the old cleared away to make room for the new. That made it a perfect city for the Jews, he said, because we were a people used to reinventing ourselves. "Reinventing ourselves?" my mother said. "We leave because people want to kill us, Abe, not because we want a change of scenery."

As I walked past the ghosts of everything that used to be here, I realized what a miracle it was that Rosen's Appetizing had survived. My father had been unlucky in many ways but lucky in one: he was the nephew of Ruben "Ruby" Rosen, an enterprising pushcart salesman who'd opened Rosen's Appetizing in a storefront on Orchard Street in 1920. Abe was fatherless and poor, so Ruby, a difficult man with no sons, took him in. My father rarely spoke about those early years when he'd worked long hours to support his mother and younger brother, Leon. If he talked about them at all, it was to say he was lucky not to be a butcher.

"Meat's a tough business," he told me once. We were sitting at the kitchen table. Abe was drinking tea out of a glass. "Most butchers are missing part of a finger or a hand. Some more than that.

"My friend Stewy Horowitz came from a family of butchers," he went on, the steam from his tea fogging up his glasses. "I was only in the back of the store once. His father was wearing this long bloody apron, and there were feathers everywhere and a wire basket full of feet. And in the middle of the floor was a giant drain where all the blood went." Abe shuddered. No, he said, in the scheme of things, he was lucky to be in appetizing.

Lucky or not, the work was hard. In nearly every memory I would have of my father, he was standing behind the counter, a white apron tied around his waist, a wax crayon tucked behind his ear. His life had been filled with long days on his feet and brushes with financial ruin. And yet here he was, still in business. "One day we'll all be gone, but for now, I'm still here."

I pushed open the door and the smell of smoked fish and vinegar filled my nose. Everything here always looked the same. Ruby, who'd been dead for more than fifteen years, would have recognized the sawdust-covered floors, the long glass counter with its theatrical display of salmon, cream cheese, olives, shriveled yellow sturgeon. The only improvement Abe had made was replacing the front window after someone threw a brick through it. When he did, my mother had convinced him to have the words "Rosen's Appetizing, Est. 1920" stenciled on the glass in gold.

Manny was behind the counter, sliding his knife carefully across a side of bright pink salmon. Some of the old timers liked to have my dad slice their lox instead; Manny did a good job, but Abe sliced the lox so thin you could read the newspaper through it. (And also, although they didn't say it out loud, they never got used to seeing a Dominican slice lox.) People in a hurry preferred the presliced packages in the back, but those who had the time—those who knew better—waited for Abe.

"Hi, Izzy. Your dad's in the back," Manny said without looking up. He wasn't being rude. Manny had been at Rosen's as long as I could remember, working his way up from stock boy to lox slicer. He hadn't gotten there without learning the first rule of lox slicing: never look up.

I found Abe in his office, wedged behind the desk that had once belonged to Ruby. "Hello, stranger," he said, rising to give me a hug. My father was a small man, narrow like a dancer. His thick gray hair was combed neatly to the side, and he smelled strongly of aftershave. He'd gotten thinner since I'd last seen him, and I worried he wasn't taking care of himself.

"Hi, Izzy." My cousin's voice startled me. Benji, Leon and Fanny's son, was sitting on a stool in the corner, a stack of purchase orders on his lap. I hadn't seen Benji for a while, not since he'd graduated from SUNY Binghamton with a degree in business or marketing or some other uninteresting thing.

"Isabel, you want anything?" Abe asked.

"Sure." I wasn't hungry, but there was no point refusing since I knew he'd bring it anyway.

"What are you doing here?" I asked Benji.

"Helping out," he said, and something about his tone annoyed me, the implication that I wasn't helping my dad or that he needed help at all.

"Oh, yeah? With what?"

"This and that. Getting organized mostly, putting systems in place." He went on for a while about maximizing efficiency, streamlining productivity, getting systems to talk to each other—a bunch of business school lingo I had a hard time picturing in the context of Rosen's Appetizing.

"Are you getting him to use that?" I pointed to the computer on Abe's desk. Someone—maybe Benji—had convinced him to buy it a year or two ago and, as far as I knew, he'd never turned it on.

"Actually, yes," he said. "I'm showing him that while it feels like more work now, it will be *less* work in the long run."

"Good luck with that. Are you working at the counter? Abe says that's the only way to learn the business."

Benji pursed his lips. "I'm not learning the business, Izzy. I'm just helping out. But sometimes, yes. When it's busy."

"Has it been busy?" I asked.

Benji paused. "Now and again."

Abe walked back in and handed me a bagel with whitefish salad, my favorite. I felt a pang of something as he and Benji chatted about a shipment that had been delayed, not jealousy, more like nostalgia for something that didn't exist anymore, that maybe had never existed. I'd never really thought about what would happen to the store when Abe retired, or died. I guess I thought he'd sell the building at some point—that's what most people like my dad did, since the real estate was almost always more valuable than the business itself. Abe said the only reason Rosen's had survived all these years was because Ruby had had the sense to buy the building when he had the chance. But now I wondered if he had other plans, and if they involved Benji.

Abe glanced up front. "Benji, there's a woman by the candy counter."

"Okay, Uncle Abe." Benji stood up, and I saw he was

wearing an apron. "Izzy, my mother says you should come for Shabbos when you get back to the city. Celia will be there too, with the twins."

"Sure," I said, through a mouthful of whitefish. "I'm not sure when I'll be back, but I'd love to come."

"What do you mean you're not sure when you'll be back?" Abe asked when Benji was gone.

"Just that I was thinking of staying in New Hampshire this summer." This was something Connelly and I had talked about briefly before I left. Roxanne was going to England for the summer, so he'd largely be on his own. The idea was both thrilling and terrifying—lazy afternoons holed up in his office or house, wide swaths of uninterrupted time to read and write. We could go for drives together, eat a meal, take a walk, things we'd never done. But I didn't have a job or a place to live and I hadn't discussed it with Kelsey, with whom I was planning to share an apartment and who would want to know why I was staying at Wilder and wouldn't let me get away with vague excuses. I didn't know why I'd mentioned it to Abe, and when I saw how panicked it made him, I instantly regretted it.

"In New Hampshire? Why? What would you do there? Where would you live? You can't stay in the dorms."

"Nothing's settled. It might not happen. It probably won't." His face softened. "You didn't tell me Benji was working here."

"Fanny asked me. I guess he needs a job to attract a nice Orthodox girl. I don't know what that degree was for." He put on his glasses and squinted at something on his desk.

"To tell you the truth, I never thought he was that smart, but he has some good ideas."

"Oh, yeah? Like what?"

"Well, we're selling takeout sandwiches, so people can eat on the go. And this computer thing. He thinks it can extend our reach. That's how he puts it: 'Extend our reach.' He thinks someday soon people will buy whitefish salad on the World Wide Web." He raised an eyebrow. "Good thing I'm not paying him that much." He tapped the side of the computer monitor. "Okay, let me finish up and we'll get going."

We were spending the holiday in Rockland County with my mother's cousin Elaine and her second husband, Sol. Leon and Fanny had invited us to their seder, an invitation Benji repeated before he left, but Abe hated spending the holidays at his brother's: "Too much praying." Elaine and Sol's seder was more laid-back and had a pleasant, bohemian vibe, lots of hand-holding and off-key singing, colorful prayer shawls and not too much Hebrew. I liked it at Elaine and Sol's. Abe did, too, although he complained about the traffic the whole way there.

"You look beautiful, darling," Elaine said, kissing me wetly on one cheek. "Like your mother. Doesn't she look just like Viv, Sol?" She wiped away a tear. "Oh gosh, look at me." Sol put an arm around her shoulders.

"How are things in New Hampshire?" Sol asked. He had a long gray ponytail and a body like a refrigerator. "Any nice boys up there?"

"She's not there to meet *boys*, Sol," Elaine said, giving his forearm a gentle slap. "Honestly."

Elaine and Sol's dining room table was set for twenty, far more than it could comfortably hold. Elaine wasn't a skilled hostess like my mother, but the room had a warm, pleasant feeling that made me feel sleepy and cared for. If there were too many rules at Fanny and Leon's, at Elaine and Sol's it wasn't clear there were any rules at all. Throughout the seder, people interrupted, had side conversations, stood up, walked around. I sat quietly, turning the pages of my Haggadah and wondering why my father had insisted I come home for this. I was distracted by the painting on the wall above the sideboard, an abstract my mother had made years before. She had never had much luck with abstracts— landscapes and still lifes were easier to sell—but Elaine had liked this one so much, my mother gave it to her.

I remembered the day she painted it. It was a few weeks after her diagnosis, long before we understood what it meant, what we were in for. She'd spent the night on the couch, which wasn't unusual. But that morning, she didn't stir as I clomped around the kitchen, getting ready for school. Abe was already gone. Before I left, I went into the living room to say goodbye.

"Mom," I said, placing a hand on her shoulder. She didn't answer. Her hair was wild, and she felt so thin through her long gray T-shirt.

"Mom," I said again.

"What time is it?" she asked. Her voice was hoarse and cracked, as if she'd been screaming.

"It's almost eight. Mom, are you okay?" I was starting to get scared. Was this the cancer? Was she dying already?

She reached for my hand. Her fingernails were dirty and broken.

"Find a man who understands you, baby. Promise me that, okay?" There were tears in her eyes. She was looking at me so intensely, I had to look away. I saw that she had taken out all of her paintings and had them leaned up against the walls. Bowls of fruit and plates of walnuts, their shells ridged and bumpy like brains. The scene outside our window, the pitted sidewalk, the greasy puddle at the curb. So many paintings, visions of the world the way she saw it. How could it be I'd never really looked at them before?

I stood up and walked over to the easel. On it was the painting she'd been working on the night before, the one that now hung in Elaine and Sol's dining room. The paint, a bright vivid turquoise like the blue of a California swimming pool, was still wet. The same color was in my mother's hair, on her cheek, down the front of her shirt.

"What do you think of that one?" she asked.

I looked back at the painting and tried to think of something to say. My mother had never asked me about her work before, but maybe I was old enough now to have an opinion. This one was different from her other work, more abstract and urgent, the brushstrokes wild and sensual. I tried to make out faces, eyes, recognizable parts of human forms, but everything was fractured, split open, like fruit or rot.

"It scares me," I said.

My mother sat up and reached for her cigarettes. The scrape of the match was the loudest sound in the room.

"That's what your father said." And then she stood up and walked into her bedroom, closing the door behind her.

We left Elaine and Sol's early to beat the traffic. When we got home, Abe went into the kitchen.

"I have some macaroons. You want some?"

"Dad, come on. We just ate so much."

He put on the kettle, then sat down at the kitchen table. I noticed there were still three chairs around it, although he needed only one.

"Did you see what's going on at Litkowski's?" he asked, setting a plate of cookies in front of me.

"I saw. He sold the building?"

"They offered him a fortune. He couldn't say no. His son's a dentist in Manhasset. He doesn't want to bake bread for a living."

"What are they building?" I asked. Despite myself, I picked up a cookie and took a bite.

"Some high-rise, with a Duane Reade."

"Fancy."

"All these yuppies need somewhere to buy toothpaste."

"I'm not sure they call them yuppies anymore."

"You ever meet with that woman from Career Services?"

He switched topics so quickly, it took me a second to catch up. "Oh. Yeah."

"Anything good?"

"No. The only jobs they have listed there are corporate jobs."

"So, what's wrong with jobs like that?" Abe asked as the kettle whistled. "Isabel, you pooh-pooh this stuff, but those are good jobs with benefits." I watched him unwrap the tea bags, place them in the mugs, pour the boiling water over them. My mother used to complain that Abe could never sit still, a criticism that always felt harsh to me—when had he ever been given the chance to relax?—but now his puttering annoyed me. "You're the one who wanted to be an English major. Now you have to figure out how to make a living." He placed the mug in front of me and pushed a sugar bowl my way.

"I know," I said. "Actually, my writing teacher thinks I have talent."

"You're a talented girl."

"He thinks I should pursue writing. As a career."

"What? A PhD?"

"No. I mean, he thinks I could be a writer."

"You can be whatever you want."

"This teacher . . ." I paused. It felt strange to conjure Connelly here, in this room. "He thinks I should take some time and just write. See what I can come up with. He thinks if I could sell a few stories, I might be able to get an agent."

"Do you get paid for that?"

"Not much. Not right away. That's why I was thinking of staying in New Hampshire. It's not as expensive there." Abe was chewing on his bottom lip, working it in and out of his mouth. "Or I could come home, live here for a while."

"You know you're always welcome, but what would you do? I can't give you any more money."

"I know that. I could do SAT tutoring, or work in the store. I won't need much."

Abe shook his head. "I don't want you working in the store."

"Why not?"

"I didn't send you to college so you could work in the store."

"Benji went to college."

"Benji is not my child."

"Then I'll stay in New Hampshire."

"And do *what*, Isabel?"

"I told you. Write."

"'Writing' is not an option."

"Why not?"

"Because you need a job." He picked up a sponge and started wiping down the counter. "You sound just like your mother, talking about your art, thinking everything will work out. But you won't have me downstairs working to pay for everything. I can't do that anymore." He threw the sponge in the sink. "I thought you were more sensible than that. You saw how it worked out for her."

"What does that mean? Mom sold her paintings."

"Sure. A couple hundred bucks every once in a while that she'd go spend on some silly thing. Your mother was not a practical woman, Isabel. She should have done more to help us, to help you."

I looked down at the pile of crumbs on my plate, remembered my mother's words. *Find a man who understands you.* I'd never understood what held my parents' marriage together. If you'd drawn a Venn diagram of them, the only thing you would find in the space where the two circles met would be me.

Abe was standing by the sink, his back to me. I could see his shoulders shaking.

"Dad, what is it?"

"Nothing." He sat back down. There was a tremor by his jaw.

"Why did you ask me to come home?" I said. My hands were cold. "What is this all about? Are you sick?"

"No. *Bubeleh*, no. I'm fine. But the money your mother left, it didn't cover as much as we thought it would." *The money your mother left*—it sounded like he was talking about an inheritance, but he was talking about her life insurance, the bulk of which had been used to pay for my education, or so I thought. "Wilder was expensive, and I had to borrow a little to get you through. Most of it in my name, but some of it in yours."

I felt something enter the room, something slithering and pale. I could feel it, winding around my ankles and shins, pinning me to the chair, forcing me to pay attention. *This*, it whispered. *This is happening.*

"How much?"

"In your name? Maybe twenty-five thousand dollars."

"Maybe?"

"That's how much. Twenty-five thousand dollars. No more."

"When were you going to tell me? Wait—how long have you known?"

Abe paused. "A year or two."

"A year or two?" I walked over to the refrigerator, placed a hand on the door. I didn't have to open it to know what was inside: a container of skim milk, a stick of butter, a carton of eggs. Nothing extra, nothing decadent. "You said this was the one thing you wanted to give me. All those years of depriving ourselves, saying no to things, it was all for this, so I wouldn't have debt. So I would be free."

Abe had his hands wrapped around his mug like he was trying to get warm. Something about the pose infused me with tenderness, but it was quickly snuffed out by anger. For more than a year, maybe two, he'd known about the money and not told me. I pictured everything I'd done in that time, turning down extra shifts at the information desk to go to Kmart with Debra or the local truck stop for a plate of toast and eggs. Movies with Kelsey and Jason, late-night pizzas and Thai food, stacks of hardcover books from the campus bookstore—all while the debt accumulated, dollars and cents piling up like snow. What would I have done differently if I'd known about the money? What would I have said yes to? What would I have said no to? It occurred to me, briefly, that this might have been why Abe hadn't told me, but I wasn't sure I liked it better this way, and I wasn't in the mood to be generous.

"I didn't have to go to Wilder, remember? You were the one who wanted that. Other schools gave me more money, but you said, no. Go to Wilder. You said it was your dream, that it was Mom's dream. You *lied* to me."

"I don't know what else to tell you," Abe said tightly. "Maybe one day you'll have a child and you'll understand." He stood up. "You'll have to meet with the financial aid office when you get back." He said some things about grace periods and credit scores, what it would mean if I wanted to buy a house one day, what would happen if I defaulted.

I heard him, but I wasn't listening. Or maybe I was listening, and I just couldn't follow.

Abe went to bed, but I stayed in the kitchen for a long time, watching the second hand move across the face of my watch. It had belonged to my mother, one of the things she'd bought herself with money she'd made selling her paintings. Her earnings traded in for jewelry, pretty plates, fancy soaps, little things to cheer herself. Abe was furious when he found out how much she'd spent on the sterling silver watch with a mother-of-pearl face: nearly eight hundred dollars. A terrible extravagance, he said. Didn't she know there were braces to pay for and college? He demanded she return it, but she refused. One night near the end, when it had become clear she would not survive, she called me into her room and pressed the watch into my hand. "I want you to have this," she said, "so you remember that it's okay to want things." She made me promise never to sell it.

I walked into the living room and remembered the summer she died, right before I left for Wilder. When it was all over, Abe stayed in his room, coming out only to get food from the kitchen, where a parade of women left a continuously replenished supply. Manny handled everything at the store, and I was alone and rudderless. A few of my high school friends were still around, but no one knew what to say to me, and I didn't want to talk to them either. The only person I wanted to talk to was Abe. Whenever I heard him come out of his bedroom, I would place myself in his path. *Talk to me*, I wanted to say but never did. When he finally emerged after eight days, he bagged up my mother's things, and when he was done, he put on his apron and went back to work.

A few days before I was scheduled to leave for school, I found him in the living room reading the newspaper. My mother had been dead three weeks and we were wobbly, like a table missing a leg. I practically ran into the room, sat down on the coffee table, our knees only inches apart. I was so close I could have reached out and touched him.

"Maybe I shouldn't go," I said.

"What are you talking about?"

"To Wilder. Maybe I shouldn't go."

"Of course you should go. Don't be ridiculous."

"I could take a year off, go next year."

"No," he said. "You are not going to put your life on hold."

"There are other schools. Less expensive ones. Maybe I shouldn't be so far away."

He lowered the newspaper. "Isabel, you've suffered a terrible loss. I wish I could change that. I can't. But I can tell you this: Go. Live your life. Get away from all this. Believe me, you won't miss it."

"What if I don't like the people?" I said.

"People are people. And what would be so bad about meeting different kinds?"

We drove up to Wilder at the end of the month, the car so full of stuff we couldn't see out the back. I cried the whole way, everything I'd hated about New York suddenly wrapped in a patina of loveliness: the subway tunnels that smelled like piss, the roaches that skittered across the sidewalk in the dark, even Rosen's. I sniffed my nails, hair, and skin, searching for the smell of lox and brine, the one I'd always tried to wash away. When we pulled off the interstate, Wilder appeared before us, rising up out of nowhere like a fairy village or a mirage. We parked in front of my dorm, carried in boxes, hung posters, made the bed. Then I waved goodbye to my father and began again, just like he told me to. Forgetting what I'd left behind, which was everything, and nothing.

15

I started my job search when I got back, did what I was supposed to: pored over listings in the Career Services office and sent my résumé to any job that had anything to do with writing. Accessories assistant at a fashion magazine. Assistant marketing manager at an academic publisher. Grant writer at an environmental nonprofit. While I was home, I'd bumped into a girl I'd gone to high school with who worked at a magazine called *Get Out!* and had just been promoted. They were looking for someone to take her old job, she said, so I gave her a copy of my résumé. None of the jobs sounded terribly interesting, and none paid enough to cover my share of rent on the apartments Kelsey was looking at, but I decided to worry about that later. Abe and I patched things over before I left, and I promised him I would find something, but in my heart, I was staying here, with Connelly. So even though I followed the footprints, I wasn't really on the trail.

Back on campus, corporate recruiting was in full swing. From my perch at the information desk, I saw my classmates rushing to interviews, carrying briefcases and wearing suits and dress shoes that looked like they came from their parents' closets. While I was dabbling with the lowest bidder, they were interviewing for jobs in advertising, consulting, investment banking; jobs with benefits, jobs that paid. One sunny Thursday, I sat there buried under my knitting, listening to the printer churn out cover letters and résumés—*dear sir to whom it may concern please find enclosed*—and thought about money. It had always been there of course, the silent drumbeat to everything, but while we were here we all lived in the same crappy apartments, ate at the same restaurants, and were all in service to the same goal—or so I'd thought. But now I saw that it had always been about money, and those who'd spent their time here with that in mind were the ones with all the answers, while the rest of us were left scrounging.

I was filing the pages that came off the printer when Bo Benson stopped by. I'd been expecting him; his résumé had just come through (government major, poli-sci minor, member of the Tunemen, Wilder's all-male a cappella singing group). We'd hung out over the weekend at Gamma Nu. I'd sat on a dirty sofa in the basement watching him fling his body around the ping pong table; he was so tall his head practically touched the ceiling. Later, when he was good and drunk, he sat next to me and told me about his mother who loved Jesus and cross-stitch, his father who liked bowling, and their elderly arthritic cat, Morris Grossman, named after their accountant. (Was he the only Jew they knew, I wondered? I didn't ask.) Bo was funny and easy to talk to. He had a laid-back quality, like a California surfer, even though he was from Ohio. There were no sharp angles to Bo; it felt like anything you threw at him would roll off, like oatmeal down a wall.

"You cut your hair," I said, handing him his résumé.

"Yeah." He ran his hand back and forth across his scalp. "I'm doing the whole corporate recruiting thing so I figured clean-cut was the way to go. Is it terrible?"

I pretended to study him. "No, it's good. You can see your face better." I paused, letting the compliment sink in. "Who are you interviewing with?"

"Goldman," he said. "Yeah, I know what you're thinking."

"What am I thinking?"

"That I'm a sellout."

"God, I don't think that at all. I'm thinking how much I wish I wanted a job like that. The jobs I'm looking at barely pay, if they pay at all." Behind me, the printer hummed. "I thought jobs had to pay, like that was what made it a job. The quid pro quo of it."

Bo smiled, revealing his most delightful feature: a slightly crooked front tooth that overlapped the one next to it. "Don't worry. You'll find something cool."

I lifted the warm pages off the printer. "I'm starting to think cool jobs are for rich girls."

"Hey, are you going to the Pine on Saturday?" Bo asked, slipping his résumé into his backpack. "A bunch of us'll be there. Rice Krispy Treat is playing."

"Maybe," I said, even though I'd already told Kelsey I'd go.

"All right. Later, cool girl."

"Maybe I should work for Goldman Sachs," I said to Connelly that afternoon. I was lying across the sofa with my head in his lap. I was wearing my favorite dress, navy with a smattering of flowers, no tights. "How hard could it be?"

"You don't want a job like that. It's just pushing money around."

"Pushing money around sounds nice," I said. "How does Bo *know* that's what he wants to do? I don't even know what those jobs are."

"Because it's what Daddy does. That's how wealth gets passed down, Isabel, how dynasties get perpetuated. A whole system of entitlement from prep school to the Ivy League to white-shoe law firms and investment banks. But come on, you know this. You're not stupid. You're the one writing about Wharton."

"I don't know. Sometimes I think I'm very stupid." I picked at a scab on the side of my knee. "Oh, I got some good news. Someone from *Get Out!* called. They want to set up a phone interview."

"What's the job?"

"Writing listings for concerts and movies, stuff going on in the city each week."

"I thought you were going to stay here this summer and write."

"I know, but I'm not sure I can swing that right now." I watched him closely to see how he would react.

He lifted my head off his lap and walked over to his desk. "Do what you want, but you can't take a job like that."

"Why not? I'd be writing."

"Barely. It's nothing more than a glorified PR job."

"Well, it's a job and I need a job." I pouted, but inside I was thrilled.

The phone rang. I lay with my legs up the wall, listening to Connelly interview someone for an article he was writing about a warehouse fire in Vermont. I hadn't told him about the money Abe had borrowed. He was always telling me not to worry about money, to concentrate on the work. After college, he'd waited tables, painted houses, sold a little pot. "You do what you have to do." It made me feel bad, like I wasn't prepared to give up everything for my art, which felt like the kind of thing a man could do more easily than a woman. Or at least didn't feel like something I could do. I wanted—no, I needed—the security that came from knowing how I was going to make that month's rent. I was my mother's daughter, yes, but Abe Rosen was my dad.

Connelly was still on the phone. I moved my legs farther up the wall, letting my dress fall down around my waist, revealing the edge of my underwear. I could feel him watching me, heard him trying to get off the phone. As exciting as it was to imagine staying near him all summer, it was also scary to think about being here alone, without the structure of school or my friends, with no one to rely on but him. I worried that what we had wasn't real and if we pushed it too far, we might see how easily it broke. But still, I wanted him to say he wanted me to stay, that he needed me to stay. In the meantime, I'd have the interview, talk to Kelsey about apartments, appease Abe.

Connelly hung up the phone as something scurried across the floor.

"What was that?" I said, pulling down my dress.

"Goddamned mouse." Connelly leaned down and checked under the sofa. "See. There's a hole under there. I've been trying to catch that fucker all winter." He wrapped his arms around my waist. "I've got to get you away from this shitty office."

"Where?" I asked, thinking of his cabin.

"I don't know. Anywhere." He kissed my knees, one at a time. "Don't take that stupid job. Stay here with me. We'll have fun."

My heart swelled: he wanted me to stay. But still I pushed. "What about what you said on the first day of class? How working at the *Citizen* was the best job you ever had?"

"I said that?"

"Yes. You said people value art for art's sake but real life happens all around us. School board meetings and droughts and all that. You don't remember?"

"I must have been having a good day. Listen, I just think you start down that path and . . . Even the tiniest decision has consequences, Isabel. Look at your mother. She walked into a deli one day and never left."

I must have looked as hurt as I felt. "I'm sorry," he said. "I shouldn't have said that."

"Yeah. You shouldn't have."

He reached for my hand and kissed it. "All I mean is, it's hard to get back on track. And every step you take in that direction, in the *Get Out!* direction, is one step further away from what you're meant to be doing. And this," he picked up a copy of the new story I was working on. "This is what you're meant to be doing."

"You like it?"

"I love it," he said, and I forgave him everything. For the past few weeks, I'd been working on a story about a store a little like Rosen's and a family a lot like mine. Connelly had read about fifteen pages, but I had close to fifty. I'd thought it was good, hoped it was, but hadn't been sure until now.

"I just don't know how you get from here to there," I said as he thumbed through the pages. "Sure, it all worked out for you. You became a writer. You didn't need a plan B."

"Neither will you."

"But how do you *know* that? How can you be sure?"

"Because I'm sure." He tossed the story aside and slid his hands under my dress. I ran my fingers through his hair, pulled his mouth toward mine.

There was a knock on the door. "Randy? Are you in there?" Without waiting for an answer, Tom Fisher walked in. I jumped off the sofa, but Connelly waved for me to relax.

"Tom," Connelly said, buttoning the cuff of his shirt. "Everything okay?"

I saw Tom take in the scene: Connelly, the sofa, my bare legs, mussed hair. Tom looked bad. His clothes were rumpled, his hair greasy; there were broken blood vessels on his cheeks. The cut on his hand was healing, but there was an angry red line running up the side of his wrist. He picked at it nervously as I stepped into my sneakers and reached for my bag.

"Randy, man," Tom said. "I really need to talk to you."

Connelly nodded at me. "Sure thing, buddy. Isabel was just leaving."

THE KNOTTY PINE was the only real bar on Wilder's Main Street. There were other places in town to get drinks—a glass of wine at the pizza parlor or a gin and tonic at the Wilder Inn when someone's parents were in town—but the Knotty Pine was where you went when you wanted to get shit-faced. It was tradition to go to the Pine on your twenty-first birthday and let people at the bar buy you shots of Jägermeister until you stumbled into the bathroom, past the condom machine and cologne dispenser, and puked your guts out. At least, that's what I'd done. Debra hated the Pine, never went. She said it reminded her of the bar in *The Accused*.

I could feel the townies staring at us as Kelsey and I pushed our way toward the back of the bar; that Wilder students found the Pine amusingly ironic was no doubt irritating. Jason was already there, sitting at a long table with a bunch of his Gamma Nu brothers, including Bo. The Pine was always crowded on Saturday nights, but it was especially crowded tonight because Rice Krispy Treat, a popular student band, was playing. The lead singer, Tabitha something, had a paisley scarf tied around her head and was wearing tall leather boots; she looked like Stevie Nicks if Stevie Nicks was from New Canaan. Tabitha was dating Doug Biaggio, a Gamma Nu brother who sang with Bo in the Tunemen; he was known around campus for his winning rendition of "Jessie's Girl." Later that summer, he'd fall off a balcony at a party in the Hamptons and become the first of our class-mates to die.

Bo slid over to make room for me on the banquette.

"It's this phone number, see," Doug was saying. "1-800-I-AM-LOST. And you can call it if you're lost."

"How does that work?" Jason asked.

"It uses GPS technology," Doug said with only the hint of a duh. "It stands for Global Positioning System. Satellites determine where you are in space. So my idea is to have this phone number—"

"1-800-I-AM-LOST," offered Bo.

"Right," Doug said. "And there'll be people working the phones twenty-four hours a day who can direct you where you need to go."

"What if you're only spiritually lost?" I asked. Doug looked confused. Bo turned to me and smiled, his snaggle-tooth visible. The words were out of my mouth before I could stop them. "Did you ever have braces?"

"You mean because of this?" He pointed at his tooth, and suddenly I felt bad for asking. "Nah, my parents are kind of cheap. You know, mow their own lawn, drive an old car. I guess orthodontia seemed like another frivolous expense."

"Oh, my dad's the same way," I said, although he wasn't. "He never throws anything out, washes plastic bags so he can use them again." What I didn't say was that Abe was frugal because he was poor and, even so, he'd never skimped on me. By all accounts, Bo's family had money; until I came to Wilder, I'd never heard of a family with money that didn't spend it.

The waitress dropped a pitcher of beer on the table along with a sleeve of plastic cups. Doug reached for it, but Bo pushed his hand away and poured a cup for me. It might have been the most gallant thing that had ever happened at the Knotty Pine.

We clinked our cups together. "Cheers, big ears," Bo said.

Across the table, Kelsey was talking to Allison Etter, my freshman-year roommate. For some reason, she and I always acted like we didn't know each other.

"The thing I don't get," Kelsey was saying, "is she isn't even that pretty."

"Or thin," Allison said without looking at me, maybe because I was the only one at the table who knew she'd spent the summer before freshman year at fat camp.

"Who are you talking about?" Jason asked.

"Monica Lewinsky," Kelsey whispered, as though she might be sitting nearby.

"Can you imagine going on a date with her?" Doug said, laughing. "Like, introducing her to your mom? 'Mom, I'd like you to meet my girlfriend, Monica Lewinsky.'"

The whole table tittered, including me. In the short time we'd known her, Monica had become every girl's worst nightmare, the equivalent of having your seventh-grade diary read over the school loudspeaker or walking into class with a period stain on your pants. We identified with her, which should have made us kinder but instead made us mean. We felt more comfortable siding with guys like Doug because their side was safer. They would never admit to wanting to fuck Monica even though they would, of course they would, but if they did it would be her fault and not theirs. Her desire made her unseemly.

"I feel bad for her," Bo said, and we all turned to look at him. "Everyone's lying except for her, but she's the one whose life will be ruined."

"Well," said Doug, "one thing I'll say, she certainly makes watching C-SPAN more interesting." He raised his cup and chugged it down as the band finished its sound check and started to play.

I lit a cigarette. Bo leaned over to grab a handful of nachos and the feel of his thigh against mine felt good. I wondered if he'd heard about me and Zev—then, strangely, if he knew about Connelly. I felt the sudden urge to tell him everything, to confess my sins the way he'd told me he used to at church. I pictured him as a little boy, sitting in a pew next to his grandmother, and wondered if I was the kind of girl a guy like him could introduce to his parents.

Up on stage, Tabitha had started singing. I'd always thought she was an idiot but on stage she was sexy, wrapping her hands around the microphone like it was a dick. I watched the guys at the table watch her—Doug, Bo, even Jason. It was easy to fall in love with a girl behind a microphone. I was about to whisper something about Tabitha to Bo when I looked up and saw Connelly pushing his way through the crowd, like Moses parting the goddamn Red Sea.

I'd never seen Connelly outside Stringer Hall and, as strange as it sounds, never thought of him out in the world doing mundane things like pumping gas or buying groceries. For me, he only existed in that office on the fourth floor, where dust motes hung in the soft, gray light. And yet, there he was in the Knotty fucking Pine, wearing a puffy black jacket and a wool hat. I saw people staring at him—how could they not? The man was too handsome for his own good, I thought, as he pulled off his hat and ran a hand through that hair, aware of the impression he made. It was, perhaps, his greatest fault, and yet I couldn't help but watch him too, amazed that out of all the people in this crowded bar, he had chosen me. I thought of a line from *The Age of Innocence*, something Newland Archer says to Ellen when he sees her for the first time in a long while: "Each time you happen to me all over again." I felt a blush run through me, from the base of my spine to the hidden part of my scalp. I brought my cigarette slowly to my lips, then my gaze shifted and I saw the woman he was with.

She was older than me, a graduate student maybe, petite and muscular with hair so short it looked like it had been painted on her scalp. The two of them squeezed into a small table by the wall, and I saw him ask her something before heading over to the bar. The woman leaned back in her chair and unbuttoned her plum-colored coat with an ease that unsettled me; she didn't seem uncomfortable being left alone as I would have been. I poured myself more beer, then laughed hard at something Jason said, a loud ridiculous bark that drew Kelsey's attention like an arrow. *Are you okay?* her look asked. I ignored her.

God was I stupid, I thought, as Connelly walked back and set a small glass down on the table in front of the woman. Believing him when he told me I was the only one—of course I wasn't, and he wasn't even trying to hide it. He leaned over and whispered something in her ear, his head so close to hers I could feel his curls tickling her nearly naked head. Up on stage, Tabitha was still singing. *One is the loneliest number that you'll ever do. Two can be as bad as one, it's the loneliest number since the number one.* Bo said something to me, but I wasn't listening. I was too busy picturing Connelly kissing this woman's strong shoulders, her small hands running up and down his back, his fingers shoved inside her and then into her mouth. His voice, echoing in the seashell cup of her ear: *I want you to know what you taste like.*

The set went on, my cup filled and drained, then filled again, my head fizzy with cheap beer and cigarettes. Bo was still sitting close to me, but the feel of him now was oppressive. His face was shiny, and there was a red spot on his jawline where he'd shaved over a zit. Whatever satisfaction I'd gotten out of flirting with him was gone, and I saw my whole life unspool before me, filled with silly flirtations and hurried gropes with boys like Bo. Why had I believed Connelly when he told me I was special? There was nothing special about me. There never had been.

"Isabel." Bo's face was close to mine. He, too, was drunk. "We're going to head over to Gamma Nu. Do you want to come?" I looked up and saw that Rice Krispy Treat's set had ended. Doug was whooping and pumping his fist as Tabitha and the bass player, who was clearly in love with her, clasped hands and took a triumphant bow.

I nodded, then stood up, trying not to stumble. The bar was packed, the air so thick with smoke I yawned to take in more oxygen. I followed Bo through the bar, keeping my eyes focused on the back of his head. We were nearly to the door when I heard someone calling my name—once, twice, three times. I turned and saw Connelly inexplicably waving me over.

"Who's that?" Bo asked, squinting through the smoke. I pretended not to hear him.

"I thought it was you," Connelly said as I walked over. His big hands were spread across the table like starfish. "Isabel, let me introduce you to Daria Azar-Khan. She's one of Roxanne's graduate students. We met on Roxanne's study abroad—when was it, last spring?" Daria nodded. "God, I can't believe that was a year ago already."

Daria held out her hand. "Nice to meet you." She had a tiny silver stud nestled in the fold of her nose and an accent I couldn't place.

"Isabel is in my writing seminar," Connelly said. "She's a very promising writer. I'm trying to convince her to take herself seriously."

"What sorts of things do you write?" Daria asked.

"I don't know. Stories?" I looked back at the door. Kelsey was peering through the window, her hands raised questioningly.

"Wonderful stories," Connelly said. He was looking at me

with a strange sense of ownership, like I was the daughter of a family friend he hadn't seen in a while and he was checking to see how I'd turned out. It made my palms itch, and for the first time in a long while, I felt the urge to steal something.

Daria smiled, showing a disproportionate amount of gum. My mother would have said she should learn to smile with her lips closed.

"Isabel's from New York," Connelly said. "Her family owns a famous appetizing store."

"Oh, really?" said Daria. "What's that?"

I started to answer, but Connelly interrupted me. "Let me try. An appetizing store sells fish and dairy, unlike a deli, which serves meat. Do I have that right?"

"Bingo," I said. Then I mumbled something about friends waiting for me and pushed my way out of the bar and onto the street where I stood for several seconds, my hands on my knees, gulping mouthfuls of cold air until my lungs hurt.

Bo was on the corner with the others.

"Are you okay?" he asked.

"Who was that?" Kelsey asked.

"I'm fine," I said, answering Bo's question but not Kelsey's.

"So, Izzy," Kelsey said, looking back and forth between me and Bo. "Are you coming to Gamma Nu?"

I didn't have any reason not to but I couldn't stand the look on Kelsey's face, like she was already planning our wedding toast.

"I think I'm gonna pass."

I could see how badly she wanted to try to convince me, but Jason placed a hand on her arm and led her away.

"Do you want me to walk you home?" Bo asked. He had a sad droop to his neck. The old me would have said yes, would have let him kiss me under a streetlight, stick a cold hand under my sweater, but I shook my head and told him I would be fine.

I waited outside the Knotty Pine for a long time. Packs of students traipsed past me, some heading toward campus, others into town. A group of freshman girls walked by, all wearing a version of the same babydoll dress whether it suited them or not, and I thought about following them and seeing where the night might lead. But instead, I stayed where I was, watching the traffic light on Main Street flash from red to yellow to green and then, finally, to a steady blinking red, signaling that it was past midnight. I wasn't waiting for Connelly, not exactly, but when he came outside—alone—I saw how it might look like I was.

"Isabel. Is everything okay? Are you all right?"

"I'm fine. Where's *Daria*?" My voice was uglier than I'd intended. Connelly didn't say anything, so I kept going. "What the fuck was that? You *introduced* me to her? Why couldn't you just ignore me like a normal person?"

"Why would I ignore you?" He was calm, which infuriated me even more.

"Why? Do I seriously have to explain that?"

"Daria is one of Roxanne's grad students—"

"Yeah. So you said. What I want to know—" The door opened and the bartender came out with a bag of trash.

He gave us a look letting us know we were not the most interesting thing he'd seen all night, but still I waited until he was gone to continue. "What I want to know is if you're sleeping with her, too."

Connelly took my arm and pulled me down the alleyway that led away from Main Street. I liked the way it felt, him touching me in anger.

"Lower your voice, please. I told you who Daria was, and I have no reason to lie to you. I didn't ask if you were sleeping with whoever it was you were hanging all over."

"You saw me?"

"Of course I saw you." He let go of my arm. "I watched you the whole time."

"I'm not sleeping with him."

"And I'm not sleeping with Daria. I'm only sleeping with you."

I covered my face with my hands, felt my eyelashes flutter against my palms. "I'm sorry," I said. "I don't know how to do this."

"Isabel." He placed his hand on my cheek. "If this is too much for you, we can stop. Is that what you want?"

"No."

"Okay." His voice softened. "Then we will find a way to make this work, whatever it is. Because what we have is extraordinary."

Extraordinary. The word echoed in my head, finding every dark place and lighting it up.

He drove me back to my dorm, parking in the place where I'd seen Joanna and Tom fighting. I reached for him, but he kissed me on the forehead and made me promise I would go straight to bed. That night, I dreamed of him going back to his office where Daria was waiting for him, naked, a metal key hanging from a chain around her neck, but by morning, I'd already forgotten.

WHEN WE GOT to Room 203 on Wednesday, there was a note on the door from Connelly telling us he would be gone for a few days and that we should move ahead with the reading. He hadn't said anything to me about being away.

I walked upstairs to his office, looking for a sign of where he might be. Nothing. On my way back down, I passed Tom and Igraine on the stairs.

"Isabel," he said, and I blushed, remembering the last time I'd seen him, in Connelly's office. He looked better than he had that day, his eyes bright, his skin clearer. Igraine looked exhausted, her gray eyes wide and serious, as if whatever energy he had had been gained at her expense.

"Could you do me a favor?" he asked. "Could you watch Igraine for a few minutes?"

Without waiting for an answer, he leaned down and kissed his daughter on the forehead. "Sweetie, wait here with Isabel. Daddy has to take care of a few things." Then he disappeared down the hall toward his office.

Igraine had on a long dress and rain boots, her hair loose around her shoulders, a mini-version of Joanna. She barely made a noise as she took off her jacket and spread it out on the floor between her parents' offices. I sat down next to her and watched her unpack her tote bag like she was setting up for a picnic. A pencil box, a black composition notebook, a plastic baggie with cut-up pieces of apple. I didn't know if I should talk to her or if I should respect her privacy. I knew so little about children, what they thought about, what they needed.

While she busied herself with her things, I took a book out of my backpack and started to read. After several minutes, I could see her sneaking peeks at me.

"Do you want to see?" She nodded and I turned the book toward her. Her eyelashes were long and pale like Joanna's, nearly translucent. Her long hair was wispy, the skin near her temples so thin you could see the veins beneath the surface.

When she was finished, she turned back to her notebook. "Can I see?" I asked.

"Sure." Her voice was small and adorable. She handed me the notebook, and I flipped through the pages. I could make out letters, lots of *I*'s—for Igraine, I supposed—and drawings of people with big heads and mitt-like hands, unicorns, and princesses with long dresses and tall triangular hats. There were several drawings of what looked like her family. She'd captured them well: Joanna with her long hair and dresses, Tom with his rumpled clothes and lazy eye. In one of the drawings, they looked like they were screaming at each other.

"What else do you have?" Igraine asked, pointing at my backpack.

I took out everything I had: a hairbrush, a sweatshirt, a couple of spiral notebooks. Igraine studied each object thoughtfully, placed it next to her, then held out a small hand for what came next. The last thing I handed her was a soft zippered pouch. I watched as she unzipped it and pulled out a tube of cherry ChapStick, mascara, a couple of tampons.

"What's this?" she asked, holding out a scrap of paper.

"Oh. My grandmother gave that to me. It's very old. Those letters are Hebrew."

She held it up to her face. "What does it say?"

"I don't know exactly. It's a prayer of protection, I think."

"She gave it to you so you would stay safe?"

"Something like that."

Igraine studied the paper again, so thin and worn it looked like a piece of muslin. Yetta gave it to me after my mother got sick. It was a copy of something her grandmother had given her, and it had been copied and recopied so many times it was nearly illegible. She'd once asked a rabbi to translate it, but even he couldn't make out what it said. It might have been written down by someone who had been illiterate, he told her, who'd copied it from someone else; somewhere along the way, the meaning had gotten lost, like an intergenerational game of telephone. Even though I considered myself neither religious nor superstitious, I always carried it with me.

"I think it's a secret message," Igraine said. One of her eyes was tipped slightly to the side, making me think it might go lazy one day. Years later, my daughter Alice would get the same look when she was on the cusp of understanding something, and every time she did, I would think of Igraine.

Just then, Tom reappeared, a stack of manila folders under his arm. "Okay, time to go."

I helped Igraine pack her bag, then turned to Tom.

"Professor Fisher. I just wanted to say, the last time I saw you—in Professor Connelly's office—"

"Isabel, please," he said, smiling. "I'm sure you had a very good reason for being there."

"I know it looked strange. The thing is, I had spilled coffee on my dress and I was trying—"

He held up a hand. "Really. No worry at all. Randy's my friend, and I would never betray a confidence."

As I leaned down to help Igraine put on her jacket, she pulled me toward her and pressed her mouth to my ear.

"I think I know what it says," she whispered. "The secret message. I know what it is." Her breath was hot against my cheek. She smelled like apples and baby shampoo.

"You do? What does it say?"

"It says." She flicked her gray eyes up to the sky and nodded, as if to say *Oh yes, I hear you now.* "It says, 'Be careful, my darling. I love you.'"

I nodded my head slowly. "Yes. I think that's exactly what it says. Thank you, Igraine. I really appreciate it."

Tom walked over and placed a hand on the back of her neck. Igraine gave me a shy wave, then followed her father down the stairs.

16

IF you had asked me where I lived in May 1998, I would have said New Hampshire, which was ridiculous because in less than three weeks I would leave and never live there again. When I was older, four years would pass in a flash—I'd live somewhere for six years and feel like I'd just moved in—but then it felt as though I'd been at Wilder forever.

I turned twenty-two. Kelsey and Jason took me to dinner for my birthday. Debra bought me *Memoirs of a Geisha*. Time marched on, the warm weather making everything sweeter—students sprawled on the grass, boys playing Frisbee, girls in shorts and tank tops, their knees and elbows winter-white and ashy. One day, Linus came to French class barefoot. When the teacher asked him why, he shrugged and said, "*C'est le printemps.*"

On Monday, I stopped by Stringer Hall to drop off the last

chapter of my thesis along with the latest draft of my story about Rosen's. It had a title now: "This Youthful Heart." I passed Daria in the hallway. I didn't recognize her at first, but then she smiled her gummy smile and I remembered. Connelly never told me where he'd been all week, and I didn't ask. Sometimes, right before I fell asleep, I imagined he'd gone somewhere with her, but in the morning, my suspicions seemed absurd. He had secrets, I knew, a life that didn't involve me. One night while he was gone, I made out in the basement of Gamma Nu with Bo Benson, maybe to prove that I had secrets, too.

"Did I tell you Jeffrey Greenbaum got into medical school?" Abe asked during our weekly phone call. I was only half listening. Debra was in the bathroom dyeing her hair with Crashy Bellwether, and it was my job to watch the clock. Crashy was Debra's latest protégée. A statuesque blonde with a high bosom and a distant stare, she looked every inch the sorority girl she'd been before Debra convinced her to de-pledge and write exposés about the Greek system for *bitch slap*, including the one that had gotten her into so much trouble with Gamma Nu. She didn't talk much, which made her a perfect match for Debra. Crashy was her unfortunate nickname, although if you asked me, her given name—Prudence—was worse.

"You did tell me," I said as the timer went off. "Time to rinse."

"What's that?" Abe asked.

"Nothing, Dad. That's great about Jeffrey. Mrs. Greenbaum must be very happy." The Greenbaums lived around the corner from us and were in the Judaica business. Jeffrey and I had kissed once in the back of a taxicab. He was the first boy I ever made cry.

"I always said every Jewish family needs a doctor," Abe said.

"Maybe Mrs. Greenbaum will let us borrow Jeffrey."

"Did you decide about the magazine?"

"I'm letting them know tomorrow."

"Did you ask for more money?"

Debra pulled off the towel, revealing popsicle-red hair. "No, Dad, but I will." I hung up as Kelsey walked in and surveyed the mess.

"Debra dyed her hair," I said.

Debra struck a ta-da stance. "Whaddaya think?"

"Well," Kelsey said, "you'll be easy to spot in a crowd."

"What's wrong with you?" Debra asked.

"Nothing," said Kelsey, as Crashy wiped her red hands on one of Kelsey's towels. "I just don't like coming home to a mess." She walked into the bedroom and closed the door. I followed her, leaving Debra and Crashy giggling in the bathroom.

Kelsey looked over at Debra's bed, unmade and piled high with clothes. I thought I saw part of a sandwich under her pillow.

"I don't like the way she's acting right now," Kelsey said. "Do you?"

"She's okay."

"Now you think she's okay? You were the one who was worried about her. I think she's up to something. I think Crashy is in on it, too."

I folded a couple of Debra's T-shirts and put them in a

drawer. I had been worried about her, but she seemed better, or maybe I had just stopped paying attention.

"I know she thinks this Crushgirls stuff is funny," Kelsey said, "but I don't. And if she's planning to do something around graduation, she's going to get in real trouble." She put a hand on her hip. "Did you ever look at the floor plans I left on your desk?" I looked at her blankly. "For the apartments my mom found. If we want to move in July, we have to choose one."

"I know," I said. "I will." Connelly had just told me about a friend who was renting a room over his garage. I was planning to look at it tomorrow. We'd talked more about our plans for the summer, ideas for my story, which he thought could be a book. I could feel Kelsey watching me. I knew she needed an answer, but I didn't have one.

"Isabel?" she said. "Are you even listening? What's going on with you these days?"

Just then, Debra pushed open the door. "Whatcha talking about?"

"Nothing," I said. "Where's Crashy?"

"She split." She plopped down on Kelsey's bed, mussing the bedspread.

Kelsey frowned. "What are you guys up to?"

Debra folded her hands across her chest, smiling like the Cheshire cat.

"Come on, Debra," I said. "Tell us."

"Oh, my God, we have a great idea. It's such a great idea. And Kelsey, we need your help to pull it off. You have a key to the art center, right?"

"Yeah. Why?"

"Do you know if the sculpture of Eleazar Wilder is bolted to the floor?"

"Debra, what are you on about?" Kelsey asked.

"Okay, so get this: the night before graduation, we drag that old coot out into the middle of the green. A couple of guys from Agora have offered to help us, and Crashy has her Jeep. Normally I'd say no to male assistance, but this plan is too good." She was practically vibrating as she described her plan, which involved spray-painting the words "womyn are everywhere" on the sculpture of Eleazar Wilder, founding father of Wilder College, then dragging it out into the middle of the green so that everyone—parents, faculty, alumni—would see it on their way to graduation. It would be, according to Debra, the greatest Crushgirls stunt ever, a way to show everyone that the patriarchy was toppling and the reign of women— womyn?—had begun. Or something like that. Honestly, the plan was poorly thought out and juvenile, not to mention derivative of previous Crushgirls stunts. I almost said as much, but it didn't seem worth it. Kelsey looked outraged, but I just felt sad. Aside from being unfeasible and, most likely, criminal, Debra's stunt wasn't fun or clever. It was, I thought, beneath her.

"What do you think?" Debra asked.

"I think you're out of your mind," said Kelsey.

"Oh, you're no fun."

"Fun?" said Kelsey. "What's fun about criminal mischief? What's fun about getting arrested, or worse, not getting your diploma?"

"What about you, Izzy?" Debra said. "Are you in?"

"Debra, I don't know. I think we'd get in real trouble for that. That piece is probably valuable. There are probably cameras, and alarms. Have you thought any of this through?" I wasn't sure why I was fixating on the details, as if that was all that stood in the way of making this a good plan. "What if we planned something else? Banners, or we could spell out something on our caps? A message or something?"

"Lame," Debra said.

"Stop humoring her," said Kelsey.

"Do we have to do anything?" I said. "I mean, it's almost over. Can't we just enjoy the time we have left?"

"Since when did you get so nervous?" Debra snapped. "I understand Kelsey wanting to prop up the system, but you? What did Wilder ever do for you? Zev's still a student here."

At that, Jason opened the door, and I was spared having to answer her.

"Sorry," he said. "I was knocking. Everything okay in here?"

"We're fine," Kelsey said and walked out.

"Better check on the missus," said Debra.

"Hey," Jason said to me, "did you hear about Professor Fisher?"

"No. What about him?"

"I don't know much, but apparently he and his daughter are missing."

"What do you mean 'missing'?"

"I heard it from Andy. He said Fisher was supposed to take her to his sister's house and they never showed up." He looked at Debra. "What happened to your hair?"

I ran over to the library, where I found Andy in his carrel.

"I don't know how much I'm supposed to say," he said, "but I guess it'll all come out anyway now that the FBI is involved."

"The FBI? Andy, what the fuck happened?"

Andy looked tired. I hadn't seen him much lately, but I'd heard he and Kara had broken up. Also, he hadn't gotten funding at his top programs and had been wait-listed at a couple more.

"Tom was supposed to take Igraine to his sister's house in Rhode Island for a couple of days. Joanna didn't want him to, but Tom convinced her it would be fine, that Igraine would get to spend time with her cousins or whatever." He reached for his cigarettes, offered me one. "So Joanna said yes. He was supposed to get there on Saturday, but he never showed up."

"That was four days ago. What does the sister say?"

"She said she hasn't spoken to Tom in months."

"Jesus." Andy lit his cigarette, then leaned over and lit mine. I noticed his hands were shaking. "Where could he be?"

"No clue. Joanna's calling everyone. No one knows where he is. Tom doesn't have much money and Igraine doesn't have a passport, as far as she knows. Isabel, it's bad. When I was living there last summer, they fought all the time. Like, really fought."

"Yeah. I saw them one night," I said. "This winter. Fighting in front of my dorm. They were yelling at each other, and then he pulled her into the car."

Andy sucked hard on his cigarette. "Tom is not a good

guy. He's always been jealous of Joanna's success. You'd never know it looking at him, but the guy's an asshole."

"You don't think he'd hurt Igraine, do you?"

"No. I think this is all about hurting Joanna." Andy tapped his cigarette ash into a paper cup. "Listen, don't tell anyone you heard this from me, okay? It's not gossip."

I promised Andy I wouldn't tell anyone, then I left the library and headed over to Stringer Hall. I didn't think Connelly would be there. Still, I walked up to his office and knocked three times on the closed door.

Tom's office was dark, as it had been for weeks. There were a few papers sticking out from underneath the door, and I bent down and pushed them all the way under. Then I wiggled the doorknob, hoping it would open and I'd find Tom inside, rolling a cigarette or holding out a bag of Starburst.

I remembered the first time I met him, when I'd come by to ask him about mentoring my thesis. He asked where I was from, and it turned out he and Joanna had lived on the Lower East Side for a few years.

"Your family owns Rosen's Appetizing? Joanna and I used to go there all the time. Joanna was addicted to the whitefish salad. And the smoked salmon." He kissed the tips of his fingers. "What a store. Those are the places that make New York so special." He paused. "So, why Wharton?"

"What do you mean?"

"I mean, is Wharton's New York *your* New York?" He walked over to his bookshelf. "Why not Grace Paley or Henry Roth? Or Malamud?" He took a book off the shelf and handed it to me. "I would think there are writers who speak more to your experience than Wharton."

I looked at the book he'd given me. Bernard Malamud's *The Assistant*. Whenever I asked Abe about his childhood, he would say, "Read *The Assistant*."

"I'm not telling you what to do," Tom said. "Just think about it."

I'd decided to stick with Wharton, although I thought about what Tom said every time I stepped into the world of characters who wouldn't have even glanced at my forebears if they passed them on the street. I still hadn't read *The Assistant*.

Igraine's face floated back to me as I passed the spot where we had sat together that day. *Be careful, my darling. I love you*. I tried to imagine where she might be right now, if she understood what was going on, if she was scared. Maybe if I had said something, this wouldn't have happened—but what would I have said, and to whom? I headed downstairs. A bird had flown inside the building. I tried to get it to follow me outside, but it kept walking down the hall, as if it were late for a meeting. I stepped out into the late afternoon sunshine and remembered Doug Biaggio's phone number, the one he'd told me about at the Knotty Pine. *1-800-I-AM-LOST*.

"I HAVE NO idea where Tom is," Connelly said. We were sitting in the front seat of his car, which was parked behind the computer science building. He'd asked me to meet him there instead of his office. With all the commotion surrounding Tom's disappearance, he thought it best that we be cautious. "Everyone keeps asking, but I promise you, he didn't say a word to me."

It was early, just past seven. The sky was the color of a peach. I sipped my coffee slowly and watched a group of birds fight over a bird feeder someone had hung from a nearby branch. Tom and Igraine had been missing for nearly a week, but unlike the story of his jump in the lake the night of the Senior Mingle, this story was filtering slowly through the campus ecosystem. When we discussed it, we did so gravely, because, I liked to think, we understood how serious it was. Maybe we felt guilty for not having recognized the danger; we'd seen at least part of what Tom was capable of that night. Or maybe I was only speaking for myself.

What little I knew came from my conversation with Andy and an article in the *Daily Citizen*, which I'd dug out of the recycling bin during a shift at the information desk. According to the article, most of what Andy had said was true: the sister, the trip to Rhode Island. The divorce, by all accounts, was bitter, the marriage troubled. Police records revealed at least two visits to the house on June Bridge Road, including once when Joanna was pregnant. The police had labeled the incidents "domestic disturbances" and left it at that. According to an unnamed source, Tom had been behaving erratically since Joanna had filed for divorce in December, more so since she had sued for custody, but there had been no indication that he'd planned to kidnap Igraine, or worse. Wherever Tom was, the authorities didn't think he'd gone far: his credit card hadn't been used since the day he left, when he'd used it to buy gas at a service station a few miles from campus. There was some grainy surveillance footage of him pumping gas—no sign of Igraine, although there was no reason to think they weren't together. After that, they fell off the map. I'd hoped Connelly could shed more light on what Tom had done. At twenty-two, I still believed adults did things because they made sense, that they had information I did not have, by virtue of being adults. I was beginning to think this might not always be the case. I would soon come to understand that adulthood was exactly this: the constant upending of everything you believed when you were young.

"Did you think he was capable of something like this?" I asked Connelly.

"No, of course not. Tom's a peaceful, gentle guy. But who knows what goes on inside a marriage? A lot of marriages fall apart when kids come into the picture, squabbles about money, who's going to take care of this or that. Some men get jealous when their wives become so devoted to this other little person. Then again, a marriage without kids loses something too. Momentum or energy. Oxygen." He nod-ded, as if satisfied to have found the right word.

I spilled a little coffee on my shirt. I opened the glove compartment, looking for a napkin, and saw the ring of keys. I started to reach for them, then thought better of it.

"Did you ever want kids?" I sometimes thought about what Whitney had told me, about Roxanne being pregnant, but had never asked Connelly about it.

He was quiet for a while, and I thought maybe I'd pushed

too far, but then he said, "I was going to say it was a long story, but it's actually pretty short. Roxanne didn't want kids and then when she did, it was too late. Women like to think they can 'have it all,' but there is a biological component to things, whether we want to admit it or not." He looked straight ahead, and a ray of sunlight glanced off his cheek. "We did get pregnant once. Twins. Roxanne thought it was absurd to grieve for someone you'd never met. She wanted to try again, but . . ." He shook his head. "It was probably for the best."

The sky brightened. "Whatever Tom's guilty of," he said, "he loves that little girl."

17

I hadn't seen Debra for a couple days when I bumped into her walking across the green with Crashy. I spotted her hair first, glowing like a candied apple in the moonlight.

"Izzy!" She ran over and grabbed me by the shoulders. It was ten o'clock on a Wednesday night, and she was already drunk. "Agora is having its leopard and lace party, and you have to come!" She opened her jacket and showed me her dress, short and black, and a pair of black lace stockings. Crashy had leopard-printed press-on nails poking out of fingerless lace gloves.

"I'm not really dressed for it," I said. "Plus, I'm wiped."

"Oh, come on! How many more nights do we have here anyway?" Debra placed a heavy arm around my shoulders. She smelled like pot and rotting flowers.

"Fine," I said. Debra squealed with delight. A feather boa materialized. Crashy pulled a leopard scrunchie out of her hair and handed it to me, then steered me under a streetlight and smeared my lips with lipstick.

"This is perfect!" Debra cried. She linked arms with me and Crashy and the three of us marched over to Agora, like Dorothy on the road to Oz.

The party had the feel of one that had been going for a while even though it was still early. In Agora's smoky main room, people were draped over each other, smoking or taking long, luxurious sips from plastic cups. Out on the dance floor, a shirtless guy in a rainbow wig was hanging off a girl in a low-cut top, his face buried deep in the line of her cleavage. Music throbbed through the creaky wooden floor, pounding bass notes that vibrated in the space behind my sternum. Three girls danced together in the middle of the room, a seductive tangle of arms and legs. One was wearing only a bra and bike shorts. There was a tattoo of an eagle across her shoulder blades; when she moved her arms, it looked like it was flapping its wings.

Amos Jackson was manning the keg. "Welcome, ladies," he said. He had on a greasy black fedora and Ray-Bans, a lace scarf tied around one ear.

"Damn I Wish I Was Your Lover" came on. "I love this song!" Debra shouted. She grabbed Crashy's hand and pulled her onto the dance floor, leaving me alone with Amos.

"Hey, I saw your boyfriend," he said, handing me a cup of beer.

"Who?"

"That professor filling in for Maxwell." He laughed. "Whitney calls him your boyfriend."

My face got hot. "Where did you see him?"

"In the general store near my great-grandpa's farm." His eyes kept moving from my face to the dance floor where Crashy and Debra were making large, slow movements with their bodies. "He was hard to miss. The only other people who hang out there wear bib overalls and are about a hundred years old."

"Huh," I said. I couldn't imagine Connelly would be that far upstate, but I couldn't ask him because I wouldn't want him to think people were gossiping about him, about us. Plus, Amos was probably wrong.

I sipped my beer, which tasted vaguely of socks, and saw Amos's eyes grow wide as Debra and Crashy moved closer together, Debra's thighs scissoring Crashy's long leg. In 1998, Agora may have been the most subversive thing about Wilder College. Once part of the Greek system—back when Wilder was all-male, it was known as the only fraternity that would accept gays—it broke away in the eighties and became a coed "undergraduate society" instead. I forgot this was why some straight boys came to Agora, because they thought the girls who partied there were kinky. Crashy was flinging her hair back and forth. I saw one of her fake nails fly off and slide under a sofa. I imagined someone finding it later, much later, after we were all gone and out in the world.

I noticed someone watching me from across the room. It was the guy in the rainbow wig, the one I'd seen dancing when I walked in. He took a swig from a small glass bottle and started walking toward me. There was something shiny on his chest, a sheen of sweat mixed with glitter. He was more than halfway when I realized it was Zev. I looked over my shoulder, but Amos was gone.

"Isabel Rosen." Zev's voice sounded thick, like his tongue was swollen.

"Hi, Zev." We hadn't spoken in a while, not since that day at the information booth, but I felt more relaxed around him now, either because I was a little drunk or because he looked so stupid in that wig.

"How come we never talk anymore?" He moved closer to me, and I caught a whiff of him.

"You're drunk."

"Yeah." He took a long swig and smeared his hand across his chest. "I am. But seriously, I thought we were friends. Now you don't call, you don't write."

I tried to catch Debra's eye. She was still dancing, now in a small group that included Amos. "Were we friends, Zev?"

"I thought we were." He scratched his head, knocking the wig askew. "I liked talking to you. You have all these opinions, things you believe, but you can't defend any of them. Your whole worldview is based on feelings. It amuses me."

I could tell he was trying to provoke me, but I decided not to let him.

"If you liked me, why didn't you ever tell me?"

"Would it have made a difference?"

"It might have. Maybe things wouldn't have gotten so messed up if you did."

"Hey, the only reason things got messed up is because of what your friend did."

"I disagree."

"You *disagree*?"

"Yeah. I think they got messed up because of you."

Zev started to respond, but then I remembered I didn't

have to talk to him, not now, not ever, so I turned on my heel and walked away.

He followed me into a big room at the back of the house. It appeared to be a kitchen—there were cabinets and a greasy range top and something that looked like a refrigerator. In the corner, a group was gathered around a large metal mixing bowl. A girl with straw-colored dreadlocks looked up as we walked in.

"Don't run away from me," Zev said.

I stopped in front of the refrigerator. "Why not? I don't owe you anything."

"You don't *owe* me anything? Nobody would even talk to me after what you and your friend did."

"You think *that's* why nobody would talk to you? Nobody talks to you, Zev, because nobody *likes* you."

From the expression on his face, I could tell I'd hurt him in some soft, secret place, the same way he had hurt me. But it didn't give me pleasure. All I felt was sad, as if this was all life was, an endless, interlocking chain of hurting people and being hurt in return.

"*You* came to my room," he said. "I didn't force you. And then, while we were . . . you didn't say anything. I thought you wanted to. I thought—"

"I know." I did know, had known it ever since that night, when Debra and I went back to his room and I'd seen his face when he opened the door. He was happy to see me, happy I'd come back, as though I were coming back for more. For him, that night might have been the start of something, while for me it was the absolute and irrevocable end.

If it was true what Roxanne said, that women cry when they're angry, perhaps it was also true that men got angry when they were sad.

"Do you really think I *raped* you?" he asked.

I leaned against the counter, felt the hard edge press into the small of my back. Did I? I didn't know anymore. Everything Zev had said so far was true: I had gone to his room. I didn't say anything. He thought I wanted to. I thought I did too. The confusing part was, this wasn't what I thought rape looked like, the thing I'd been taught to steel myself against ever since I was young. This was sex in a dorm room in New Hampshire, a room with a river view. And I didn't even say no.

"Do you, Isabel? Do you really think that?" Zev's face was so close to mine I could count every eyelash. It felt like the old days, Zev challenging me to explain myself, presenting a hypothetical for me to puzzle over. And now, like then, I couldn't. My belief system was fuzzy, even when it came to my own body. I thought about all the times Zev had sought me out because he wanted to talk to me, because he thought I was interesting, different from the Sally Steinbergs and Gabe Feldmans, different from the Debras. I sometimes wondered why he tolerated me when he found everyone else at Wilder unbearable. Maybe because I was poor and my father sold smoked fish for a living; he told me once I had a "shtetl mentality" he found refreshing. Sometimes it seemed like Zev was the only person here who saw me, really saw me, and maybe I'd let him fuck me to thank him for that.

The refrigerator door was hanging open, the mildewed shelves bare except for a bottle of vermouth, a carton of milk, and a jar of maraschino cherries. Zev's face looked bluish and pale in its light. I knew he was waiting for an answer, but I didn't have one. If he had accused me of only knowing how I felt about a thing, in this case he was right. I didn't know what to call what he had done to me. I only knew how it had made me feel.

"I don't know," I said finally.

"You don't know?" he said. "Then why'd you go to the dean?"

"The dean? I didn't go to the dean. I thought you did."

"Why would I go to the dean?" He took a step back, like he smelled something bad. Maybe it was whatever they were mixing in that bowl. Maybe it was me. "You know what, have a nice fucking life, Isabel Rosen. Oh, and by the way, there's a rumor going around that you're sleeping with a professor. I thought you might like to know."

The words landed the way I imagined he wanted them to. My breath became short and shallow. There was a sharp pain under my rib cage. Zev pulled off his wig, and I realized that no matter what he had done to me, I would always be the one unpacking that night, wondering what I might have said or done differently. Even then, I could taste the shame that would follow me for a lifetime. It was gritty, like sand on my tongue. I wiped my mouth with the back of my hand and thought I might be sick.

Zev balled up the wig in his fist and tossed it across the room. "Score!" he yelled as it landed in the mixing bowl with a plop.

"What the fuck, man?" The girl with dreadlocks looked up, a tongue stud glimmering in the dark cave of her open mouth. "Hey," she said, pointing at me. "You're bleeding."

I touched my face. My nose was bleeding. I covered it with the boa and ran out of the kitchen. Debra and Crashy were still on the dance floor, slow dancing with Amos. He was cupping Crashy's ass with his hands.

"I'm leaving," I said to Debra. She looked up sleepily, then saw my face.

"What happened?" She pushed Crashy away as Zev came out of the kitchen holding a roll of paper towels. "Wait— did he *hit* you?"

"Debra, no—"

"Of course it would be you," Zev said, raising his hands to the ceiling.

"Why are you even talking to him?" Debra asked me.

"Debra, stop." I wiped my face with my hands, refusing the paper towel Zev offered me. Somewhere in the middle of everything, Amos slithered away. This was not the kink he was after.

Zev turned to Debra. "You're a real piece of work, you know. What you did, it basically ruined my senior year."

"Oh, boo-hoo, it ruined your senior year," Debra said. "How do you think her senior year was, after you *raped* her?"

"Debra, stop!" I said again.

"Why don't you ever let her speak for herself?" said Zev. "Isn't that what you feminists are always on about? Women's voices, women's choices?"

"You don't know shit about feminism," Debra said, taking a step toward him.

"Shut up," I heard someone say, quietly at first and then louder. "Shut up, shut up, shut up." The string of words echoed through the room, rising over the music and the din. It took me a second to realize it was me.

"You heard her," Debra said, folding her arms.

"No," I said. "*You* shut up. You never stop talking. You never listen. You're like a wall of sound." She reached for me, but I pushed her away. It felt good to put my hands on her.

Outside, the air smelled fresh, like grass and daisies. I sat down under a tree, felt the wet ground seep into my jeans. My hands were sticky and coated with glitter and blood. I pulled off Crashy's scrunchie and let my hair fall over my shoulders. The tickle of it down my back reminded me of Connelly, and for the first time all night, I allowed myself to think about him, to wonder what he was doing, if he was thinking of me.

After a few minutes, Debra stumbled outside, cradling the roll of paper towels. Her eye makeup was smudged and there was a run in her stocking.

"So, what? You're mad at *me* now?"

"I don't know, Debra."

"I can't believe you're letting him off the hook. It's like you're *friends*."

"I'm not—" I put my face in my hands. "Forget it."

"Forget what? Stop being so passive-aggressive."

"There's no point in even talking to you because you never listen."

"What are you talking about?"

"Like that night with Zev. I just needed you to listen to me."

"I *did* listen."

"No. You didn't. You pounced." I unwound the boa from my neck. "I don't know what happened that night. Zev just did what guys do, you know? He had the chance to fuck me so that's what he did. And I let him."

"Well, that's the saddest fucking thing I've ever heard." She sat down next to me. There was glitter in her hair, embedded in the line of her part. She sniffed several times before speaking. "I'm sorry, Iz. I was just trying to protect you."

"I know. But I don't need you to." I looked down at my hands and shirt, both streaked with blood. "Despite all evidence to the contrary."

Debra laughed. Her face, wide and smooth and full of everything, shone in the moonlight. Above us, the sky was dark and vast, dotted with tiny pinpricks of light. I would never have the words to describe this part of Wilder, the quiet, majestic part, but it was the part I wanted most to remember.

"You know why I wanted to come to Wilder?" I said.

"I have no fucking clue."

"Because it had its own T-shirt."

"I think a lot of schools have their own T-shirts. You could've saved yourself a lot of trouble."

"Yeah, but it's the only place where people actually wear them. When I first visited with my dad, I remember seeing all these kids in their Wilder T-shirts, and I wanted to be a part of that."

"Yeah, so?"

"It's just, this place, Debra—it isn't all bad. You always talk about changing it, 'burning it to the motherfucking ground,' but I actually kind of love it."

"I love it, too." I looked at her. "No, I do. What I hate is that it feels like it will never be ours. I thought being here made us equal, you know, but we're always on their turf, playing by their rules. I worked just as hard as Zev did to get here, as hard as all these assholes. So did you." She sniffed again, louder this time, and I realized she was crying.

I reached for her hand and held it as she told me how she was feeling. The ground was slippery, she said, and she was losing her footing, the way she had freshman year. It started the night we'd gone back to Zev's room, and I realized there was a pattern: Debra usually broke down after a stunt like that, as if the things she thought would destabilize Wilder only succeeded in destabilizing her.

"I'm so angry, you know?" Debra said, and I put my arms around her and told her that I forgave her, of course I forgave her. Because even though Debra was impossible and difficult and messy and careless—not to mention certain about things she knew nothing about—she was also my friend and even then I knew she always would be, even when I didn't like her very much. Later, I'd drop people for far less, but Debra had imprinted on me. It's like that with the people who know us when we're young, when we're still figuring out the world and how we might fit into it.

After a while, we headed back to the dorm. Fireflies were passing secret messages to each other, and I thought about something my grandmother's rabbi said when I asked him what happens to us after we die. His answer was unsatisfying to me at the time, something about stardust and energy and how nothing is ever wasted. "Yeah," I said, "but what does that *mean*?" I didn't care about energy; I just wanted to know if I would see my mother again. But now I thought he might have been on to something. I could feel a kind of energy swirling around me, not just my mother but Debra and Crashy and Zev, Connelly, even Amos. We would all leave parts of ourselves behind after we were gone. Nothing we'd done here would be wasted.

WE NEVER FOUND out who told Dean Hansen about the spray paint on Zev's door—a janitor, Debra thought; there were probably procedures for things like that. And I never saw Zev Neman again. I heard he moved back to Israel, went to work for his father, married Yael. This last part I read about in a Hillel newsletter that arrived the day Bill Clinton was acquitted by the Senate. When I imagine Yael telling their origin story—dinner party, candlelight, glass of merlot—I have nothing whatsoever to do with it. I am facedown on the floor at their feet.

18

ABE was coming for graduation. Benji was ready to watch the store, along with Manny, and Abe was looking forward to getting away.

"Are you sure?" I said. "It's such a long drive and it's not like I'm doing anything special."

"Isabel, there's enough *tsuris* in this life. Let's celebrate when something good happens. Besides, it'll be good for Benji. I can see how he does without me."

Abe had gone to check out an apartment Kelsey's parents had found, a junior 4 in a doorman building in Alphabet City; I'd agreed to take the smaller bedroom in exchange for lower rent. "Not horrible" was Abe's review. "Small, but lots of light. And it's not Brooklyn. I don't know what you girls were thinking. I thought everybody wanted to leave Brooklyn." Kelsey's parents were laying out the security deposit and first month's rent, which I promised to pay back, and come July 1, it would be ours.

Kelsey had landed a job at an art gallery in SoHo; we'd celebrated by taking her to get her eyebrow pierced. She spent the evenings leading up to graduation flagging items in the Pottery Barn catalog, wicker baskets and throw pillows and a bright kilim rug. Jason would be in New York too, in law school. He would be sharing an apartment on the Upper West Side with Bo and another Gamma Nu.

After our talk at Agora, I'd encouraged Debra to reach out to her mother. Marilyn swooped in—of course she did—and Debra's psychiatrist adjusted her prescription. I think she might have gone to see Dr. Cushman a couple of times, although she never said. She seemed quiet, chastened. She hadn't mentioned the sculpture stunt again and had spent the past couple nights at home with Kelsey and me. The two of them were even getting along. It was almost like it used to be, but I wasn't upset she was moving to San Francisco. My head was quieter without Debra in it.

As for me, while I was moving ahead with the Alphabet City apartment and the job at *Get Out!*, which I'd finally accepted (and for the salary they'd offered, although I told Abe I'd negotiated fiercely), I was also looking for rooms to rent in town and circling want ads in the local *Pennysaver*. Connelly didn't know about my New York plans. As far as he knew, I was staying at Wilder with him. We'd started meeting in his office again. He'd finally caught the mouse under the sofa, but he still talked about taking me some-where. "I want to make love to you in a real bed," he said.

We would spend the summer together and he'd send me back to New York with a finished manuscript I could shop around. He'd worked with students before, he said, but none of them had what I had. I just had to want it badly enough. "I can taste it," he said. So could I, how easy it would be to slip into a life he created for me instead of having to make one of my own.

One afternoon, I found myself alone in our dorm room for the first time in a long while. I stepped over the cardboard boxes Kelsey had brought us; Debra had already started packing a couple. I thought back to the day we'd moved in, carrying everything up the stairs, sweating and cursing. It didn't seem that long ago. In a few days, we'd carry it all back down again. It hardly seemed worth the trouble. We'd always been on our way out, I could see now, even from the start, Wilder shedding students the way a snake sheds its skin: slowly but inexorably, the edges moving out to make way for the new.

I lit a cigarette, let it hang from my lips and walked into the bedroom. I opened one of Debra's overstuffed drawers and pulled a sweater over my head, studied myself in the mirror, then took it off and put it back. I did that with a few more of her things, then noticed Kelsey's jewelry box was open. I reached in and took out the silver bangle Jason bought her for Valentine's Day, felt its cool heft against my skin. Then I picked up the ring her parents had given her for her twenty-first birthday and slipped it on my finger.

I rolled the ring around my knuckle and thought about the day I stopped stealing. It was the fall of my senior year of high school. My mother was home again after spending the summer in and out of the hospital, but she wasn't painting.

Every day I came home from school, hoping I'd find her at her easel, but instead she'd be exactly where I'd left her, in bed, her coffee cooling on the nightstand, the sandwich my father had brought her for lunch uneaten. I dreaded coming home, so I started walking instead of taking the subway, finding longer and longer routes so I could put it off a little longer.

One day, I stopped in a store on lower Broadway, the kind that sold vintage clothing but also new clothing made to look old. The store was empty; the lone salesgirl sat behind the counter reading a magazine. She barely looked up as I walked into the dressing room with a pair of jeans and a blouse. The jeans were nothing special, but the blouse was magical. I was beginning to learn how clothing could turn you into someone else, at least for a few moments in front of a dressing room mirror. I checked the price tag, but it didn't matter how much it cost. I couldn't afford it.

I stayed in the dressing room a long time. I had a rusty taste in my mouth, a prickle of sweat between my breasts. I'd never stolen anything from a store before. After a few minutes, I unbuttoned the shirt and placed it carefully in my backpack, then piled my books and folders on top.

"Thanks," I said to the salesgirl as I placed the jeans on the pile and headed for the door.

"Hold on." She looked up from her magazine. "How many things did you bring in with you?"

"Just the jeans," I said, but I could hear my voice quaver. I was a good thief but a terrible liar.

The girl stepped out from behind the counter. She was older than me, with a short haircut and a nose ring.

"Give me your bag," she said, resting a hand on her narrow hip. I passed it to her and watched as she dug out the shirt.

"I'm sorry," I said, and I burst into tears, gasping, ugly sobs like something inside me had come loose. I was ashamed and scared and embarrassed, but mostly sad that the beautiful shirt would never be mine.

"Go," she said, tossing the bag at me. "But if I ever see you in here again, I'll call the cops."

I ran all the way home, stopping briefly to throw up between two parked cars. When I got home, I put everything I'd ever stolen in a black garbage bag and tossed it in the dumpster behind Rosen's.

I slipped off Kelsey's ring and held it in my hand. It was beautiful: gold with two tiny diamonds nestled together like twins in utero. If it were mine, I would have worn it every day, wouldn't leave it languishing in an overstuffed jewelry box. I tightened my fist around it and placed it in my pocket. I held it there for a minute, my heart pounding, breath quickening, that rust taste tangy in my mouth. Then I threw it back in Kelsey's jewelry box and slammed the lid shut.

ON FRIDAY NIGHT, I found myself following Ginny and a group of rowers down to the river. It was late, and I'd lost Kelsey and Debra somewhere between Gamma Nu and a party at the River Ranch, an off-campus house perched above the river in Vermont. I'd had quite a bit to drink, although not as much as Ginny, who stumbled as we headed down the narrow, wooded path that led to the Connecticut River, the body of water that separated Vermont and New

Hampshire. Ginny and I had never really hung out before, but as graduation drew near it felt like everyone was my friend.

Up ahead, someone started singing the alma mater. Back when I was in Glee Club, we used to sing the alma mater for groups of Wilder alumni, old, white-haired men in kelly green jackets and plaid pants. As we sang, their rheumy eyes would fill with tears; some would struggle to their feet, gripping tightly to their canes. I always thought there was something cultlike about the alma mater, vaguely Hitler Youth, but now, walking arm-in-arm with Ginny on a cool spring night, my heart swelled with feeling and I thought I might cry.

"*We will remember Wilder, the rolling hills of Wilder, our happy years at Wilder nestled in our memory and our hearts,*" we sang.

"That song is creepy," Ginny shouted. "I don't want Wilder nestled in my heart."

"It's a metaphor," I shouted back.

"A metaphor!" Ginny tossed her head back and laughed as if it were the funniest thing she'd ever heard. "I love you, Iz," she said, winding her strong arm around my waist. "I don't think I've ever told you that. I always wished we were better friends."

"Aw, thanks, Ginny. Yeah, me too."

"I know a lot of people don't like you," she said, "but I think you're a badass." And then she leaned over and kissed me on the lips. It wasn't entirely unpleasant, but maybe it was just that kind of night.

The rain from earlier in the day had stopped, but the sky felt heavy and swollen. After a few yards, the path narrowed, then opened up into a grassy field that sloped down to the river. I kicked something with my foot. It was a T-shirt. Up ahead, a trail of clothing led to the water's edge.

Ginny kicked off her sneakers, then looked at me as if to say, "Why not?" I watched as she pulled off her clothes and ran toward the water, her strong pale body glowing in the moonlight. All around me, people were doing the same. "Come on, Isabel!" Ginny shouted. I looked around, then carefully removed my shorts and T-shirt, underwear and bra, and placed it all neatly in a pile on a rock. And then, before I could think about it too much, I plunged feet first into the black water.

There were people for whom the river had been at the heart of their Wilder experience, much as the library had been at the heart of mine. Ginny, for example, and the rowers who came here every morning in the fall and spring as mist rose off the water like dry ice. In the winter, when the river froze over, some traversed its length on cross-country skis. In the summer, they floated down it in big rubbery inner tubes. I'd only been to the river a couple of times and I'd never swum in it. I'd always thought of it as belonging to that part of Wilder that didn't feel like mine, but now, suspended in the water's soft embrace, I wondered what I'd been waiting for.

I floated for a while, thinking about Connelly. Roxanne was going to a conference, and he'd invited me to spend the night at his house. I wanted to go, but I also wanted to do this, float aimlessly through my final few nights here. The Tunemen were performing in their last big concert, and Bo

had asked me to go. I felt stuck between two paths, one leading toward a future I could understand, the other leading—
where? Nowhere good. There was, I can see now, a kernel
of self-preservation at my center, a belief in myself and my
future. I wanted more than what Roxanne and Connelly
had, more than what my parents had had. I wanted something close to what Kelsey and Jason had, what I'd thought
Joanna and Tom had. I wanted love. I wanted it all. I dipped
my head under the water and, weirdly, thought about Bo.

A breeze rippled through the trees, ruffling the water
and raising goose bumps on my skin. I looked up and saw
I had floated far away from everyone else. A few people
were climbing back onto shore, whooping and hollering
and scrambling for their clothes. A guy named Rod was
holding Ginny's bra high above his head. She was jumping
for it, one arm held across her chest. Someone was sitting
on the rock where I'd left my clothes. As I swam closer, I
saw it was Andy.

"Nice swim?" he asked.

"Yeah, really nice," I said. "Were you at the River Ranch?"

"No. I've been with Joanna all day."

Joanna. As soon as Andy said her name, I realized I hadn't
thought about her, about any of them, in days. *Tom and
Igraine are missing.* The thought would drift through my
mind from time to time, then get pushed aside by something more pressing. I'd begun to think of them the way I
thought about victims of accidents or crimes, as people for
whom violence was part of their destiny in a way it was
not, and would never be, part of mine. But now, Tom's and

Igraine's faces floated before me and I wondered how it was I hadn't been thinking about them the whole time.

"How is she?" I asked.

"How do you think?" he said sharply. "She's terrible."

"Of course. I'm sorry. Has there been any news?"

He shook his head. "No sign of them either. It's been almost three weeks."

"It's so weird."

"Weird. Sure." He picked up a pebble. "The cops still don't think they've left New Hampshire."

"How do they know?"

"Tom didn't have much cash, and there's been no activity on his credit card. Besides, there are posters all over the place. I'm sure you've seen them."

I nodded. I had seen them. MISSING posters with Tom's and Igraine's faces were everywhere, on the bulletin board at the supermarket, post office, bookstore. Every time I saw one, I did my best to avoid Tom's lazy eye and Igraine's shy grin.

Andy tossed the pebble into the water. It landed with a plop. "And no one's called. No one's seen them anywhere. It's like they're ghosts."

"Do you think they're—"

"Dead? They could be. But if they aren't, they've found a pretty good place to hide."

A light rain started falling. Up on the grass, someone with a guitar started playing "Layla." I could hear Ginny's voice loud above the others. The water was getting cold, and my legs were tired. I wondered how much longer I'd have to wait before I could get out and get dressed. I wanted to look for Kelsey and Jason and Bo, wanted to find them sitting together in Gamma Nu's basement, could already hear Bo saying "Hey, cool girl," when I walked in.

"I think someone knows where they are," Andy said. "I think someone's helping them, giving them money or a place to stay."

"Who would do that?"

He picked up another pebble. "What about Connelly?"

"What about him?"

"They're good friends, aren't they? And Tom was always hanging around our classroom. And remember how Connelly didn't come to class that week? That was right before Tom disappeared."

"Oh, my God," I said. "What are you, Scooby Doo?" Andy didn't say anything, kept studying the pebble in his hand. "What does Joanna think of your theory?"

"I haven't told her yet."

"That's because you know it's nuts. Look, I know you like to gossip, but don't you think you're going a little far? Accusing a man of—I don't even know what to call it. Aiding and abetting?"

Andy tossed the pebble in my direction. It cleared my head, but barely. "I'd say the guy has some secrets, wouldn't you?"

"What's that supposed to mean?"

The rain picked up.

"Come on, Isabel." He held up my T-shirt, placed two fingers in the small pocket over the breast.

"Come on what?" I felt a chill run through me. More people were climbing out of the water. I could see Ginny up on the grass looking around, maybe for me. After a few seconds, she started up the hill back to campus.

"Everyone knows." He said it so softly, it felt like a kindness, although of course it wasn't. "Hey, I'm not judging you."

"Andy, I don't know what you think you know, but—"

"What if he hurts her?" He let the words hang for a moment, a strange expression on his face. Later, I would realize it was fear. "I understand not wanting to get involved, but this is pretty fucking serious. Maybe Connelly doesn't know anything, but it doesn't hurt to ask, does it?"

I didn't say anything. A car moved slowly over the bridge, its headlights sweeping across the water like a searchlight. Andy put down my T-shirt and picked up my bra.

"Look," he said, "I don't know what Russian novel you think you're in, but you're just fucking a professor. And not even a tenured one." Then he stood up and tossed my bra in the water. I grabbed it before it sank.

19

CONNELLY said it was only six miles to his house and that the road there was mostly flat. I'd hung on the words "only" and "flat" as I headed out on Saturday night on a bike I borrowed from Kelsey. (I'd told her I was having dinner at a professor's house; I didn't tell her I was the only guest.) I'd always envied the way people at Wilder rode bikes, the effortlessness with which they navigated the uneven country roads. I thought I was too old to learn what they instinctively seemed to know, but now, guiding Kelsey's mountain bike over the smooth black road that led out of town, I felt invincible. I felt like I could ride for days.

I pulled up to Connelly's house, a small yellow ranch at the end of a quiet leafy street. He'd told me a little about the house he'd lived in with Roxanne for five years. There was a garden that was constantly being raided by a family of rabbits who lived under the porch. "Mint's taken over

everything," he said once, as if this was something everyone knew about mint. There was a sofa on the back porch
where he liked to sit and read on summer nights and an elm
tree in the front yard that was under the care of a tree doctor. Such a thing existed? I'd asked him in delight, picturing
a man in a white coat pressing a stethoscope to the tree's
thick middle.

As I turned into the driveway, the front wheel of my bike
skidded out from under me. One of my sneakers flew off
as I sailed over the handlebars and slid across the driveway,
coming to rest at the place where the asphalt met the grass.

The screen door slammed open, and Connelly ran out.

"I'm fine," I shouted as he hurried over. My knees were
stinging, the right more than the left, but my hands had
borne the brunt. I picked a pebble out of the fleshy part of
my palm as Connelly kneeled down next to me, but I could
barely look at him.

"Come on," he said, helping me to stand. "Let's get you
cleaned up." He picked up my sneaker and led me into the
house. He brought me to the bathroom and sat me down
on the edge of the tub while he rummaged through the
cabinet under the sink.

"What's that?" I asked as he pulled out a bottle of something.

"*Cállate*," he said. He shook the bottle, then sprayed my
hands with some sort of antiseptic.

"Ow!"

"Oh, stop. This'll keep them from getting infected." He
gave my knees a quick squirt, then took a couple of Band-
Aids out of a waterlogged box.

"I can do it," I said.

"It's easier if I do it. Hold still."

I sat back and let him tend to me. He took his job seriously, and I could see, for a moment, the kind of father he would have been: tender, gentle, a little overprotective. As he dabbed my knees with a washcloth, I looked around the room. The walls were covered in pale yellow wallpaper, and there was a bathrobe hanging behind the door. On the edge of the sink, there was a ceramic soap dish full of jewelry.

"That should do it." He sat back on his heels to admire his handiwork. My right knee was covered with a crisscross of bandages; the left had three in a row, like a ladder. It was too difficult to bandage my hands, so he gave them an extra spray of antiseptic.

"Thanks," I said. "I wish you could have seen me before I hit the driveway."

He smoothed the bandages with his fingers. "Yes. 'Hit' the driveway is exactly what you did."

I punched him lightly on the shoulder. "I'm here, aren't I?"

"You are indeed. And I'm sure you were amazing."

I followed him into the living room, a cluttered room with low ceilings and a worn gray sectional. My eyes moved quickly around the space, trying to take in everything: the flowered curtains, the antique sideboard, the laundry basket in the corner. Connelly went into the kitchen, and I walked over and studied the bookshelves. There was an entire shelf devoted to Roxanne's books; another housed a collection of Bibles. One was bound in navy-blue leather, the pages tipped in gold. A couple looked as if they'd been swiped from hotel rooms. I took one off the shelf. Its cover was soft, like an old leather jacket; on the lower right-hand corner, the initials RHC were stamped in gold. I flipped through the pages: Exodus, Leviticus, Deuteronomy. Ezra, Joshua, Samuel, John. It sounded like a poem, or a fraternity house roster.

"Come," Connelly said, handing me a glass of wine. "Let's eat." I put the Bible back on the shelf and saw there was another one behind it, pressed flat against the back of the bookcase.

In the kitchen, more signs of life: dishes drying by the sink, a calendar hanging on the refrigerator, a lazy Susan stocked with vitamin bottles. Copper pots dangled from a rack above the stove where Connelly stood, stirring something.

"What's that?" I asked, peering into the pot. "It smells amazing."

"Soup. And there's salad and fresh bread. I hope you're hungry."

He insisted I sit while he finished cooking. The window was open, and a soft breeze blew through the room along with the sound of crickets. I watched him add salt to the pot, deftly toss the salad with a pair of tongs. I wished I'd brought him something—the scarf still wasn't finished—but I had the feeling he wanted to do this for me and expected nothing in return. When I was older, I would learn that there were other men like him, men who would bandage your wounds and make you dinner and hold your injured hands across the table. But at twenty-two, I thought he was the only one, and I wondered how I would live the rest of my life without him.

He placed two bowls on the table and lit a candle. I took

a sip of wine and it felt as though the light of the candle was moving through my chest, down into my legs. We ate and talked until the soup grew cold. We talked about my book and the work we would do together this summer: changes to the time line, his thoughts on the ending. I watched the candle drip rivulets of wax onto the tablecloth and decided that I would untangle myself from my other plans and stay here with him because this was where I belonged.

We made love that night in the bed Connelly shared with his wife. I never asked whether he and Roxanne still had sex. The closest I came was when I asked if he ever worried she would smell me on him, and he said, "She never gets close enough to notice." In Connelly's telling, their marriage was over. They'd been close to negotiating a separation several times, but the timing was never right. I understood, although he'd never told me, that they stayed together for financial reasons. He worked only part-time at the *Citizen* and whatever money he'd made from his books was gone. As for teaching, those jobs were few and far between and arranged by Roxanne. I may not have understood the intricacies of a long marriage, but I knew what it meant to have your choices constrained by financial realities.

I fell asleep and dreamed I was in Room 203. Everything looked the same except Abe was sitting in Connelly's spot at the head of the table. We were discussing my story, the one about Rosen's, and Abe asked what I meant by something I'd written about him. I tried to answer, but my mouth felt stuck, stopped up like a clogged drain. I reached inside and pulled out yards and yards of thick white cloth.

I woke with a start. Connelly was still asleep, snoring with one arm thrown across his face. I tiptoed into the bathroom and splashed cold water on my neck. I pulled at my cheeks, stretched the skin under my eyes, the thin skin my mother said to touch only with my ring finger, a habit I never outgrew. The bathroom cabinet looked like every bathroom cabinet I'd ever investigated, and I'd investigated many—a bottle of rubbing alcohol, cold medicine, a pair of tweezers. Under the sink, another typical collection: toilet paper, Epsom salts, a tangle of Ace bandages. I sifted through the soap dish full of jewelry and picked up an earring, an amber stud on a silver post. I held it for a moment, then put it back and left the room.

The living room looked prettier in the moonlight, all the rough edges smoothed out. I poked through the books piled on an end table, Dostoyevsky and Tim O'Brien, a dog-eared copy of *Harper's*, a half-finished crossword puzzle. I opened drawers, lifted pillows, checked behind curtains. In one drawer, I found an envelope of pictures from London— Connelly and Roxanne and a group of smiling students, including Daria. In one, Connelly and Daria sat shoulder to shoulder in an English pub; while everyone was look- ing at the camera, she had her gaze directed toward him. I put the pictures back and walked over to the bookshelf. I didn't know what I was looking for, but I was looking for something. It wasn't just the thief in me. This was the most intimate thing I could imagine, this communion with the material. I fantasized about Connelly doing the same thing at my house, poking through bookshelves, investigating my sock drawer, my diaries, the secret stash at the back of my closet. I would have watched, breathless, as he did.

Somewhere in the distance, I heard a dog bark, then another. I pulled out the Bible with Connelly's initials on it, then reached for the one hidden behind it. I opened it and something fluttered to the floor—a daisy, pressed between the onionskin pages. I picked it up carefully, the petals threatening to crumble in my hand, and placed it back inside the book. That's when I saw the photograph, tucked deep inside the pages of the Bible that was itself tucked behind the others. Whoever put it there didn't want anyone to find it. You didn't have to be a thief to know that.

I turned the picture over slowly, letting my eyes blur before focusing them. Outside, the dogs were still barking, politely now, each one waiting for the other to finish before starting up again. The picture was of a girl sitting cross-legged in the grass. She had a pale-pink hoodie zipped up to her chin, a crown of daisies resting atop her blond head. And even though I hadn't seen her in years, I instantly recognized Elizabeth McIntosh, the girl Debra and I used to see coming out of Dr. Cushman's office, the one who'd been taken away by an ambulance a few days before graduation. Behind her was a cabin, Connelly's cabin, the one I'd read about in *Time* magazine.

Why did Connelly have a picture of Elizabeth McIntosh? And when had she gone to his cabin? I tried to remember everything I could about Elizabeth. Pretty, quiet, an English major, one of those girls who'd read everything. Kelsey said her parents were awful. She had a brother who'd died at boarding school. She ate so many carrots that year her skin turned orange, and her arms were covered with a thin layer of down, her body's attempt to conserve heat. We'd watched her feed herself with her scabby fingers, just enough to stay alive another day, disgusted but also oddly entranced by the discipline it took to starve yourself and the strange beauty it conferred.

I looked around the room. Had Connelly brought her here, too? Made her soup, poured her wine? Told her she was extraordinary, that she was the only one? I looked back at the picture, studying the cabin this time, the one that stood in a quiet corner of New Hampshire, a place where no roads led and no people came. The cabin where he used to go to write and drink, where he'd smashed a window with his fist and almost bled to death. I imagined Elizabeth there, picking daisies for her flower crown, Connelly watching from an Adirondack chair as she twisted one for him. Then I pictured her in Connelly's bed, his big hands moving across her wasted body. I remembered the day the ambulance came, sirens piercing the campus quiet. We hadn't actually seen Elizabeth loaded into the back. Had she walked? Been carried? Was she alone? I fell onto the sofa. How many girls had there been? Was I just one of many, as I'd suspected? And why me? Why Elizabeth? I'd chosen to believe Connelly when he told me I had promise, but maybe it was my weakness that he loved, the same sort of weakness he saw in Elizabeth. Or maybe he just knew we were both good at keeping secrets.

The dogs had stopped barking. I heard only one of them now, crying, a low steady whine. I looked back at the photograph, a Russian nesting doll of lies. I remembered suddenly what Amos had said about seeing Connelly at the general store near his family's farm, remembered too Andy's suspicions, which I'd laughed off as insane. Now it became clear: Connelly hadn't brought Elizabeth here so they could be alone, so he could make love to her in a real bed. He'd brought her to his cabin, where he might have brought me, except somebody else was there.

I brought the picture close to my face. The front door of the cabin was barely visible, but I could just make it out. It was a heavy Dutch door with a big iron lock, just the right size for an old rusty key.

The keys. When had I last seen them? In the glove compartment of Connelly's car a week after Tom and Igraine had gone missing. I pictured Connelly meeting them by the side of the road, or maybe at the gas station where they'd last been seen, Tom's strawberry-blond hair tucked under a dirty baseball cap, Igraine in the back seat covered with a blanket. Did Connelly wave to her, ask how she was doing? Or did he just hand the keys to her father and drive away?

I would never betray a confidence.

I flicked on the bedroom light and waited for Connelly to stir. I thought about something my mother used to say when I forgot my lunch money or bled through my pants at school: "For a smart girl, you can sure be dumb sometimes."

"Isabel?" Connelly said, blinking into the light. "What time is it?"

"Do you know where Tom is?" My voice was quiet, barely a whisper.

"What?" He fumbled for his watch. "What are you talking about?"

"Do you know where Tom is?" I said, louder this time.

"Jesus Christ. What's gotten into you?"

"Andy." I was having trouble catching my breath. I still had the picture of Elizabeth in my hand. "He thinks you know where they are. He thinks you're helping them."

"Andy? What does he have to do with this? Did you tell him about us?"

I shook my head.

Connelly pushed himself up on one elbow. "Of course I don't know where they are. Why would he think that? And why would you believe him?"

I thought about all the reasons Andy had given, but none of them felt important. "I don't know."

Connelly got out of bed and directed me to a chair by the window. I slid the picture underneath me.

"Oh God, you're shaking." He kneeled at my feet and wrapped his arms around my waist. "People always want to find someone to blame when things like this happen. I'm not sure why Andy wants to turn *me* into the villain." He sighed. "Look, I don't know why Tom did this, but trust me—he will come home soon."

"Are you sure?"

"Yes, I'm sure."

I took a deep breath. When I exhaled, the tears came, streaming down my face. Connelly hugged me tighter, kissed the tops of my thighs. Despite everything, I wanted him.

"Andy shouldn't have involved you in this," he said. "He shouldn't be involved himself."

"He's been talking to Joanna."

"Joanna's very upset, understandably so. Why she's talking

to an undergraduate about it, I have no idea." He reached under my shirt, ran his fingers along the knobs of my spine. "What Tom's done is terrible, but Joanna isn't blameless. She's always had trouble with boundaries."

I pushed his hands away. "What does that mean?"

"I just mean—it's complicated."

"What's complicated about it? He kidnapped his daughter."

He sat back on his heels. "I think 'kidnapped' is a bit of a strong term."

"Really? What would you call it?"

He stood up and walked back to bed. I looked out the window. There was a hose coiled up on the patio; in the dark, it looked like a snake.

"Andy thinks Tom might hurt her."

"That's ridiculous. Tom would never do that."

"There are MISSING posters all over town with their faces on them, Connelly. I think we're past the point of knowing what Tom would or wouldn't do."

"He would never hurt her."

"He's already hurt her."

"You know what I mean."

"Maybe they're dead," I said, feeling underneath me for the picture.

"Come on," he whispered. "They're not dead."

"How do you know?"

"Because I know."

"But *how?*" I pulled out the photo and held it toward him.

"What's that?"

"Is this your cabin?"

"Where did you get that?"

I walked over and handed the photo to him. He studied it for minute.

"Yes, that's my cabin."

"And is that Elizabeth McIntosh?"

"Who?"

"Fuck, Connelly. You know who."

He looked back down at the photo. His eyebrows drew together slightly. "Did you know Elizabeth?"

"Don't change the subject. I know it's her."

He handed the photo back to me. "Isabel, I don't know what you're talking about, and I don't appreciate your tone."

"Are they there? Are they at your cabin? Is that where they're hiding?"

He looked at me, then down at the floor. I could feel something fracturing, like the first time you ask your parents a question they can't answer or the first time they don't catch you in a lie. The moment you recognize your separateness.

"Tell me." I saw him look at the photo, measuring what a lie would cost him and what he might still get away with. Maybe he thought I would use the photo against him, show it to someone—who? Joanna? Roxanne? The police? I had no such intentions, but I believe the threat is what caused him to say what he said next.

"Yes. They're there." He rested his head in his hands, as if it had become too heavy for his neck, and for a brief moment, I felt sorry for him. But then I remembered Igraine and the smell of her hair and the sound of her cries at the party when Roxanne pulled her away from her mother, and I didn't feel sorry for him anymore.

"What happened?"

Connelly was rocking his head back and forth. The gesture sickened me. "What happened?" I said again.

"Tom called me."

"When?"

"I don't know. Two weeks ago?"

"*Two weeks?*"

He looked at me. "Isabel, please." He took a breath. "He needed money. Joanna was acting crazy. He said she was going to sue him for full custody. She was going to say he abused the little girl."

"Did he?" I asked, but I didn't want to know. Connelly didn't answer. "What did you do?"

"I told him he could go to my cabin for a few days, until he figured things out. And that's where he is. As far as I know."

"We have to tell Joanna."

"No." He grabbed me by the wrists. "Isabel, no. They're fine. The girl is fine."

"Igraine. Her name is Igraine."

"Igraine is fine," he whispered.

"But Joanna needs to know where she is! She's her mother."

"Goddamnit, Isabel! We can't tell Joanna!" His eyes were crazed. He smelled like sweat and something I didn't recognize. "Tom knows he messed up. He just needs a little more time and he will bring her home. I promise." He was still holding my wrists. I looked down at the fingers that had probed every part of me. I'd seen every inch of this man, and yet I didn't know him at all.

"Isabel, please. Promise you won't say anything." He put his hands on my face, pressed his knuckles against my cheekbones. He knew my architecture, my soft spots. He knew the places I would buckle.

"Can he just let Joanna know where he is?" I said as he reached a hand under my shirt. "Can you ask him to do that?"

"Yes," he said. He grazed my nipple with his hand, kissed me along the hairline. "I will. It will be all right. I promise."

What was a promise anyway? Just a string of words. I knew as well as anyone they didn't always mean something.

I watched the shadows move across the ceiling as he came inside me, crying out the way he couldn't when we were in his office. I realized I hadn't asked him about Elizabeth, but it didn't matter anymore. I understood well enough what had happened, understood too why he had asked me, back at the beginning of things, to be clear about what I wanted, to articulate my desires. *So there are no misunderstandings*, he'd said. *Because the stakes are too high.* He had seen the end embedded in the beginning in a way I hadn't. It was how adults behaved, I knew now, and I would never again not see the world in the same way.

After he fell asleep, I went into the bathroom and fished the amber earring out of the soap dish. I imagined it looked nice on Roxanne, golden honey against her pale skin. Over the years, I'd come to recognize what people would miss and what they wouldn't. This earring felt like exactly the sort of thing she would, its abandoned twin forever reminding her of what she had lost. I squeezed it tight in my still-tender palm, then tucked it in the pocket of my shorts. Before I left, I placed the photograph facedown on the sink. The road home felt longer in the dark.

20

SUNDAY. I spent the whole day in bed, waking only when Kelsey and Debra came in. "Rough night?" Debra asked. Kelsey placed a cool hand on my forehead. My head hurt, my hands stung, and my knees ached, but there wasn't anything wrong with me. Not anything they could fix.

The midday sun leaked through the blinds, painting stripes across the wall. The phone rang: Debra's mother, Jason checking in, then two hang-ups, which I imagined were Andy wanting to know if I'd spoken to Connelly.

Before he fell asleep, Connelly had made me swear, again and again, that I wouldn't tell anyone what I knew about Tom and the cabin.

"So you're saying we should do nothing?" I said.

"We aren't doing nothing. We're giving Tom a chance to do the right thing. And he will, believe me."

After wrestling with my pillow all afternoon, I dragged

myself to the bathroom. The clock on the bell tower rang five times as I peeled back the Band-Aids on my knees; bruises were starting to form, like continents under the skin. The phone rang again, and I thought about picking up and telling Andy everything. Or maybe I would call Joanna, call the police. Or maybe I would do nothing. I closed my eyes and let the feel of nothing sink in. It felt good. Nothing felt good.

A memory came to me then, clear as a mountain lake. It always happened this way; just when I thought I'd run through every memory I had of my mother, a new one would rise to the surface like sea-foam.

"That's the great thing about knitting," she said. She had her hair in a loose knot at the nape of her neck. "You can always start over."

The great thing? I'd thought. I'd been working on the sweater for weeks, a complicated cable pattern, increases, decreases, yarn overs. Somewhere along the way, something had gone wrong and I couldn't find my way out.

My mother leaned over and inspected my work. "You have to take it out. Down to here." She pointed to a spot just above the ribbing.

"To there?" I whined. "I might as well take out the whole thing!"

She paused, peering over the top of her glasses. "Yeah. You might as well."

I did what she suggested, complaining the whole time. But she was right, as mothers often are, particularly in the years we are least inclined to listen to them: you can always start over in knitting, something you can never do in life. There is no such thing as a clean slate. We take our decisions with us, no matter how much we wish we could leave them behind.

I looked at my face in the bathroom mirror. Elaine was right: I looked more like my mother every day.

I wasn't sure where I was going, but I took my time getting ready. I put on a short-sleeved button-down shirt, khaki shorts, a pair of gold studs. I brushed my hair, put on lip gloss, placed a dab of perfume behind each ear. I went to look for my mother's watch, but it wasn't there. Then I pictured it, on the floor of Connelly's bathroom, resting in the space between the toilet and the sink, and that was when I started to cry because I knew even then that I would never get it back.

The phone rang again. This time, I decided to answer it. If it was Andy, I'd tell him—well, I wasn't sure what I'd tell him.

But it wasn't Andy. It was Abe.

"Isabel? Is everything okay?"

"Yeah, everything's fine." It was a relief to hear his voice. Abe went over the details of his upcoming trip. He'd found a room at a motel off the highway, nothing fancy but it was okay. Should we make a dinner reservation for Saturday night? And did he need a jacket for the brunch Kelsey's parents were hosting on Sunday?

"You don't sound good," he said in response to another one-syllable answer.

"I don't know. I guess I'm having a hard day." And then, to my surprise, I started to cry again.

"Isabel, what is it?"

"Dad, I think I might have made a mistake."

"Okay." He sounded nervous. "Do you want to tell me what it is?"

"I can't."

Abe took a deep breath. I pictured him in his office in the back of the store, a store he opened and closed each day, then opened and closed again. A desk where he sat and reconciled his receipts, a record of everything he'd been given and everything he'd given away.

"Well," he said, "here's what I do when I think I've made a mistake. First, I ask myself if it's something I can fix. And if it's not, I ask if it's something I can live with."

"And what if it isn't something you can live with?"

"Then I go back and ask myself the first question again."

THERE WAS A street in town called Memory Lane. It sounds like a joke, something the alumni office made up to manufacture nostalgia, but it isn't: maps dating back to the 1890s show the horseshoe-shaped lane running perpendicular to Main Street—a dead end, fittingly enough. On reunion weekends, alumni flocked to take pictures in front of the street sign, their arms linked together or swung over shoulders, clinging to each other like survivors of a shipwreck. We loved making fun of them, these paunchy middle-aged mostly men reliving their youth. Sometimes they'd shout at us as we ran by, ask if we were having fun, if we loved Wilder as much as they did, if we were enjoying every minute. As soon as they were out of earshot, we'd burst out laughing and promise each other we'd never be that lame. But of course we would be. We were the ones who didn't understand how it worked, pathos, the pull of the past. The sting of regret. Memory Lane didn't interest us because we didn't believe in memory. We believed in now.

I didn't pass any picture takers as I ran through town on my way to the Grand Union, the large, brightly lit super-market at the end of Main Street. As cold as a walk-in freezer and as big as a convention center, the Grand Union was as far from Rosen's Appetizing as you could get. Whenever I told Connelly that no one would want to read a book about my dad's store, it was because of places like this, where no one touched the food or sliced it or weighed it, where everything was tucked inside packages that fit neatly into brown paper shopping bags, where the food didn't leak onto your hands or leave a smell on your skin. I wandered the wide aisles, past packages of Lender's bagels and Philadelphia cream cheese, thinking, for some reason, about Lauren Fishman, Barbara's daughter, the girl with the tire swing and playroom, the girl whose life I wanted so badly when I was eight. The thing about Lauren Fishman, the thing I sometimes forgot, was that she died. An allergic reaction to peanuts when she was fourteen, or maybe a bee sting. Barbara and Stanley divorced a few years later. It was hard for marriages to survive the death of a child, my mother told me at the time. I thought about Lauren whenever I wanted to feel that I had cheated fate, that by not trading lives with her I had somehow earned the life she didn't get. Or was mine the life destined to go on while Lauren's fate, peanut or bee be damned, had been to die? Either way, hers was a life I thought I wanted and now it was over. Be careful what you wish for and all that.

But I hadn't learned my lesson, it seemed. I'd never stopped wanting things that weren't mine.

I finally found what I was looking for: the MISSING poster on the bulletin board behind the registers at the front of the store. Tom's and Igraine's faces peered out at me, and this time I looked right back. Outside, the late afternoon sun burned the thin line of scalp where my hair was parted. I walked over to the pay phone on the corner, stuck a dime in the slot, and dialed the phone number I'd scribbled on my hand. The phone rang, and I thought about the time my grandmother's rabbi stood in front of the congregation on Yom Kippur and squeezed an entire tube of toothpaste onto a plastic tarp. "There are some things you can never take back," he said. "That is when you must ask for God's forgiveness."

This may not have been something I could fix, but it wasn't something I could live with.

The world will not fall apart if you tell the truth.

The phone rang twice more, then a woman answered and I told her what I knew.

EVERYTHING HAPPENED QUICKLY after that.

A few hours later, based on an anonymous tip, state police were dispatched to a cabin near the Canadian border, where they found Igraine. The little girl was huddled inside a sleeping bag, hoarding what was left of their provisions, severely dehydrated but alive. It appeared they'd been in Connelly's cabin for a while—the police found flashlights and blankets, a hot plate, a battery-operated radio. When the officers asked Igraine where her father was, she told them he'd gone to get firewood. "When was that?" they asked. "Four sleeps ago."

It took them several days to find Tom. The area around the cabin was thickly wooded, and the recent rain made the terrain soft and treacherous. He hadn't gone far; his body was found at the bottom of a ravine no more than a mile from the cabin. Whether he'd slipped or jumped, no one knew; an autopsy showed no sign of drugs or foul play, only that Tom had died as a result of injuries sustained during the fall.

Most of this I learned later, after I was back in New York. Between compiling listings for one-woman shows and cover bands for *Get Out!*, I followed the case on the *Daily Citizen's* fledgling website. There was little in the news coverage about Igraine, which didn't surprise me. I imagined Joanna wanting to protect her daughter from the glare of outsiders curious about the little girl who had survived. From Andy, I learned Igraine had spent a few days in the hospital but had been, for the most part, unharmed. The only photograph I saw of her from that time was taken at Tom's memorial service, which took place at a Quaker meetinghouse later that summer. In it, Joanna held tightly to her daughter with one hand; with the other, she clung to someone's arm as if for dear life. I zoomed in closer and saw it was Roxanne.

As for Tom, despite everything, I could never bring myself to believe that he would have left Igraine alone to fend for herself. In the end, I believed—I chose to believe—that his death had been an accident. But what was clear was that Igraine would have died if the police hadn't found her when they did. She might have wandered off to look for her father and gotten lost in the woods or simply died because she didn't have enough to eat or drink. I didn't think about that much, or the part I had played in her rescue. It was only later that spring, the spring after I left Wilder, when news coverage crescendoed with the release of the final report before petering out to nothing, that I allowed myself to think about Igraine, always at the end of the day, when the late afternoon sun moved across my desk like a beacon. And when I did, I often thought about calling Connelly. Once, I even dialed the first six digits of his phone number before remembering that I couldn't. It felt like dreams I used to have after my mother died. The phone would ring and it would be her. "Where have you been?" I would ask her. "I have so much to tell you." And I'd fill her in on everything she had missed. Because of course I couldn't call Connelly. After what I had done, I would never talk to him—he would never talk to me—again.

OUR LAST DAYS at Wilder were hectic, filled with finals and packing and trips to Kinko's to get our theses printed and bound. The English department honored Jason and Andy for their work on *The Lamplighter*, and there was a reception for studio art majors where one of Kelsey's photographs was on display. And then a few days before graduation, a class ceremony where Debra was presented with an award for her contribution to women's lives on campus.

"Total crock of shit," she said, tossing the plaque in the trash as soon as we got home. "They're thrilled to see me go." I was happy for my friends, swept up in the excitement of their accolades even though none came my way. In the end, Andy won the department prize for excellence in creative writing, and Amos Jackson's thesis about his great-grandfather was named Outstanding Thesis. I was disappointed, but not surprised. "There should be a word for that emotion, or at least a German phrase," I said to Debra as we packed up the room one afternoon. "It doesn't matter. I'm just happy to be done."

Debra threw a pair of boots into a box labeled More Crap. She had a Blow Pop in her mouth. "That's because you're a crumb eater, Isabel, and you think you deserve scraps. I can't wait to see what you do when you realize you deserve a place at the fucking table."

I never told Kelsey what happened that spring, but I did tell Debra. After graduation, she moved to California, studied acupuncture, toyed with becoming a therapist, but eventually became a lawyer instead. She spent time in Mexico, where she met Luis. The two of them moved to New York with their daughter, Anka, and I found the intervening years had mellowed her. I told her the story one night at her apartment while on the baby monitor we watched Anka sleeping. I told it simply and without embellishment, beginning with the night of the Senior Mingle all the way to the bitter end, or what I thought was the end. Debra listened thoughtfully, didn't judge or probe. "I'm sorry you went through that," she said when I was finished. "I'm sorry I wasn't a better friend to you." The way she said it, I thought she might have made a good therapist after all.

BUT BEFORE ALL of that, graduation.

I met Abe in front of the bookstore on Saturday afternoon. He looked only slightly out of place, reading the *New York Post* on a bench under a green-and-white striped awning. He had on khaki-colored pants I'd never seen before and a navy sweater.

I gave him a quick hug. "Where'd you park?"

"By the supermarket. It was hard to find a spot. The town is jumping."

Wilder was at its picture-perfect best, everything manicured and clean, all dressed up for company. We had time before dinner, so I took Abe on a tour of campus: the library and student center, the information desk where I'd spent so many hours. It was simultaneously thrilling and unsatisfying to see Wilder this way, like listening to the greatest hits album of a band you loved—the songs were great but without the B-sides and liner notes, something was missing. Most underclassmen had already gone home, and the few who remained ran past us seniors like we were a virus they might catch. I already envied them, the way they moved around campus with a sense of ownership I could feel slipping away.

At five o'clock, the bell tower played an extralong set of songs—the alma mater, "Auld Lang Syne," Aerosmith's "I Don't Want to Miss a Thing"—and I remembered the first time I saw Wilder, on that long-ago high school visit. It was one of those glorious spring days that always came at the end of a long winter. Everyone was in motion, biking or jogging or slicing across the road on long, skinny skates— training skates for Nordic skiing, I would learn, which was

different from alpine skiing, as I would also learn. Abe, seeing what I saw, turned to me and said, "Are you sure this is
the place for you?"

Our tour guide that day was a hyperfriendly junior in a
green-and-gold Wilder sweatshirt and track pants that made a
swishing sound as she walked. I caught a glimpse of myself in
a window and saw that my look—motorcycle boots, ripped
501s—was all wrong and made a mental note never to wear
any of it again. I was seventeen years old and thought my life
was over. But here, I could taste the possibility. There were
other ways I could live. There were other people I could be.

On our way back into town that graduation weekend,
Abe and I stopped in front of the Arts Center, where the
Tunemen were giving an impromptu concert. Bo stepped
forward for his solo in "Oh, What a Night," and I waved at
him but he didn't wave back. We hadn't spoken since the night
we'd kissed in the basement of Gamma Nu. It was only a few
weeks ago, but it felt like a lifetime. Later, when we started
dating, he'd tease me about it, those weeks he'd pined for me
and how I'd ignored him. It was the best round of hard-to-get
he'd ever seen played, he said; he even mentioned it in his toast
at our rehearsal dinner. But that afternoon I could tell how
hurt he was. I felt bad about it somewhere distantly, but it was
hard to know because I felt bad about so many things.

After the Tunemen finished their set, Abe and I headed
to dinner. On our way, we passed a copper bust in front of
the Admissions building. Wilder tradition held you were
supposed to rub its nose each time you passed for good
luck.

"Let's rub it," Abe said.

"Really?" I wasn't sure I'd ever rubbed it, other than maybe once or twice freshman year.

"Yeah, why not? We could use a little luck, couldn't we?" Our hands touched as we reached for it at the same time.

We'd made a reservation at a Middle Eastern restaurant in town. It was the night before graduation and most restaurants had been booked for months; Kelsey's parents had made their reservation at the Wilder Inn freshman year. Abe and I were shown to a table in the back, and I felt a kind of kinship with the people there, who I imagined lived the way we did, without boundless optimism for the future and the blessings it was sure to bestow.

"So, you're going to take that apartment," Abe said after the waiter took our order.

At the table next to us, a kid in orange glasses was playing tic-tac-toe with a woman in a jewel-colored sari.

"Yeah. You said it was nice."

"It is nice. I just worry you won't have enough money. That job doesn't pay much after taxes."

"Kelsey and I agreed I'd pay less because my room is smaller."

"It's hardly a room. And there's more than rent, Isabel—there's electricity, heat, health insurance." He didn't mention the student loan payments. When I'd met with the financial aid officer, I found out that, starting in January, I'd be responsible for paying back $175 a month. For the next ten years. It was a sum I couldn't contextualize at the time but would turn out to be just enough to keep me from joining

Kelsey and Jason for dinner or being able to buy a new pair of boots or a handbag. In other words, just enough to keep me from enjoying my life in the city.

"I thought we agreed I could swing it," I said, "if I was careful."

"You'll have to be more than careful. You'll have to be a magician." He tore off a piece of pita bread. "Benji's living at home. The commute from Crown Heights is terrible, but at least he's saving money."

"You think I should live at home?"

"No. It's just—these glamour jobs, Isabel. They're for rich girls, like your friends. I know you want to be a writer, but it's a hard road."

I watched him squeeze a lemon into his drink. Why was he bringing this up now, I wondered, when I'd already agreed to take the apartment and the job, when I'd ruined whatever hope I had of staying here with Connelly? I thought about "This Youthful Heart." Without Connelly's help, would I ever finish? Abe was right, it was a hard road, and while there was no point in bringing it up again now, he hadn't made it any easier.

We were quiet until the waiter returned with our entrées. At the table next to us, the boy had lost his tic-tac-toe partner. I watched as he made big swooping spirals on the paper tablecloth.

"I'm sorry I haven't lived up to your expectations," I said, popping a piece of broccoli in my mouth. It tasted charred and bitter, like tears.

"What are you talking about?"

"Do you ever hear yourself? You're always going on about how great everybody else is doing—Casey Hurwitz, Jeffrey Greenbaum—"

"Jeffrey Greenbaum is a schmuck."

"Well, he's Doctor Schmuck now. Even Benji, so sensible and clever, living at home to save money. And then there's me, taking some stupid job I can't afford to take, pursuing a dream that'll never come true. You don't believe in me, just like you never believed in Mom."

He looked wounded. "I'm sorry you feel that way. It was never my intention. Your mother was a great artist." I rolled my eyes. "No, she was. She always said I held her back, and maybe I did. But she didn't believe in herself. I don't know how you become a writer. It isn't a life I ever imagined for myself and I don't know how you get from here to there. But I don't want you to be like your mother, with dreams that don't come true. Or like me, who never had time for dreams."

The waiter came by to refill our water glasses. "Do you remember that game we used to play?" Abe said when he was gone. "How Small Is Isabel?"

I nodded, remembering the game my parents and I used to play when I was little. A version of hide-and-seek in which I'd squeeze myself into as small a space as possible and wait for my parents to find me. It started when I was a baby. My mother had gone in to check on me and, in my father's telling, had run back screaming, "Abe! She's gone!" They looked for me everywhere—in the closet, in the bathroom, even on the fire escape, until, finally, Abe spotted me, wedged into a corner of my crib under a blanket. After he got my mother to laugh about it, it became part of the story they told about me. Isabel the magician! The shape-shifter! Able to transform herself into a speck of dust!

"That was a weird game," I said, laughing.

Abe didn't laugh. "After a while, I told your mother I didn't want to play it anymore because I could see you doing it even when we weren't playing. I don't know how to explain it," he said, "but I could see you making yourself small. And I didn't like it." He picked at his rice pilaf. "It's silly to blame it on a game, but over the years I've wondered if I ever made you feel that you weren't allowed to take up space in the world. Because you are."

"I know that."

"Do you?" He was looking me straight in the eye. "So maybe that's what I'm telling you when I talk about other people doing great things. Because if Dr. Schmuck can go to medical school, you can, too."

The waiter cleared our plates. The people at the table next to us raised their glasses. "To the graduate!" Abe ordered dessert—two of them, an unheard-of extravagance. As we dug into our chocolate mousse, I wondered if this was why he'd come, to tell me this and make sure I heard him, really heard him. Maybe he'd always been telling me and I'd just chosen not to hear him. Why did I believe Connelly when he told me I was special, but not my father? In the candlelit glow of the restaurant, I saw Abe as others might have seen him, as a man free to decide what to do with the rest of his life. I thought about how he'd insisted we rub the bust's nose. *We could use a little luck, couldn't we?* Abe had never been allowed to have dreams of his own and so he focused on mine. It was the one thing he could give me that no one could take away.

A light rain was falling when I walked Abe back to his car. We went over, in great detail, where he would meet Debra's parents in the morning before the ceremony and where we would all meet up when it was over.

"By the way," he said, "did you fix the thing you were asking me about? The mistake you thought you'd made?"

"Yeah," I said. "I did. Wait. I have something for you."

"For me?" He unwrapped the package I handed him. It was the scarf I'd been making, wrapped in the front page of that day's copy of the *Wilder Voice*. He held it up in front of him. Blue, yellow, gray; wool, cotton, polyester—it was a crazy, patchwork mess of a thing.

"I had a lot of extra yarn," I said as he wrapped it around his neck, once, twice, three times. From tip to tail, it was taller than he was.

"I can see that," he said, laughing. "Thank you."

I smiled. A scarf was a project with no clear end, a way to outrun my mother's words, and so I'd kept knitting until I'd run out of yarn. The whole time, I'd thought I was making it for Connelly, but it turned out it had always been for Abe.

He placed a bag of leftovers in the back seat. "I only worry about the money because I wish I could have given you more."

"Stop it. You've given me so much."

"Well, I wish it could have been more." The rain picked up. Abe got in the car and turned on the windshield wipers. Before he pulled away, he rolled down the window. "If you want to be a writer," he said, "I know you'll be a great one."

21

THREE years later, Abe walked me down the aisle. Isabel, the motherless bride, handed off from one man to another in a dress Kelsey helped me pick out. It was white, which Debra derided as outdated and anachronistic, tangled up in patriarchy and the suppression of female sexuality, but I liked it. It was the white of new beginnings and fresh starts, driven snow and the blank page.

Bo Benson and I got married in a country club in Shaker Heights, Ohio. His family took up twenty tables while mine took up only four. That should have told me everything. There were clashes over invitation wording and menu planning, religion and money, of course money. Clashes that indicated future clashes, but Bo and I were young and hopeful and in love, both looking for something in the other person we hoped would make up for our own deficits, wide gaping holes that were far too cavernous to fill, but who knows that at twenty-five? Who knows that ever?

We moved into a one-bedroom apartment on the Upper East Side not far from Kelsey and Jason. We had dinner parties and bought shower curtains. We talked about getting a dog or maybe a cat, but in the end we had a baby. While Kelsey suffered miscarriages and Debra slept her way through San Francisco, I had an easy pregnancy and, at the end of nine months, a fat, beautiful baby girl. Alice had ten fingers and ten toes and a soft, velvety head I couldn't stop kissing. I had embraced optimism and this was where it got me. Was this how life was going to be from now on? I felt certain that it was.

Benji was working full-time at Rosen's, and Leon, Abe's brother, offered to pay off my student loans in exchange for Abe taking Benji into the business. Despite my feeble protests, Abe agreed, and I was released from my monthly obligation. Bo and I were engaged by then, and he probably would have offered to pay them off for me, but I let Leon do it instead as payback for my father's long years of service, for the life he'd never chosen. In exchange, Benji did what he said he would do: extended Rosen's reach. The store is listed in several New York City guidebooks and you can now buy whitefish salad on the World Wide Web; you can even buy a T-shirt that says "Rosen's Appetizing, Est. 1920." Abe doesn't let success go to his head, though. "I don't care how much money we have, Isabel. I still put on an apron and sell people a half a pound of cream cheese and a container of herring."

Bo and I had money. We hired a nanny. I worked, first

at *Get Out!* and then at Westview Day School, where I was a part-time librarian, or media specialist, as my job would eventually be called. In the afternoons while Alice napped, I started writing again. When she was three, I had a story published in a small literary magazine, the kind that paid in prestige. That's when the letter arrived.

I hadn't heard from Connelly in years. I didn't know what he was up to, only that he was still in New Hampshire and still married. I'd read somewhere that what he'd done—helping Tom hide Igraine—was a criminal offense and that he could have been charged with aiding in felony kidnapping or conspiracy. That didn't happen, as far as I knew, but he never taught at Wilder College again, which I imagined Joanna, in her position as English department chair, had had something to do with. It wasn't clear what he was doing; other than a few stories in the *Daily Citizen*'s online archive, he barely existed on the internet, although in those years I wasn't looking that hard. I didn't like thinking about that time in my life, those afternoons in his office behind the locked door, his big hands, the leather sofa. I thought I saw him sometimes, riding the 6 train or hailing a taxi on Third Avenue or once, standing in front of EJ's Luncheonette where I used to take Alice for pancakes bigger than her head. There was a band teacher at Westview who reminded me of him, and one summer, when Bo, Alice, and I were in California, I could have sworn I saw him riding a bike down the boardwalk in Venice Beach, zigzagging through the skateboarders, stoners, and snake charmers. After he passed, I gathered Alice in my arms, buried my face in her hair, and remembered I wasn't that girl anymore. I had outrun her.

The letter wasn't a letter, it was a story about a woman, newly divorced, living in a mansion in the Hollywood Hills. It's wildfire season and she has to decide whether to evacuate. We learn she is an actress, her ex-husband a director who left her for some young starlet. The actress and her ex never had children: he hadn't wanted them. Now the starlet is pregnant.

It wasn't a perfect story. I remember wanting to like it more. It was clear Connelly had never been to Hollywood and knew nothing about the movie business. He once told me he liked writing from a woman's point of view, and I thought that made him romantic and liberated. It only occurred to me now that he didn't know how to do it. But despite its faults, the story was beautiful—the menace of the approaching fire, the flames licking the hillside, the scream of sirens. And through it all, the slow sifting of memory as the woman wanders the empty house, deciding what to take and what to leave behind. In the end, it isn't clear if she saves herself or dies, if she leaves the house or stays behind to burn.

I turned on a television show for Alice and read the story again. There was no note, no return address. Both margins were justified so the story sat on the page like a wall of text. I marked it up, made notes, underlined parts I liked— "writer porn," we used to call it back in English 76—but I didn't know if that was what he wanted. I didn't know what he wanted. Was he sending me a message or a warning? Was I this woman, or was she Connelly? Or was she Rox-anne and I the young starlet he'd left her for? But he hadn't left Roxanne, not for me, not for anyone. I wondered if he knew I was married and had a child. Did he know I was writing again? Did he want me to know he was writing, too? I hadn't touched "This Youthful Heart" in years, not since I'd graduated. I didn't know how to do it without him. Did he know that, too?

After I marked up the story, I threw it away and wrote him a letter instead. I told him how good it was to hear from him and everything I'd been up to since we'd last spoken. I'd intended to keep it short and businesslike but found myself telling him everything, about Bo and Alice, my work and my writing. I didn't ask many questions about him. Then I sent the letter to Wilder College, hoping someone there might forward it to him, and for a good year after that, I thought he might try to contact me again. I'd open the mailbox expecting to find another story or a package or one of the love letters he'd once promised me. I'd come home and expect to find him waiting on my doorstep. But he never wrote back.

A few weeks after I got his story, I booted up my old computer, the one with "This Youthful Heart" saved on it, and started working. I worked for three years and at the end of the fourth, found someone who wanted to publish it, now a book. Bo was proud of me; Abe was thrilled. The book came out to a couple of nice reviews but mostly silence, which was okay because I was already on to the next one. The book had done what it was supposed to do, sparked something, opened the portal. I sent Connelly a copy of *This Youthful Heart* when it came out, along with an essay I wrote for the *New York Times* about my father and *The Assistant* and the parallels between Abe's story and Malamud's fictional shopkeeper, which brought even more business to the store. I never heard back. I wrote another novel, and then another, each time sending Connelly a copy along with reviews and articles about me and my life, my husband and daughter, my skin-care regimen. It was what he'd always told me I could do, and now I had done it.

It was around that time that my marriage to Bo started feeling small, like a pair of shoes you buy because they're on sale; they don't really fit, but you can't pass up the deal. Bo wanted another baby, but I didn't, so I started taking the pill without telling him. I could feel myself falling back into old habits. Unraveling. Throughout this period, I thought about Connelly's wildfire story more and more. I hadn't kept it, so what I remembered was a sort of Frankenstein version, what he had written mixed up with what I had read into it. I know you, I imagined him saying. You might have fooled everyone with your classic 6 and Vuitton purse and KitchenAid mixer, but you haven't fooled me. Was his the house on fire, or was it mine? Either way, I was about to burn it down.

When Alice was nine, I had an affair with one of the fathers at her school, a sexy erstwhile sculptor who stayed home with his daughter while his wife stormed the barricades at J.P. Morgan. I fucked him every morning for a year, while our girls played foursquare at recess. I'd forgotten how good it felt, not just the sex but the secrets, and through it all I wondered how Connelly had been able to manage it. Because once I started, I couldn't stop. By the end of the year, my marriage was over. I wrote to Connelly again and told him. He had both made me and ruined me.

Jason and Bo were still friends, so while Kelsey stuck by me, would never abandon me, she needed to make sure her own house didn't burn. And so I leaned on Debra, who was back in New York with Luis and Anka. We took long walks pushing Anka in the stroller, talking while she nursed. Why had Connelly done this? I asked her. Placed a bomb in my life and then retreated? I wondered if he was watching me, if he knew that what he had predicted for me had, in some ways, come true. By then, I'd written to him a dozen times or more, and he'd never answered. I'd had a dream that he was dead, I told Debra. He could be, for all I knew.

"Set a Google alert on your phone," she said, moving Anka from one breast to the other.

"A what?"

She reached for my phone. "Here. Type in 'R. H. Connelly' and 'obituary,' and it'll alert you as soon as he dies." Anka gurgled. Debra stroked her cheek. "I've done it for all my old boyfriends."

Times were changing, or maybe it was just me. We were reimagining things we'd taken as givens, scrutinizing the wreckage of our collective past, and I thought a lot about what Tom Fisher used to say about us being products of our time. Young women took "slut walks" and talked about rape culture, and when I considered what had happened with Zev through their eyes, I felt an outsize rage that made it hard for me to function. Even Monica Lewinsky had emerged from exile. I watched her TED Talk one night while Alice did her homework, and I could see how luminous and intelligent she was, understood implicitly why powerful men would have been drawn to her. I could also see now how young and fragile she had been and how badly we had treated her. She was lucky to have survived. I suppose we all were.

I wrote *Crushgirls* during those years, in a kind of fever dream after my divorce was final. Bo had Alice for half the week so I had more time to myself, time I filled with this strange, angry story about Eliza Cherry and her posse of girl vigilantes who systematically torture and kill the men who have oppressed and demeaned them. I remembered what Connelly told me about those long days and nights in his cabin, how he started talking to himself, drank too much, punched a window until his hand exploded. Alone in my apartment, I could feel myself beginning to succumb to my own dark thoughts, but instead I poured them onto the page. I wrote to Connelly only once during that time, a long, meandering letter about art and solitude and madness. He never wrote back.

I'd written *Crushgirls* partly as a joke and partly as an homage to Debra and the girls we had been, so I was shocked when someone wanted to publish it. "No, dear," my agent, Matilda, said after reading it. "This is the kind of book publishers *want* to publish." She pitched it as *Heathers* meets *Death Wish*, and it sold at auction for more money than I thought it deserved. Matilda got annoyed whenever I talked this way. "I don't know a man alive who would say that. He'd say he earned every damn penny, and so should you."

Crushgirls sold well, very well, and I became, in my own small way, famous. One night at a reading in Union Square where five hundred people showed up, some dressed as Eliza Cherry, I felt certain Connelly was there, watching me. I still remembered how he walked into a room, the way his shirt stretched across his shoulders, how he stood more on his left foot than his right. I could almost smell him, woodsmoke and peppermint. When the reading was over, I looked for him but he wasn't there. Gone again, like a ghost.

I bumped into Andy at a dinner party one night a few months later. He'd moved to New York after grad school and started working at a literary agency; he was now one of their top agents. We saw each other sometimes here and there. He wasn't married but had lots of girlfriends, including the one he was with that night, a young Asian woman with arms roughly the circumference of a silver dollar. He still wore his hair long, although it was thinning on top. Over cocktails and canapés, he told me about Joanna's new book, a memoir called *Daughter* about the kidnapping and the abuse she had suffered in her marriage. Early reviews were stunning, and there was talk of a movie deal. Igraine had graduated from Wilder and was writing now, too. Andy hoped she'd sign with him when her novel was ready.

It was January 2017, a few days after the inauguration. We were shaky and brittle, and it felt good to be among friends, even Andy. It was late when I got home, so I was surprised when the phone rang. I thought it might be Debra canceling our plans for the weekend or maybe Abe calling to check in. Alice was with Bo so it was just me and our cat, Sidney Fine (carrying on the Benson family tradition, we'd named him after our accountant). I opened a can of cat food and picked up without checking the number.

"Is this Isabel Rosen?" a woman asked as Sidney turned figure eights between my legs.

"Yes, this is she."

"This is Roxanne Stevenson. From Wilder College."

I tossed Sidney the can and forced out a hello.

"I'm sorry. I'm not sure how to do this." She sounded nervous. "I'm Randall Connelly's wife. I wanted to tell you—I need to tell you that Randall's dead. He died a few months ago."

I blinked a couple of times, trying to identify the feeling that washed over me. Shock, sadness—whatever it was, it was powerful. I fell back on the sofa and fumbled for my phone, searching for the Google alert that hadn't come.

"What happened?"

"Heart attack, they think. He crashed his car over by Corness Pond. It was raining, and he really shouldn't have been driving." She ran through the details quickly, and I could tell she'd told the story many times before.

"When?"

"October. Anyway, I thought you should know. I know you've been trying to reach him."

October. That was three months ago. I tried to remember the last thing I'd sent him. An article that put *Crushgirls* in the context of female anger surrounding the election. I wondered if Roxanne knew about everything I'd sent him over the years. I imagined she did.

"We hadn't seen each other in a long time," I said.

"You don't need to explain," she said curtly. "I just didn't want you to wonder why he hadn't answered."

"I'm so sorry. I should've said that first."

"Thank you." She let out a breath. "It's a lot to take in. To tell you the truth, I have a hard time believing it sometimes. This morning, a flying squirrel came down the chimney, and I called out for Randy to do something."

"After my mother died, I used to come home and wonder why she wasn't there. I always felt so stupid when I remembered."

"Sounds about right," she said. "Well." She sounded like she wanted to get off the phone.

"We used to watch you on TV," I blurted out. "In those documentaries. My mother—she loved the royal family."

"It's amazing how many people watch those." I heard the whistle of a kettle in the background and I realized she was in her kitchen, the one I'd sat in with her husband almost twenty years ago. "May I ask, how did you know my husband?"

"He was my professor."

"Ah." Roxanne was quiet for a minute. I could hear Sidney's noisy eating from the kitchen. "Things weren't the same for him after he stopped teaching. The last few years were hard. He was writing again, stories mostly, a little poetry, but he really missed teaching."

"He was a good teacher," I said and as soon as I did, I realized it was true.

"Are you a writer?"

"Yes."

"Do you love it?"

I answered without pause. "Yes."

She sucked in her breath. "That's the secret, isn't it? They want us to think it's hard, maybe so we'll stop. But we know it's a gift."

As we talked, I pulled up a picture of her on my phone. Her face was thinner, but she had the same piercing eyes, same strong brow. Her hair was completely gray. The last time I'd seen her, she must have been the same age I was now. I'd thought she was ancient. I remembered what Connelly used to say about her, that she wasn't a writer, not like we were: "She's an academic. It's not the same." But listening to Roxanne now, I felt she understood something he didn't. I'd always wondered how he could walk away from it. I still wondered.

"My husband didn't talk about it much," she said, "but he liked being famous. The interviews, reviews, the fans. He liked seeing himself through other people's eyes, what they projected onto him. Once that took over, the writing got harder. He used to go up to this cabin where he could be alone. The muse, he said. He was afraid of anything that might scare her away."

My breath caught in my throat at the mention of the cabin. I wondered what had happened to it, if he still had it, if he'd been forced to sell it. I wondered how much Roxanne knew about what he had done, and what she thought about it. It was clear what Tom's actions had cost his wife. Now I wondered what Connelly's had cost his.

"But those long nights," she went on. "The darkness and quiet. It weighed on him. I thought he'd found a way to balance the writing with his life in a way that felt healthy.

But when he stopped writing, that need spilled out into other areas."

She didn't have to say it, but I knew she was talking about the girls. Daria, Elizabeth, me—how many had there been? In the years that followed my conversation with Roxanne, in the full glare of the #MeToo movement, I would find out about at least two more, including Whitney Shaw, who confessed to me at our twentieth college reunion, which took place a few weeks after Elizabeth McIntosh published an essay about her affair with an unnamed English professor and Wilder's alleged cover-up. When I was young, I thought the sacrifices Roxanne had made for her marriage were unique and terrible, but now I knew the kinds of compromises you had to make as a wife, things you couldn't ask about and things you didn't want to know. I didn't ask about the fire in her house the same way I never asked about the fire in my own.

"He always wanted to be famous," she said, her voice breaking finally, "but when he died, no one cared." I navigated the call to its end, then let her go. It was the least I could do.

After we hung up, I searched the internet for Connelly's obituary. There hadn't been one—hence, no Google alert—just a news item in the *Daily Citizen*: "Local Resident Crashes Car into Pond." The article listed only the facts: the time of the accident, the weather that night, the names of the officers on duty. There was a brief mention of Connelly's career as a writer, no mention at all of his teaching career or his connection to Wilder.

But Roxanne hadn't told me the whole truth. She said

that Connelly had crashed his car by Corness Pond when in fact he'd driven it into the pond. When the police pulled him out, he still had his seat belt on, leading them to conclude he was dead when he hit the water, but there had been no autopsy. I didn't blame Roxanne for her omission: we tell ourselves what we need to to survive. This was what Roxanne needed. Who was I to say otherwise?

Sidney walked into the living room and started cleaning himself with a slow, raspy lick. I remembered the last time I'd seen Connelly. Graduation day. The rain had stopped—a miracle, everyone said—and the two hundred or so members of Wilder's Class of 1998 walked together for the last time under a clear blue sky. Dean Hansen, wearing a Wilder-green bow tie decorated with gold keys, handed us our diplomas, and then it was over. Abe left after brunch. Debra went home with her parents. Kelsey and I would finish up packing before heading to New York in her parents' minivan. When we got back to the dorm, we peeled off our graduation dresses and put on T-shirts and cutoff shorts, our bare feet black with dust. I felt giddy but strangely empty, unmoved by the ceremony that had marked our passage from student to graduate. Nothing had changed really, it was just time, which had run out on us at last, the escalator flattened to a line of metal teeth and there was nothing left to do now but step off.

We were carrying boxes down to the street when I saw him, standing under a tree in front of Fayerweather Hall. I placed the box I was carrying in the trunk and told Kelsey I'd be right back.

"Who's that?" she asked, squinting into the sun.

"My professor," I said. She nodded, and I walked away before she could say anything else.

Connelly was wearing blue jeans and a faded black T-shirt with a bleach stain by the heart. I realized as I walked toward him that I'd never looked at anyone as much as I'd looked at him. If I were an artist, I could have painted him from memory: each wave of hair, the contour of his knuckles, the way his cock curved slightly to the right. He was still the most beautiful man I'd ever seen.

"Were you going to leave without saying goodbye?" he said.

"I wasn't sure you wanted to see me."

"I wasn't sure either." He nodded at the minivan. "Is that your ride?"

I looked over to where Kelsey was standing, watching us. "Yeah. We're leaving this afternoon. Are you okay?"

He kicked the ground with his sneaker, sending up a plume of dust. "I'm sure you heard."

"I heard. I'm sorry about Tom."

He gave a tight nod. "He was my friend. You don't get that many in life."

I didn't say anything.

"He made a mistake," Connelly said. "A big one. But we all make mistakes."

Just then, a car drove by with the windows rolled down. "Isabel Rosen!" Ginny McDougall shouted, waving from the passenger seat. "You're a fucking badass!" She pumped her fist at me as the car peeled off.

"I know you think you did the right thing," Connelly

said. "But life is complicated. It isn't always so black and white."

"Sometimes it is."

He took a step back, pushed his hands deep into his pockets.

"I wanted to ask you something before you go." He pulled a piece of paper out of his pocket. It was a page from my story, from "This Youthful Heart." "A line you wrote that I always wondered about." He cleared his throat and began to read. "'We were girls in the bodies of women. We bought condoms with our father's credit cards, drank sloe gin fizzes, and slept with stuffed animals on our beds. We didn't know how to fold a fitted sheet.'" He looked at me. "Is that how you see yourself, a girl in the body of a woman?"

I was about to say no, that the character in my story is only seventeen when she says that, but then I thought about my friends—Debra, Kelsey, Whitney, even Ginny, all of us about to be shot out into the world, ready or not. What made a girl a woman? Through what mechanism did we pass from one state to another? Had I become a woman the day my mother got sick or the day she died? When I came to Wilder or when I met Connelly? Did it happen that night in Zev's room or was it happening right now, in front of Fayerweather Hall as the sun rose higher in the sky? In just a few moments, it would begin its imperceptible descent. I always thought there would be boundaries or milestones, something to mark the transition, but I was beginning to think the process wasn't binary, that, like consent, it existed somewhere along a vast continuum. The lines were there only until you crossed them. I looked at Connelly. There was a hard set to his mouth. I knew I'd never be able to explain this to him so all I said was "Yes."

He laughed. "You know what? I think people use youth as an excuse. Who says I have more power than you do? Because I'm older? Married? Because I was your professor? Everyone's vulnerable, Isabel—the twenty-year-old student, the forty-year-old professor. The question is, who has more to lose?"

"I guess we aren't all one thing or another."

"That's right. But the difference between a child and an adult is an adult knows that what she does has consequences." He looked across the street at Kelsey and waved. She waved back. "You want to know what I think? I think you knew exactly what you were doing."

He folded the paper and stuck it in his pocket. Part of me wanted to ask for it back. "Isabel, I wish you luck in New York. I have a feeling you'll do well there." He started to walk away, then stopped. "And just remember, later, when you write about all this and say you were the victim, you weren't. You were never the victim."

Sidney jumped onto the sofa, walked back and forth across my lap before settling into the curve of my hip. I appreciated the feel of him against me. It felt like the only thing keeping me from floating away. I heard voices outside, someone playing a saxophone. After a while, I reached into my handbag and took Roxanne's earring out of the zippered pouch where I'd kept it all these years, folded inside my grandmother's prayer of protection. The amber stone was only slightly dulled after so much time in the darkness. I don't know why I'd kept it, perhaps to remind me of something I might try to forget. Or maybe to remind myself I'd been lucky, so lucky, given chances I didn't deserve.

I sat there for a long time, watching the streetlights flicker through the blinds. The saxophone player was still playing, low, aching notes that filled me with melancholy. I closed my eyes and pictured Connelly driving his car into Corness Pond, not far from Joanna and Tom's house. Was he thinking about them and the part he'd played in their unraveling as the car sank beneath the surface? As it filled with murky water—was there a chance he was thinking about me? For just a moment, I allowed myself to see him, one last time, seat belt fastened around his middle, water rising slowly past his waist, chest, chin, the space above his upper lip, before swallowing him whole. I let the image hang there, pressed on the bruise of it, coaxing out the ancient ache. When I was done, I felt different, not lighter, just hollow, as if someone had scooped out my insides, leaving only a shell. One flick and I would crack.

I dreamed that night of the women I knew and the girls they'd once been and the girls I knew and the women they'd become, a slow gradual morphing of one into the other. In the end, there was only me, standing in sunlight, a girl in dusty sandals and denim shorts, chipped nail polish and cigarette breath. She was alone and a little bit sad, hopeful, the way young girls are. I could see her future spooling out before her, brilliant and terrible and vast. I looked right at her so she would know I saw her. Right before she faded away, I raised my voice and called out to her, that faraway version of a girl who no longer existed, not on this earthly plane anyway. I wanted to tell her something, anything, but for the life of me, I couldn't think what.

ACKNOWLEDGMENTS

One of the benefits of writing a novel in your forties is that you're old enough to know what voices to listen to and which ones to ignore. I have had so many wise and wonderful voices guiding me throughout the writing of this novel, and it is my sincere pleasure to acknowledge them here.

I thank my lucky stars every day to have met Suzanne Kingsbury, whose way of approaching writing and creativity was life changing for me. Without her, there would be no book, full stop. Thanks also to Diana Whitney for introducing me to Suzanne, and to the Gateless Writing community, especially Sheena Cook, Terri Trespicio, and Becky Karush, for years of friendship and inspiration.

Huge thanks to Susan Scarf Merrell for her friendship and expertise and for letting me spread my pages across her kitchen floor—literally and perhaps figuratively. Thanks to the entire BookEnds crew, especially Meg Wolitzer and Jennifer Solheim. Special thanks to Sue Mell and Haley Hach for their astute and thoughtful feedback.

Margaret Riley King believed in this book from the beginning and knew exactly how to make it better. Suzanne Gluck graciously read an early draft and offered wise counsel. Caroline Zancan is a wise editor and a kind friend. I am so grateful this book found its way to her. Thanks to everyone at Holt, especially Amy Einhorn, Chris O'Connell, Sarah Fitts, Vincent Stanley, Kelly Too, and Nicolette Seeback. Special thanks to Lori Kusatzky for her assistance and good cheer.

Thank you to the Writing Institute at Sarah Lawrence College and Kathryn Gurfein for the scholarship that brought Marian Thurm into my life. Marian read much of this book in its earliest stage and encouraged me to keep going. Allison Boyle, Jeannie Suk Gersen, and Erika Meitner offered insight on campus policy surrounding sexual assault. And to the many writers who read parts of this book over the years in workshops and classes, including Stephanie Newman, Dani Shapiro, Julie Buntin, and Rufi Thorpe, I offer thanks as well.

Many, many thanks to Mirna Ibarra for caring for my house and children, so I had the time to write. With eternal gratitude to the Alpert and Florin families and to those I've lost along the way, especially Peggy Tagliarino, who told me to write.

I write in memory of my mother, Ellen Alpert, who missed so much but whose spirit is woven into these pages. Mom, I have so much to tell you.

To my children, Sam, Ellie, and Oliver, my sweetest creations. My love for you is forever and always.

And finally to Ken, the beating heart of everything, who believed in me long before I believed in myself. The next one's for you, my love.